Game of Hearts

Cindy,

Enjoy!

Steph

By
Stephanie K. Deal

SK Deal

A Lyssa Winfield Mystery

ISBN-10: 0615693377
ISBN-13: 978-0-615-69337-8

A very special thank you to First Mate for lending her panties for the cover!

Cover Inset Photo of "Lyssa" by SavchenkoJulia

For the most patient and understanding man in the world.

My husband Drew.

XOX

1

"Good morning Dr. Winfield."

The greeter immediately received a light smack upside the head.

"For the last time, don't call me that Jay."

"But that's your name."

"Can't you just call me Lyssa?"

"You have a doctorate's degree."

"In anthropology. This isn't anthropology. This is... well, babysitting, mostly. Some bullshitting. A smattering of bribery and blackmail. Ahhh, the life of a production manager."

"Doesn't matter. You earned the right to your title and you should be proud."

She rolled her eyes and continued past the programmer's cubicle to her office nearby. Her second home, as she affectionately referred to her office, was a comfortable space with a faux cherry desk, large leather swivel chair and matching guest chairs. The room was also large enough to house a love seat and coffee table. Lyssa spent so much time in this office she thought of requisitioning a carpenter to install a galley kitchen. Knock out a hole in the wall to the women's restroom next door and she'd never have to leave.

Crossing to her sparsely decorated desk, she set her purse down and stopped to admire it. It was her latest purchase. A red leather Michael Kors shoulder bag. They called it lacquered pink, but it was so bright it looked more red. Either way, it added just the right touch of color to her ensemble today. White blouse, black skirt, and her favorite black Nine West pumps.

It cost more than seemed appropriate for a shoulder bag, but that was why Lyssa worked long hours. To fund her strange

1

obsession with handbags. And shoes. And exotic foods. And occasionally the latest in high-tech, battery-driven boyfriends.

Despite being top of her class at Penn State, Lyssa found the field of anthropology to be dull. It was fun while she was a student but upon entering the working world she grew to despise it. That was when she came to a sudden and startling discovery about herself.

I hate people.

Still, a job at a university or research department probably could have afforded her a social life, a respectable husband, some cute kids, a couple of low-maintenance pets. All conveniently sheltered in a well-organized split-ranch in an upper-middle-class housing development outside the hectic city!

But not a Michael Kors shoulder bag.

Besides, she hated kids and most pets too.

Instead, she utilized her minor field of study in Computer Programming and took a high-paying, uber-stressful job with Markison Industries. She'd always enjoyed computers to people, so it was just as well that she spent almost twelve hours a day, five (sometimes six, occasionally seven) days a week with them.

God. I need a hobby. And maybe a date. Or at least a friend with benefits.

"Hey cutie."

But not that badly.

"Hello Chase," she reluctantly greeted the man that had just stepped into her office.

Chase did programming, but not on any projects she worked on. He was from the security side whereas Lyssa worked almost exclusively in the gaming line of the business. Their paths had crossed the first time a year ago when he was assigned to assist with the experimental Vortex Gaming System. Not five minutes into their professional relationship he'd hit on her three times.

While Lyssa was quite flattered by the attention she received from the sandy-blond rogue, she was well aware of his reputation with the ladies (if that's what you wanted to call most of them). She hadn't been inadvertently celibate for over two years to catch an STD from a co-worker. No matter how spectacular his biceps were.

"Why do you never look happy to see me?"

"Because when you come to my office it means you're either horny or you're going to drag me to a meeting or both."

He frowned.

"Really? Both?" she squinted at him, not liking where this was going.

He nodded.

"I'm not even sure which is worse."

"It's a meeting with the boss too."

"*The* boss?"

"Yeppers!"

CEO Bryan Markison took over the company business at the young age of 32. The company was faltering badly and Arthur Markison was weeks away from putting the company up for sale or declaring bankruptcy when his son Bry begged to be given a chance to save it. In a moment of weakness Arthur gave into his son's request. It was the smartest move that man ever made.

Bryan's first decision was to add the PC gaming line to their software development business. At the time it was suspected he merely wanted to give his friends fun jobs --- a fair assumption since most of them were computer geeks and growing bored with security software --- but it wasn't long before Markison was once again a thriving business. This was mostly due to the success of the gaming software, which made it possible to financially-back their other interests, which they also excelled in. No one had ever stopped to notice that they were *excellent* computer geeks.

Chase was one of those geeks.

"I don't wanna," Lyssa whined quietly.

"Ah, come on. Bry asked for you personally. Don't make me pick you up over my shoulder and carry you there. I wouldn't have the willpower to keep from nibbling your ass, which would be perched so close to my--"

"Chase! Hello?!"

"Sorry."

"You really are horny."

"Yeah, but this time the boss was serious. Let's go."

"Ok," she relented and rose, picking up her tablet and planner, following him out the door.

"You still have that planner?"

"Yes."

"You work for a computer software manufacturer and — "

"I know!" she cut him off.

"Kelty's gonna pick on you for that."

"Why? Is he horny too?"

"I'm gonna pretend I didn't hear that," he mumbled.

Lyssa had wondered why they sent Chase to get her but she figured it out soon enough. The meeting was being held in the Penthouse North Conference Room. She didn't have security to access the penthouse floors of the business district high-rise. These were where Bryan and the executive board had their offices. It was the central hub for the base of operations for all businesses that Markison Industries owned or had a hand in. And there were several. Automotive Design, International Relations & Government Contracts (Lyssa didn't even want to know what that entailed), Organic Agriculture, just to name a few. Computer Software Development was just the tip of the billion-dollar iceberg.

"Hello Lyssa," Patrick Kelty greeted her warmly. He was the vice president of the software division and Lyssa's direct boss. She saw him about as much as she saw her favorite vibrator. Once every two weeks, sometimes twice on Fridays if she was desperate for attention.

She smiled and returned the gesture, then proceeded to say hello to everyone she knew and be introduced to those she didn't. The selection of people in the meeting was odd. The vice president of marketing, the network manager and his assistant, the security desk manager and a member of his staff, plus Bryan, Patrick, Chase and herself totaled nine. They fit around the large redwood table with one leather-bound chair to spare.

Lyssa got settled and caught Patrick eyeing her planner. She slowly slid it off the table into her lap. He rolled his eyes and she curled up her nose at him. She'd been carrying the planner around with her for over five years. He should have been used to it by now. Thankfully the entire incident passed without anyone else seeing it.

"Thank you for coming on short notice," Bryan began. "I'm afraid I have to skip the pleasantries and get right to the matter at hand. I'm expected in New York for an intimate luncheon with the Mayor and roughly fifty of his favorite rich friends so I don't have a lot of time to spend here this morning."

He tapped on his laptop and the large-screen monitor on the wall behind him came to life. What they could all easily view was an email. A very colorful and threatening email.

MARKISON - I WILL DESTROY YOUR LITTLE PET PROJECT. GAME of HEARTS WILL fail. YOU WILL fail!!!

Most of the technical staff recognized the Ransom font that was used and the rest could easily guess what it was.

"It's not unusual for me to receive threats on occasion," Bryan continued. "Most are generic. Things like, 'You will burn in hell you greedy capitalistic pig.' This one was quite specific in mentioning the name of the project. Which is still Game of Hearts?"

He glanced up at Lyssa.

"It's just the project name. Not the game name," she explained.

"And the game name is???"

"A surprise!"

"Still don't have one, do you?"

"I will. I always do."

"I know," he gave in with a small nod. "Anyway, given the details in the email and the fact that it came to my personal email address, which few people know, we're taking this very seriously. Chase, what else did you find out?"

"The email was sent from a bogus Hotmail account that's already been deleted. It was sent thru a proxy which dead-ended at a public library in Vancouver. I'm trying to get my buddy at Hotmail to give me details about the account, but as you probably know they are unwilling to hand out information. Especially when there's really been no crime committed at this time. I think we're gonna have to produce a dead body before they'll give us additional help. I highly doubt they'd have any more information for us anyway."

Bryan took over again. "This has the potential to become a critical situation. That's why I'm assigning Alexander Dane to head up the internal security here at Markison. Unfortunately his flight last night from Belfast was delayed but he should be in early this afternoon. He's already been fully briefed on the situation and will be in touch with each of you to explain the plans to prevent someone from sabotaging this important project. I have no doubt he will have this situation completely under control. He's one of my best security details."

Everyone nodded.

"This could very well be nothing. If so, consider it an emergency exercise for in case something does happen in the future. Thank you."

They all followed his lead and stood.

"Oh Lyssa," Bryan added as a last minute thought, "Alex will be working most extensively with you. Please don't abuse him too much."

Her jaw dropped. She could sense Chase next to her chuckling.

"I'll return your boy unharmed," she assured Bryan with a

smile.

"I know you will," he replied with a smile of his own.

As they left the conference room and headed back to the elevators...

"You ass," she grumbled at Chase, slapping him in the arm.

"Ow."

"You told him I like to slap, didn't you?"

"Sorry, I couldn't resist."

"I can't help it. It's just a reflex."

"It's harassment."

She glared at him.

"Ok, I'm the one usually doing the harassing so I deserve the slap. But you slap when you're happy too."

"Yeah, but you like those."

"Probably too much."

"Harassment!"

"Exactly!"

They split up when they reached the elevators. Lyssa didn't need security to get back off the floor, just onto it.

* * * * *

It was three in the afternoon when Lyssa felt herself starting to nod off. This was the worst time of the day for her. She knew she'd get her second wind at about four and end up staying until probably eight. On her way home she'd pick up a grilled chicken salad from her favorite Greek restaurant on Massachusetts Ave. Once in her apartment she'd change into her favorite house clothes -- a t-shirt and yoga pants -- and be eating in front of the TV by nine, to bed by eleven, and up the next day at six to start the whole thing all over again.

"I'm totally getting that pair of leopard-print Vince Camuto pumps this weekend," she mumbled to herself when she thought about her weekly schedule. "I deserve it."

As she stood and stretched to wake herself up, someone tapped on her office door, which was almost always open.

"Lyssa Winfield?" a deep voice requested.

"Yes?" She tugged on her blouse to straighten it again.

"I'm Alex Dane. Your security for the game project."

She looked up and was pleasantly surprised to find a very attractive man walking up to her. 6'2". Mid-thirties. Dressed in a well-fitting business suit. Built like a tanned Greek god. Or was it Egyptian? There was definitely some Middle Eastern in his heritage.

His hair was so black the crappy lighting in her office made it look like he had blue highlights. It was cut the perfect length of short with the bangs side-swept, partially dangling down to the middle of his forehead. He had a closely cropped mustache and goatee, the sides of which trailed along his jawline.

But what was making her stare was his eyes. They were a deep, dark brown. So dark that they looked almost black. And his gaze was intense.

"Yes, they're real," he sighed.

She wasn't sure if he was irritated at her or just annoyed that people always assumed he was wearing contacts.

"Sorry," she said quietly and turned back towards her desk to fiddle with anything in arm's length, embarrassed at having been caught staring at his eyes.

"Not a big deal. I'm used to it," he tried to make light of it. The curvy, long-haired brunette was quite attractive herself and he suddenly wished he hadn't been so blunt.

"You are?" She grabbed her tablet and turned back towards him.

"When I'm not jet-lagged, yes. I apologize, but you aren't catching me at my best."

You get better? Wow.

"My flights got bounced all over the place. I haven't slept in almost thirty-six..." he paused to glance at his watch, "...thirty-seven hours, and I haven't stopped moving since I got here."

"No wonder you're off your game," she finally allowed herself to smile. "Do you want something to drink? Coffee? Tea?" *Me?*

"Actually, some coffee would be great," he sighed again, this time from exhaustion, and ran his hands thru his hair, flexing his neck. Lyssa swore there was a puddle forming around her feet.

"Well," she managed to find her voice, "do you want regular or high test? Sugar and cream?"

"Thank you, but I can go get it. Who's the main programmer for this game?"

"Jerome Connors."

"Don't think I know him."

"Black kid in his late-twenties. Tall, skinny. Thinks grilled cheese sandwiches are meant to be eaten in nothing but boxer shorts."

"Really?"

She nodded. "Best to avoid the lunchroom on Wednesdays."

"Good to know."

"He prefers to be called Jay, actually."

Alex shook his head. "I think Chase has mentioned him, but I definitely don't know him. Can you call him in to meet with us?"

"Sure. I haven't told him anything."

"If you can catch him up-to-date while I get some coffee then hopefully when I return I'll be able to make a much more impressive entrance."

You get more impressive???

"And I'll try not to stare," she smiled up at him, fully aware that she was staring again.

He turned up the corner of his mouth in a little smirk that made her panties disintegrate, gave her a nod, then left. Lyssa took a deep, deep breath.

"Get a grip," she said to herself, then buzzed Jay's desk for him to come into her office.

It only took her a couple minutes to brief her lead

programmer, whom she liked to refer to as her second-in-command. Despite his young age and care-free attitude, Jay was quite level-headed in an emergency, enjoyed a challenge, and was an excellent assistant manager when one was needed.

By the time she was finishing up Alex was just returning.

"Good afternoon." He seemed much more awake and upbeat than the first time he entered her office.

"Hi Alex," she gave him a huge smile. "Welcome back. How was Belfast?"

"The airport's a shithole," he said with the same enthusiastic smile and sat down with them.

Lyssa giggled. It was an honestly adorable giggle. One that with the right lingerie could make her breasts jiggle. A small fact she wasn't absolutely clueless about.

"Alex Dane, this is Jay Connors. Jay, this is my bodyguard, so keep your hands to yourself."

"Me?" he threw his hands up in the air. "I'm pretty sure I'm the only guy in this whole building that hasn't tried to feel you up."

"I know. I'm a little hurt."

"Even the gay guy from the mail room tried to cop a feel the other day."

"He wanted rough measurements for falsies."

"Wow," Alex said. "I'm definitely gonna need more coffee for this job."

They discussed the plans to protect the project. It started with a separate backup server just for the current programming. The server would be housed in Lyssa's office. No one would know it was there except them and Chase, who was backup security for the project.

A half-hour later they had completed reviewing everything and Alex's coffee was wearing off.

"Sorry," he apologized for yawning. "I'm exhausted."

"That's understandable. You haven't slept for two days. We have to stop anyway. Jay has to back-up today's work."

"Oh snap," the programmer glanced at the clock. "I didn't realize it was that late."

"Go. Wrap up for the day. I'll see you tomorrow."

"Gotcha boss lady. See ya."

He darted out to meet the daily deadline. Alex stood to toss his Styrofoam cup in the trash.

"Do you think you can hold off the perverts for another day without me?"

"Sure." She stood before him.

"Chase will be around to install the server later."

"Oh, I can definitely handle him."

"So I've heard," he mumbled.

"What did he tell you?" she cocked her eyebrow.

"Nothing!" he blurted out. "Doctor."

She reached out and slapped him on the arm. It wasn't as light a tap as he was expecting from what Chase had told him but it wasn't hard enough to make him stop chuckling at her either.

"I couldn't resist," he said.

She rubbed her forehead, partly because being called doctor really did piss her off but mostly because she just slapped the sexiest guy she'd ever met. A guy who was also the best security agent in the building. A guy who could now confirm to the millionaire they worked for that she did indeed harass him.

When she looked up again he was staring down at her. And well below her eyes.

"Yes, they're real," she said quietly.

He looked up sharply, mortified that he'd been caught staring at her impressive cleavage.

"Go get some sleep Alex," she added with a faint smile.

He nodded with a little smirk and a lot of blushing. "I'll see you tomorrow."

"Bye."

He left and Lyssa didn't sit in her chair. She melted into it.

* * * * *

"He was hot."

"How hot?"

"Very."

"And he's your security detail?"

Lyssa nodded.

After her meeting with Alex, Lyssa decided to leave work early. It was still an hour later than the standard 8 to 5 job called for, but it was still earlier than normal for her. She'd arrived at Val's yoga studio just as her evening class was ending. The two Greek salads she was carrying and the look on her face that screamed *"We need to talk!"* convinced the yoga instructor to cancel her dinner date so she could eat in with her friend.

"What's he securing? Obviously not your hormones."

"Nope. Those are wildly out of control at the moment."

"This is so unlike you."

"I know. I probably just need one of those probiotic yogurts or something."

"Or a serious all-night shagging."

"You're not helping," Lyssa grumbled.

"It's the truth. So, what's his job anyway?"

"Oh, we got an email threat towards the current project the team and I are working on and the CEO assigned Alex as a precaution."

"Seems serious."

Lyssa shrugged. "Hard to tell. Bryan's a millionaire CEO of a billion-dollar company. Threats can't be new to him."

"What's the project anyway? Or is it a big secret?"

"No secret. I mean, we haven't released information about it but everyone has to know it's coming. It's a follow-up to Mutation. It was our most popular game so the sequel is highly anticipated. The project's called Game of Hearts, but honestly, I hate that title."

"Isn't that a card game? Hearts?"

"It was a joke someone threw out at the first development meeting and for some reason it stuck. No one's been able to think of a new name."

"Why not call it Mutation 2?"

"We are, but it needs something else to go with it. Mutation 2: Kill More Undead Things. Or Mutation 2: Rise of the Zombie Empire. Something like that."

"Oh."

"Anyway, Alex is going to make sure no one messes with the project. That's all."

"If that were *really* all, you wouldn't have needed to buy new undies."

Val gestured to the corner of the Victoria's Secret bag that was sticking out of the top of Lyssa's purse.

"I thought you didn't care for their women's intimates."

"I don't. Normally. Their lace doesn't always agree with me. But Natalie's Naughties was closed and I wanted something new."

"He was really that hot?"

"Oh yeah," Lyssa nodded wildly. "By the way, who did you cancel your date with tonight for me?"

"Reg."

"Which one was he?"

"The Red Sox pitching trainer."

"Oh. Sounds hunky."

"He is, but he likes to bite. I honestly could use a week without having to wear long sleeves to hide the marks."

"Ew."

"Hey, don't knock it until you try it."

Val was what Lyssa loved to refer to as a felony dater. The tall, thin yogini had a handful of guys that she saw on a regular basis, all of them well aware of each other. After thirty plus years of being married to a shallow, loveless man, Val decided she wanted to start enjoying life along with some nightly entertainment. That's when the native New Yorker decided to move to Boston and fulfill her lifelong dream of opening a yoga studio. Despite the fact that she'd told them for years she was going to do this, her long-since grown children were slightly mortified by their divorced mother's sudden decision to lead a hippy lifestyle.

Ten years later Val was still loving life, her men, and her yoga practice. She'd outgrown the original tiny yoga studio she bought a decade ago and had since moved to East Concord Street. It was a much larger space, in the middle of which they currently sat eating their salads, sharing a bottle of wine, and discussing Lyssa's sudden urges to molest a guy she'd only just met.

"I need to stop thinking about Alex. He's off limits."

"Who says?"

No one, really, but… isn't he? He's my co-worker. He's my project security. He's my new wet dream.

"Lyssa?" Val brought her back to Earth.

"He just is," Lyssa added quickly. "For now. I need to focus on work."

"Oh, my God! You've been focusing on nothing but your work for half a decade! You know you are allowed to focus on yourself once in a while."

"I know," she mumbled. "I got laid a couple years ago. Besides, I like my work."

"And you're very lucky for that. Most people don't."

"And most people are miserable."

"Yes, but most people still find time to enjoy themselves. And each other."

"I'm not most people."

"How well I know that," Val laughed.

* * * * *

Home was a two-bedroom apartment in the Bay Front Apartment complex, which wasn't actually on the bay front. It was eight blocks away. Despite the misleading name, Lyssa chose to live there for the security and convenience. The complex had its own workout center and swimming pool, saving her the expense and hassle of a gym membership that she wouldn't likely get to use due to her extreme work hours. As it was, Lyssa only seemed to manage one trip a week to the complex's facilities.

"I need to start working out more often."

After dinner with Val, Lyssa came home and stripped down to her bra and panties. She was currently looking herself over in the bedroom's full-length mirror. The only time she ever really looked this closely at herself was after she was dressed for work or the rare night-out with the girls or the even rarer date. And then it was only to make sure her tags were tucked in and there were no frayed fringes hanging off anywhere that needed to be cut away.

"I should do some crunches," she poked at her abdomen. "Lift some weights. Work on my kegels, maybe."

She rolled her eyes at herself. Lately all her conversations seemed to come back to that. She couldn't even have an honest discussion with herself without bringing up sex.

"Maybe I should do something different with my hair."

Most people considered her hair to be long, reaching down to a few inches past her shoulders. The color was usually light brown. When she spent time in the sun, which wasn't often, it turned near blond.

"I think it's actually getting darker," she mumbled to her hair in the reflection. "How boring."

At least it had a slight natural curl to it, and when she parted it to the side it looked almost cute.

"Nah. Still boring."

She'd been tempted to change it drastically but she didn't really see the point in it. In the past she'd tried different cuts, including a short, sporty one like Val's own salt-and-pepper do. On Val, it was sophisticated and mature. On Lyssa, not so much. She looked like the captain of the softball team.

So she just let it grow long and wavy and continue to be

boring, only getting it trimmed once every other month to prevent split-ends.

"I wonder what Alex likes. Red heads? Blonds? Probably mysterious black-haired beauties in shawls with domineering fathers, whom they have to sneak around from. Rendezvousing at the oasis where they swim nude in the clear, crisp waters for hours until—"

What the hell is wrong with you??? Seriously, you have got to get a grip!

"Ok," she sighed pathetically to herself.

Turning, she reached for the t-shirt and yoga pants that she liked to wear around the apartment. Her bedside stand caught her attention. Opening the drawer, she glanced down at her small selection of intimate bedroom toys.

"Sorry Brad, but not tonight," she addressed her favorite among them. "I have a headache."

Liar.

She closed the drawer and walked out of the bedroom, shaking her head.

"Great. I feel like I'm mentally cheating on my vibrator. I need therapy."

Or a serious all-night shagging.

"Shut up Val," she mumbled to her yogini's words which ran through her head.

Sitting down to her PC, she connected to her office computer at Markison. Accessing the company public personnel files she wasn't surprised that Alexander Dane wasn't listed there. He was part of the Security Department. In fact, from what Chase had told her, he was the upper echelon of the unit. Bryan Markison's right-hand man for all things scary. She imagined his job description included the words, 'probably illegal, borderline unethical.'

The only other thing she knew about Alex came from a conversation she had with Chase over one of their lunches together. About once a month he would come find her for a lunch date. He was a social guy that liked to keep in touch. She didn't mind because he was generally speaking a happy guy to talk to and he usually paid. He'd also toned down the sexual innuendos a lot since they first met.

"What time is it?"

"Twelve forty-five."

"I have to go. Gotta meet Alex at the airport to drop off a package."

"Sounds mysterious."

"Probably is, knowing Alex."

"It's not dangerous, is it?"

"No. Well... not intentionally. Alex is my brother-in-arms in security. He's also my best friend. I trust him. But you never know what crap he's embroiled with all for the sake of Markison Industries."

"Say no more."

"I can't. Or I'd have to kill you," he stared intently for a couple seconds, then laughed. "Kidding. But I do have to go. Thanks for coming to lunch with me."

He kissed her on the cheek, then darted off.

"I bet you're not kidding... "

She shuddered when she remembered the conversation, then closed the window on her monitor and cut off the VNC connection to the work PC.

"I have to forget about him and just concentrate on work. That's why he's been assigned to me in the first place. And the sooner this gets done, the sooner he'll go away and I won't have to worry about my vagina internally combusting."

This argument would continue for another two hours until she finally decided to end the conversation by going to bed with Brad in the hopes that 'he' would be able to satisfy her lust. Or at least take her mind off 'the other man' for a few minutes.

It worked.

Or at least she thought it did until she realized she'd called out Alex's name.

"Dammit."

2

"I kicked Jerry out temporarily last night."

"Temporarily?"

"Yeah. I accidently skipped a pill."

"Why didn't you just take two the next day to make up for it?"

"I did, but I'm taking no chances! I can't afford to get knocked up again."

Lyssa sat patiently in her office listening to the trials and tribulations of Marlene, a woman in her early thirties who discovered after many children and a matching number of failed relationships that falling in love and getting pregnant right away was not a plan that was likely to lead her down the road of happiness.

"I love my kids, but… "

(A lot of her stories started off like this.)

"… if I was going to sell any of them off, it would be Michael."

"Why him?"

"He's started masturbating."

"Oh, um, yeah, good luck with that."

"My laundry looks like something the Ghostbusters would capture and lock in a containment unit."

"Gross!"

"I know. At least he isn't hiding his soiled socks between the mattresses like my brother Oliver used to do when he was fourteen. That was vile."

"Can we go back to talking about Jerry please? How long is he kicked out for?"

"Until he buys some condoms."

"Seems simple enough."

"He hates them. He's gone to sleep on his brother's couch for the week instead."

Lyssa felt a little sorry for Jerry. He was the only relationship Marlene's had where he hadn't fathered something running around her house. He was good with her kids and he had a decent job working for the Boston Water & Sewer Commission. Still, he probably needed a break from them all. She just hoped his brother's couch wasn't too comfortable.

"Speaking of getting some, I hear we have a security guy working in our department now. Hmm?"

"Alex Dane. He's been assigned to ramp up the security around here, that's all."

"If that was all then why did your pupils just dilate to the size of my nipples?"

Lyssa was trying to give her 'the glare' but it wasn't working today. It was too early in the morning to muster up the energy.

"And after the number of kids I've had they're the size of buffet platters."

"TMI," Lyssa groaned.

"What's he look like?"

"Tall, dark, handsome."

"Ha ha. No really."

"Yes really. He's over six feet tall, his skin is dark complexion, and he's very handsome."

"Dark complexion? Like my Jerry? I mean, how dark are we talking about here? Billy Dee Williams, Ernie Hudson, or Michael Clarke Duncan?"

"None, actually. Middle Eastern dark. Maybe Indian. Although I'm of the impression he might have been in the sun recently. I'm not sure."

"You're not sure? How did you get a doctorate in anthropology?"

"Hey! I paid off that college degree! I own it; it's mine. And I don't have to use it if I don't want to."

"Fair enough. Either way, I cannot wait to see him."

"Well, wait no longer."

As if on cue, Alex walked into the office.

"Ladies," he nodded to them. His voice was extra low – extra deep – extra sexy.

"Eep!" Marlene squeaked, staring wide-eyed at the well-fit bodyguard with good DNA.

"Did you just ovulate?" Lyssa asked her.

"I think so."

"Oh, my God. Alex, this is Marlene. And Marlene, this is... off limits!"

Lyssa threw a pen at her as she reached for his hand, causing her to stop mid-shake.

"Alright! Chill. I was only going to shake his hand."

"I'm taking no chances. Especially when he's still got morning voice."

"Fine," Marlene sighed, looking over Alex again. "Definitely fine."

"Go! Leave!" Lyssa blurted out.

"Why?!"

"I don't need you trying to distract our massively overqualified security guard."

"Alright," she pouted, glancing up at Alex for help.

Standing at an even five feet tall, Marlene's head didn't even reach Alex's shoulder. The short, heavy-set woman with long black frizzy hair which was always pulled back in a bun, orange-tinted skin, and mammoth breasts looked like a strange distant cousin to the beautifully-built bodyguard. She'd be one of those cousins from the freaky side of the family. The side that would constantly wonder why their end of the family gene pool was so shallow and murky.

Even though she was three-quarters-Italian and one-quarter-Oneida, Marlene described her nationality as Jersey. It was fitting and seemed to cover any other questions people would have about her, like why someone with the blood of the Italians and Native American Indians running thru her veins would spray-tan.

The real reason was that her fourth cousin twice removed on her mother's side was currently in her third year of Cosmetology school and Marlene often volunteered to let her bring homework over to try out on her. The fact that the Cosmetology school curriculum was only seven months long, after which students normally received a completion certificate, was not a good sign. Neither was the fact that Marlene's fingernails were seemingly permanently stained aquamarine.

"Sorry, but I can't help you," Alex shrugged to the melodramatic, pouting assistant. "She's the boss."

Marlene left. Alex raised his eyebrow in question.

"Marlene has four kids with three different last names, two pending paternity tests, and a dog with a nervous bladder."

"She's quite productive."

"I think of her as terminally fertile."

Her comment made him chuckle just a little bit. She was pleased to see that he had some kind of sense of humor.

"I adore Marlene, but she does have more personal issues than anyone I've ever known."

"And what does she do? Her job, I mean," he quickly clarified, which was a good thing because Lyssa didn't want to have to explain to him about Marlene's bedroom trick involving body chocolate, petroleum jelly, and a dollar store Swiffer knock-off.

"She's the administrative assistant for the Programming Department which means she mostly works for me. She has Tuesday afternoons off to run errands and take kids to doctor's appointments, which is why you didn't meet her yesterday. Aside from the occasional emergency, it just works better that way for all of us if she has one designated afternoon off for those types of things."

Lyssa sighed, then changed her tone back to its normal

cheery self, trying to get passed Marlene and back to business.

"You're looking much more awake today."

He smiled. "Yes. Thank you for being so understanding about that yesterday."

Lyssa nodded. "What's on today's schedule?"

"I'm supposed to shadow you to your meetings and learn more about Game of Hearts."

"Well, I can start by telling you it's the stupidest project name ever."

"I can't argue with that."

"I have meetings all morning. If you haven't had your coffee yet, get it. If you have, get more."

"Sounds like good advice," he nodded and left.

While he was gone she gathered up her meeting implements. Upon standing she was immediately reminded that she overdid it on the treadmill that morning. She was grateful he wasn't there to see her wince.

First, they sat in on a Financial Department meeting…

"Is that why you carry a planner with you still? So you can doodle?"

"I get bored."

"What's the doodle?"

"An idea to put an expansion bridge between the mountain spans in the game."

"That's an expansion bridge?"

"It's crap, I know. That's why I'm production manager and not the lead art designer. That's Simon. But I like to have visual reminders. I know what it's supposed to be."

Alex gestured for the planner and she gave it to him. Three minutes later he handed it back.

"Wow," she squealed, clutching her hands together in front of her chest.

It was one helluva doodle. An expansion bridge between two mountains, complete with clouds, alien detailing, and a couple cars in transit.

"Thank you!"

She was so excited she gave him a quick hug.

"Oh, sorry." She immediately apologized. "I got a little overexcited there."

He chuckled. "I guess you like it."

She squealed, clutching the planner to her chest. "How did you do that?"

"I was an Art Major at NYU in a previous life. I still dabble now and again."

"I love it."

So did he.

…a Project Projection meeting…

"The name is kind of irritating. All in favor of changing the name to Project Forecast meeting, say Aye."

"Aye!"

"Let the record show that the motion was passed by unanimous vote."

…a meeting with HR about staffing concerns…

"I don't have any concerns."

"Our records show that the Programming Department is currently understaffed."

"We're doing just fine with what we have."

"The department is charted for fourteen full-time personnel and six part-time personnel. Its current compliment consists of fourteen full-time personnel and four part-time personnel. It would appear to be undermanned."

"Have you been watching a lot of movies with boats in it recently?"

"No."

"Oh. Well, fourteen and four works just fine for me. I don't have space for two more, even if I wanted to, which I don't."

"It's my understanding that one of your full-time staff members is currently out due to a medical condition."

"Some people call childbirth a medical condition, yes. I prefer to think of it as a lifestyle choice."

The woman from HR stared at her.

"She'll be back in two weeks," Lyssa quickly added.

"So you have no concerns about her work in her absence?"

"No."

"So, you don't have any staffing concerns?"

"No! I don't have any concerns!"

...and a meeting with the Sales Department to discuss the crappy title for the game...

"Where is everyone?"

"Apparently no one had any new ideas for the title."

"Dammit."

Alex even sat in on a lunch meeting with Lyssa, Bryan, Sales V.P. Tom O'Riley, Marketing V.P. Sally McKettrick, and Evan Gerhardt from TransAce, a global shipping contractor who was wooing Markison for their international business.

"I have no idea why I'm going to this luncheon," Lyssa said to Alex just before they entered the private dining suite on the penthouse patio.

He wasn't entirely sure either. It didn't seem like her business or technical skills would be required for this. But somewhere between the salad and main course Alex figured out the production manager's role in the process easily enough and decided to keep that information to himself for the time being.

By the end of the meeting an oral agreement had been

reached. Markison would give TransAce all their international shipping business for a 15% cut in prices and the addition of a valuable enhanced tracking service for free. The fantastic deal didn't have so much to do with Tom's negotiation skills as the fact that Gerhardt was fascinated by Lyssa's legs.

"Probably because I didn't shave well enough," she commented when Alex pointed it out to her on their way to back to their offices. She was either terribly naïve about the power of her sexuality or completely brilliant.

In truth, she was in denial. Gerhardt kinda creeped her out.

"Gerhardt's probably back in his hotel room surfing leg porn to satisfy himself," Alex found himself uncharacteristically commenting.

"And O'Riley's probably doing the same thing right now with the service contract."

"You're a little filthy-minded."

"You brought it up first," she pointed out.

"Must be Chase's influence," he mumbled to himself in conclusion.

"I tried being a good girl once," she continued. "It didn't really work out well."

There was a hint of regret in her voice that he picked up on. He decided to let it pass for the time being.

"When's the next meeting again?" he asked instead.

"We have an hour reprieve. I'm going to my office to hide. Catch up on email. You can tag along and nap on the couch if you want."

He furrowed his brow at her in confusion.

"Isn't that what guys do? Try to touch things you shouldn't and nap?" she picked.

"You're not my only job here, you know," he rolled his eyes at her.

"God I hope not. You'd be massively overpaid if it were."

As they reached the intersection in the hallway Alex said to her, "I'll see you at three," then patted her behind, pushing her straight through the intersection while he traveled down the left corridor to catch the penthouse elevator that would take him to his office.

He could hear her giggling almost all the way to the elevator.

Chase's influence is gonna get me fired for harassment...

The attitude at the three o'clock meeting was sullen.

Marketing.

This would be the most important meeting of the day and everyone was dreading it. V.P. Sally McKettrick put it best...

"I'm drained. That lunch sucked the life out of me. I should have scheduled this meeting for tomorrow morning."

"I don't even know why I was at lunch," Lyssa said. "Alex thinks it's so Gerhardt could stare at my legs."

"It was."

"What?!"

"Why do you think I told Markison to add you to the guest list?"

"You sneaky bitch," Lyssa said calmly and quite plainly.

Sally laughed. "I'm good."

Lyssa looked back at the snickering bodyguard behind her.

"She is good," Alex agreed.

"Shut it, you," she mumbled to him.

During the marketing meeting, Lyssa started to feel ill. It must have shown on her face too because she caught Alex looking at her with concern.

"Ok?" he mouthed to her.

She gave a small nod and tried to focus on the meeting. Thankfully there was over a dozen people in the room so no one really took notice of her. They were trained on the speaker and his presentation.

A minute later she shifted her gaze to Alex, who was still

keeping an eye on her. She gave a small shake of her head this time. He nonchalantly pulled out his cellphone, type a quick message, and slipped the phone back into his pocket.

A moment later Lyssa's phone buzzed, causing everyone to look at her. She glanced down to the new text.

"Forgive me," she carefully interjected, "but I have to cut out of here a little sooner than expected. Bryan's paging me."

"Oh! Well, the CEO trumps all!" Sally laughed.

"Yes he does. Everything sounds fantastic though."

"I'll email you the full detailed plan."

"Great. Thanks."

She gave them a smile, a quick goodbye, and she left, followed by her shadow. As soon as they were outside the conference room and the door was closed...

"What's wrong?" Alex asked quietly.

"I don't feel good. I need the ladies' room."

"Is it your stomach?"

She shook her head.

"Your head? Something you ate? Drank?"

"No. I just want the bathroom."

They traveled back to the floor her office was on and she ducked into the ladies' room while Alex waited outside. After a couple minutes with no one else going in or out, he cracked open the door.

"Lyssa? You ok?"

"I'm fine," she answered.

He walked in tentatively. Except for the production manager with her head over the sink, the room and all three bathroom stalls were empty.

Lyssa had a damp paper towel in her hand and was patting down her face.

"I'm fine," she stressed, standing up straight again and throwing the towel out.

She straightened her top and turned to face Alex.

"You're in the women's room," she stated flatly.

"I was concerned."

"You don't need to be."

"I do. It's my job."

"Then you're fired."

He smirked at her. She was cute even when she was being pissy. Unfortunately his smirk only pissed her off more and it gained him 'the glare', which to be frank, was kind of scary.

"I'm sorry to report that you can't fire me."

"You said I was the boss."

"Of Marlene. Not me. Although I have a feeling you often still manage to get your way."

She nodded to him slowly with a faint grin that bordered on psychotic.

He walked up to her and spoke calmly, hoping to quell her anger, because while 'the glare' was kinda scary, 'the grin' was starting to freak him out.

"It's my job to make sure nothing happens to this project, and you are vital to its success. Your welfare is my chief concern at the moment. Given the nature of the threat, it's possible someone might try to harm you and if that's the case, then—"

"It's my underwear, ok?" she suddenly blurted out, stopping him cold. "I wore a brand new pair of undies this morning and I'm allergic to them. I have a rash all over my naughty bits."

He just stared at her, trying to figure out where to go from here. For once in his life he had nothing.

"It happens sometimes, ok?" she continued. "Sometimes immediately, sometimes it doesn't bother me until later in the day. I don't know why it happens. It just does."

He was still staring; still trying to think of something to say.

"Look, if you don't believe me…" she started to hoist up her skirt.

"I do!" He closed his eyes quickly and looked away, putting out one hand to stop her. When she said nothing more, he opened one eye towards her. Her skirt was back down, her arms crossed in front of her, and she was still glaring.

Marlene suddenly walked thru the door. "Whoa! Sorry. Didn't know this conference room was booked."

She backed out of the room and Lyssa followed close behind.

"I need two Benadryl and a bottle of water."

"Oh, is it the thing with the panties again?"

That question garnered her 'the glare' this time. And this time it worked.

"Ok. Right away." Marlene turned tail and hurried to comply with the order. It seemed everyone was afraid of 'the glare'.

Lyssa headed into her office with Alex right behind her.

"Lyssa—"

"I don't have any other meetings this afternoon. You can shadow Jay for the remainder of the day to learn more about exactly what they're doing to complete the game. He has a status meeting with the other programmers at three."

"Ok, but—"

"Here Lyss," Marlene hurried in with the pills and water.

"Thank you. If anyone asks, I'm unavailable for the rest of the afternoon."

"Gotcha. Anything else I can do for you?"

"No."

Marlene left as quickly as she arrived. Lyssa popped the pills into her mouth, then struggled with opening the water bottle. Alex walked over and took it from her, opened it, and handed it back. She downed the pills.

"Thank you," she said quietly, recapping the bottle and setting it on the desk next to her.

Alex looked down at Lyssa, waiting for his command.

"You might as well go too," she said. "As soon as these pills kick in my inflamed crotch and I are going to take an involuntary nap."

He very carefully put his hand on the back of her head. Leaning forward, he kissed her lightly on the forehead.

"You should take a couple aspirin too. You have a slight fever," he said softly.

He stared into her eyes for a moment, then turned and left, closing the door behind him.

Lyssa stood in the middle of her office, stunned. It would be a full two minutes before she would move. And then it would be to lock her office door.

* * * * *

It was almost five-thirty when Lyssa woke up, still stretched out on her office sofa. Looking up, she saw Alex sitting in the chair across from her. He'd kicked his shoes off and his legs were stretched out and crossed, his feet perched up on the small coffee table. He'd shed his jacket and rolled up his sleeves. His tie was pulled loose and his collar unbuttoned. He looked relaxed as he read something on his tablet.

"Feeling any better?" he asked without looking up.

"I locked the door. How did you get in?"

"What kind of security expert would I be if I couldn't pick a cheap door lock?'

Made sense.

"How are you doing?" he asked again, shifting his eyes to look at her.

She pushed herself up, noting that her nether region did feel quite a bit better. She also quickly checked to make sure she hadn't been drooling in her sleep, then praised the heavens she hadn't.

"I'm fine," she finally answered.

"You said that before."

"Because when I say I'm fine it means I may or may not be but I can handle it, so as far as you're concerned I *am* fine."

He set his tablet aside and sat up, leaning forward to stare at her intently. It reminded her of the previous day when they'd met for the first time and he'd been annoyed with her. She decided just to ignore his attitude this time around.

"How did things go with Jay this afternoon?" she asked as she pulled her hair back into a ponytail. It was late in what turned out to be a very long day and she wanted it away from her face.

"The team has made some very impressive progress."

"My guys are good."

"You have girls too."

She nodded. "Two, actually. Marla, as you're painfully aware after today's HR meeting, is out on maternity leave and doesn't count at the moment. And Kim doesn't like to be reminded she's a girl. She just wants to be one of the guys, despite the fact that she doesn't look anything like one. So I let her. She's one of our best graphic designers so whatever makes her happy and won't land anyone in a sanitarium, hospital or prison is fine by me."

"Well, it works."

"The relaxed atmosphere around here isn't a fluke. I could have just as easily been a screaming lunatic, but they work better when I'm not. As do I."

"It's a testament to the company and your leadership that they trust you enough to know what's best, and you do it."

She cocked her eyebrow at him.

"I'm just trying to understand the dynamics of your department."

"I thought maybe you were sucking up."

"Did it work?"

She shrugged. "A little."

"Bonus."

Her eyes narrowed slightly. "Why are you here?" she asked quite seriously.

"You know why."

"I also know that there's no way in hell they would have pulled you off whatever secret agent espionage job you normally do to protect the game."

He smiled at her. She was a very bright girl with an even brighter personality that tended to make people forget just how brilliant she really was. What he couldn't figure out was if she did it on purpose or not. He didn't think so. At least he truly hoped not.

"The first email Bry got was the usual rampaging threat that he's more used to. Threatening his demise, that sort of thing. The second threatened the company in general. The third was a little more cohesive, which triggered a few alarms. Rambling nut jobs rarely follow-up on anything. The thinkers are the ones that you gotta watch out for.

"The fourth email was the one you saw. It was much more specific, especially in mentioning the Game of Hearts project, a name which was never made public."

"Never will, if I have my way."

"Yeah, that title really sucks."

"Is that all? The four emails?"

He nodded.

"Thank you for telling me."

"Does that mean you trust me?"

"My mother said there are only two types of men you can trust in this world. One of them just happened to be men with tan lines."

Alex chuckled. His collar and wrists were exposed, revealing that he was indeed a little darker toned on the face and hands.

"My last mission was in Saudi Arabia. I spent a number of hours in the desert sun."

"So you didn't get that in Belfast?"

He shook his head. "That was just the last plane connection. I never even left the airport in Belfast. Just as well. Rumor had that it was raining."

Lyssa stood and stretched while Alex put his shoes back on.

"Incidentally," Alex started, "what was the other type of man that your mother said you could trust?"

"Gay men. A girl can always trust a gay guy."

He chuckled again, finished tying his shoe, then stood to say goodbye.

"Alex," she started first, "I'm not completely ungrateful. I do appreciate the fact that you're looking out for me, even if it's only part of your job."

He started to talk and she put up her hand to stop him.

"But when I truly need your help, I'll let you know. I might even sometimes say please." She lowered her hand. "With that said, thanks for the save."

He questioned with his eyebrows.

"The text at the meeting."

He nodded, remembering now. He smiled down at her. "I'm still going to ask how you are."

"I know. And I'm fine."

"Not that I don't believe you... "

He placed his hands on either side of her jaw and tilted her head towards him. Pressing his lips gently to her skin, he made no noise as he lightly kissed her forehead. He lowered his hands and remained standing close to her, looking down into her sparkling light gray eyes.

"... but I like to check for myself."

"Anytime," her lips said while her brain screamed, *"Kiss me! Please kiss me!"*

For a moment it seemed like he might, but a beep from the laptop she'd left open on her desk caught both their attentions, killing the tension. It was the beep from a new email.

I WILL DESTROY YOU BITCH!!!!

3

The tired vice president of software entered the conference room and took a seat to the right of his favorite production manager. While Lyssa had been escorted home by Chase upon receipt of the previous night's email, Patrick had been called in for a late impromptu meeting to discuss the situation with Bryan, Alex, and other members of security.

"How are you doing this morning?" he asked Lyssa.

"I'm fine."

"Your version of fine or mine?"

She squinted at him.

Alex, who was already sitting on the other side of her, muttered, "Mostly hers."

Without looking over at him, Lyssa slapped his leg under the table. Alex smirked.

"How many times have you been hit?" Chase asked from across the table.

"Today or in total?"

"Today."

"Twice."

"Only once," Lyssa corrected.

"So far," he glanced down at her. He had a teasing smirk this morning. And that damn deep voice again!

While Chase entered into a conversation with Tom O'Riley about the game last night, Alex took the opportunity to lean in towards Lyssa and ask very quietly, "How are your bits and pieces today?"

"Much better, thank you," she smiled, glancing up at him.

He smiled back and a sweet scent caught his attention. It

was faint and very lovely.

"Jasmine?"

She nodded to let him know he'd guessed correctly. He secretly wondered how many dollars an ounce she paid for her perfume. He had no idea but was willing to admit it was worth every penny.

"It's an essential oil. My yogini says it's to promote relaxation and ease anxiety."

"That's not all it does."

"Your morning voice should be illegal."

She looked down at the planner in her lap, pulling it closer, just trying to avoid eye contact at this point.

Alex sat up, cleared his throat, and reminded himself that he needed to focus on the job and not be distracted by the production manager who looked good, smelled good, and was probably pretty flexible.

"Yoga?" he found himself asking despite his internal dialogue telling him not to.

She nodded.

"I haven't done yoga in a while."

"If you decide to take up practice again I recommend The Lotus Blossom."

"The Lotus Blossom," he repeated to seat the name in his memory.

"On East Concord. The yogini is Val Tucker. She does have other yogis that rent her space if she doesn't offer a class you're interested in. The schedule is listed online."

"Thank you for the recommendation."

He didn't ask anything further but she knew the question that was burning in his mind right now.

"I go on Thursday nights," she offered freely.

Bryan entered the room, saving them from having to continue this conversation.

"Thank you for clearing your calendars this morning."

He sat, turned on his tablet, then looked up to address them.

"Last night at five-thirty Lyssa received a threatening email."

He again hit a button on his tablet that brought up the email to the large screen monitor.

"Wow," Sally McKettrick muttered. "That's rude."

"Very," Chase added.

"Lyssa's email isn't as private as mine," Bryan continued. "Everyone's well aware she's the production manager. It isn't something we advertise, but it's not a secret either."

"If you wanted to ruin the project it only makes sense to go after its manager," Tom suggested.

"True."

"They're just trying to scare you," Sally said. "They obviously don't know you if they think an immature threatening email will work."

"No, they don't," Lyssa smiled.

"All possibilities are being taken into account but the general consensus is that it's just meant to scare Lyssa. Throw her off her game. Bring more stress to the project."

Lyssa wanted to laugh. Alex was doing more of that than the email was and he probably wasn't even trying to.

"At this time we will not be involving the authorities. My decision is based solely on the fact that I think we can handle this better in-house. We have some of the best IT people in the world. If anyone can figure this out it's us. Boston's finest are great men. I wouldn't want any other police force in my backyard, but I don't necessarily want them playing in the house."

Everyone was in agreement.

"Tread carefully and just keep up the work momentum. Things are going great. Lyssa, you and your people are at the top of their game and I have great confidence in you.

"With that said, I want everyone on their toes. You get anything suspicious or have concerns, please bring them to our attention immediately. We have any and all resources at our fingertips so we might as well use them."

The meeting dispersed. Patrick, Chase and Alex trailed behind to talk to Bryan.

"Seriously, how is Lyssa doing?" the CEO asked.

"She's ok," Alex confirmed.

"She seems a bit off."

"That might have more to do with the fact that she was under the weather yesterday."

"She was sick?"

"She had an allergic reaction."

"Was it the thing with the panties?" Patrick asked.

"Ouch," Chase grimaced.

"How does everyone know about that?" Alex asked.

Patrick explained. "The first time it happened I was in a meeting with Sally and Chase. Marlene freaked out and called me screaming that Lyssa's underwear was attacking her."

"We all heard it," Chase admitted.

"Marlene's kind of dangerous," Bryan snickered.

"She has her moments. To her credit, it scared the hell out of her. She is nothing if not completely dedicated to Lyssa."

"Patrick, can you talk to her privately? See how she would be about a personal security detail. I don't really think it's necessary at this point but I'd like to know how she feels about it. I want her to feel safe and comfortable, and I think she might be more willing to tell you than the rest of us."

"I have a meeting with her at ten. I'll discuss it with her then. I'm sure she'll be reasonable about it."

"No way."

"Lyssa."

"I mean it."

"Come on."

"No."

"Bryan's men are very good."

"I know."

"They'd be quiet and unobtrusive."

"I know that too."

"They would take the intimate details of your personal life to their grave."

"I believe you."

"And they can keep you safe."

"Probably."

"So, you'll let them tail you?"

"Not a chance in hell."

"Lyssa!"

"Patrick!"

"Give me one good reason why not."

"I'm horny."

As soon as she said it she regretted it.

"Wha???" he was dumbfounded.

"Dammit," she sighed.

"You're horny? I didn't even know that was possible."

"Well, of course it's possible," she grumbled.

"So," he crossed his arms with a big smile. "Confess. Who is it?"

"I'm not telling you."

"Come on."

"You're my boss."

"I'm also your friend. And Janice adores you. We're practically family."

It was true. His wife had been one of her closest friends. They didn't spend much time together anymore since she had demonic small children torturing her now, but whenever Lyssa needed a friend Janice had always been there.

"It isn't anyone in particular at the moment--"

"It's Alex, isn't it? You've got a thing for the Great Dane."

"No," she said rather unconvincingly and he wasn't buying

it for one second.

"Well, you picked the best one of the bunch. As far as security goes. He's got a very dark side about him though, and I'm not referring to his tan. He doesn't talk much. Very private. He and Bry are very close, but it seems tense sometimes."

"Does he have someone?"

"You mean a girlfriend?"

"Or wife. Or boyfriend. Or concubine."

"Ah, no. None of the above. Well, that I know of. Like I said, he's a private guy. Chase occasionally tries to fix him up, but he always passes. I would too if it was one of Chase's recommendations. But for you I bet he'd make an exception."

She rolled her eyes at him.

"He commented in last night's meeting that you were an exceptional manager."

"Stop it."

"No joke. He said you were very intelligent, highly attractive and... how did he put it?... wise enough to know exactly how to use it."

"He did?"

"Yes."

"I wonder what that meant."

"It means you have the power to lure him into bed."

"I doubt it," she mumbled. "Especially after yesterday."

"I heard your underwear tried to kill you again."

"Oh, my God! Did Marlene call you?"

"No! It was just mentioned that you were ill yesterday. We guessed the rest."

"So embarrassing."

"How badly did he pick on you?"

"Not at all really. He was very caring and concerned. Probably scared the hell out of him."

"I give the guy credit. I would have razzed the hell out of you. If you want me to tell Bryan to assign Alex to you, I –"

She grabbed him by the tie and pulled him down so she could look him straight in the eye.

"Ack!" he choked.

"You tell anyone what I just told you and I swear to God I will take Janice shopping for the biggest, meanest vibrator on the market."

"O... k..." he gagged.

"Not only will it put your small dick to shame, but she'll be screaming *my* name."

"I... promise."

She let him go. He took a deep breath and stood, straightening his tie.

"Besides," Lyssa continued in her more normal, controlled tone of voice. "I have a dinner date tomorrow night. It's going to be difficult enough so the last thing I need is to bring a bodyguard."

"Who told you I have a small dick?"

"Your college roommate."

"You know Pete?"

She nodded.

"Did he tell you about that spring break trip to..." he trailed off as she was nodding wildly at him. "Yeah, ok. I think you'll be just fine on your own. I'll let Bryan know that until we have further reason to worry a personal bodyguard won't be needed."

"Thank you... Pattycakes."

Lyssa gave him a devilish grin, turned on her heel and left.

"He told you that too? Shit."

The rest of Lyssa's day went relatively quiet compared to the beginning of the week so far. She saw no one from security or upper management level. Most of her time was spent reviewing the recent changes in the landscape coloring. This was what she liked doing best. Reviewing the game with the designers and artists. This was why she put up with the rest of the job.

Now she could enter a peaceful night of tranquility and

enjoy her yoga practice.

Or at least try to.

"So, how's the hottie?"

"No offense but I really don't want to talk about it tonight Val."

"Oh, why not? My love life is getting redundant. I was hoping to spice it up via a little hormone osmosis from you."

"That sounds disgusting."

"Ok, maybe it was a little. Still... what went wrong?"

"I had an issue with... you know... new underwear."

"I told you that was a bad idea!"

"Yeah, well now he knows it was a bad idea too."

"Really?"

"He followed me around all yesterday. He knows just how boring and weird I am."

"I prefer to think of you as dedicated and spontaneously quirky."

"And then my groin decided to abandon its post on deck."

"It declared mutiny?"

She bent over to stare at her private parts. "Traitor!"

"Well, that isn't all too bad. He's seen the worst of it anyway."

"And then I got a threatening email."

Val was finally shocked into silence.

"It's nothing I'm worried about but my boss Patrick wants one of the goons to follow me around 24/7. That is not happening! I have enough problems."

"Are you sure it's nothing?"

"Yeah. Probably."

"You poor thing. I'm sorry I picked on you."

"That's ok. I just need a nice relaxing night of yoga," Lyssa smiled.

Val hugged her. "Then I'll give you a nice relaxing fuuuuck."

"Excuse me?"

Lyssa stepped back to find Val staring across the room.

"Hello handsome," Val growled.

Lyssa looked behind her. "Oh, dammit." She slapped her hand over her face. "I can't believe he followed me here."

"Is that him?" Val smiled widely.

"Yes. And do not say anything to him about the email!" she whispered urgently. "I shouldn't have said anything but — "

"It's ok. I understand. That's why we're yoga sisters," Val smiled at her.

Long ago they'd made a pact that they could share everything with each other. All girls needed to vent once in a while. They vowed to keep everything they talked about a secret.

"You didn't know he was coming tonight?"

"Don't you think if I knew I'd have worn something better."

Val looked down and had to admit it wasn't Lyssa's nicest yoga outfit.

Alex walked over to them. "Hi Lyssa."

"Hey. Alex, this is Val. Val, this is Alex."

They shook hands and exchanged a nicer greeting than she gave him. Then Alex turned his attention back to his sulking co-worker.

"Happy to see me as always, I see."

"Did Patrick send you?"

"No. You did."

"Excuse me?"

"You told me to come here."

"Not tonight! You have to come on a different night."

"This night works better for me."

"You have joint custody of me?" Val asked.

"But it's my one night without work!"

"I'm not here about work. I'm just here for yoga."

"Mom and Dad!" Val threw her arms up. "Why can't you just get along and love each other like you used to?"

They both stared at her.

"Do it for the kids," she added, pleading.

Lyssa relented and walked over to the wall to get her yoga mat and blanket.

"Poor thing," Val sighed. She should have been a better friend to Lyssa, but the girl was being a little unreasonable.

"I should go," Alex said.

"No. Stay. It'll be good for her."

Val proceeded to explain the studio and class to him.

"You've done yoga before?"

"Years ago. I can catch up pretty quickly though."

Alex rolled out his mat next to Lyssa. She sat on hers, cross-legged, staring somewhere out over the floor. He couldn't begin to fathom what she was thinking about, but he was sure how much she hated him right now was somewhere in that pretty head of hers.

"It was Jay."

This finally got her attention and she turned to look at him.

"I was checking on the server today and ran into Jay. He said he was worried."

"Jay never worries."

"Apparently he's never had a reason to. He asked if I'd pay extra attention. That's all."

"Have you ever really done yoga?"

"Yes. I didn't lie to you. I can be a bastard for a lot of reasons, but lying isn't one of them. I do really need this too. A little meditation might help the next time I'm stranded in an airport and have the urge to murder someone."

"Belfast must have been really bad."

"Not really. I was just impatient to get back home. I didn't want to miss the meeting that morning. I didn't lose my cool at the ticket desk, but for once I really wanted to."

"It's a good thing you're here then."

"So I can stay?"

"I'm not your boss, remember?"

"This isn't about work."

"Yeah yeah yeah. Just don't..." she trailed off, wishing she hadn't started that sentence.

"Just don't what?" he urged her to continue.

"Just don't sleep with Val."

He looked at her like she was insane.

"She has lots of guys already," she explained.

"I'm sure there's a good reason for it but I'm not interested in finding out what it is."

"She likes younger guys too. Well, younger than her."

"She's not my type."

"I just—"

"No!" he stressed.

"Ok. Jeez."

"You recommended this place."

"Well, I didn't think I'd have to bear witness."

"If she comes near my johnson, I swear, I'm rolling over on top of you to protect it."

She started to laugh and stifled it.

"In fact, if she even looks at me funny... like she is now... come here."

"No."

"Fine, I'll come to you," he started to move.

"No!" she screeched, then laughed.

He sat back down with a chuckle. "Ok, but next time you better be ready."

Class started. Alex struggled to remember the moves at first, but he caught on soon enough as he'd said. Lyssa performed everything perfectly, mostly with her eyes closed. It was like she was doing sleep yoga.

During child's pose, Val would travel to each class member and press down on their backs and hips, making adjustments. Then during reclining cobbler's pose Val came around to Lyssa only and whispered, "How's the joints today?"

"Good."

"Want an adjustment?"

"Please."

Val stood at Lyssa's feet and bent over, putting her hands on her thighs, slowly pressing down.

"Tell me when it hurts."

"It doesn't today."

After she was done, Lyssa hugged her knees to her chest and Val pressed on her legs as well.

At the end, as they entered shavasana, they all lay on the floor, feet at the corners of their mats, arms to their sides, hands opened up to the heavens. Val came around and gave them little face massages using lemongrass oil.

"You did a good job today sweetie," she smiled down at Lyssa.

"Thanks."

Val moved onto Alex.

"Are you allergic to any essential oils or scents?"

"No."

As she massaged his face, Lyssa rolled over to her side and her arm landed on Alex's. She'd fallen asleep.

"I think she's a little tired," Val snickered.

Lyssa squirmed a little, getting more comfortable on her mat. Her hand was draped over his bicep.

"She's a Leo, you know. Kitties like to possess by touch."

Val patted his shoulder with a smile and moved onto the next student.

Minutes later, the class was over. Alex gently woke Lyssa.

"Am I home?" she mumbled, sitting up.

"No," he chuckled.

"Dammit."

"Come on, I'll drive you home."

"I brought my car."

"I didn't."

"Then I should drive you home."

"No. I'll drive you home, then I'll take a taxi."

"Alright. I'm not arguing with you anymore. I'm too tired."

He picked up both their gym bags. "It's been a tough week so far."

Lyssa struggled to stay awake for the drive home. It helped that Alex wanted to talk.

"So, which came first? Yoga or Val?"

"What do you mean?"

"Did you meet Val when you started doing yoga, or did you start doing yoga because you knew Val?"

"Oh, I met Val doing yoga. My physical therapist suggested I try it. I was in an accident a few years ago and injured my hips. He thought yoga might help. It does. I barely notice anymore."

That explained the special attention Val paid to her and the words of encouragement.

At the complex, she gave him the instructions to pull into the underground parking garage then they took the elevator to the lobby.

"Hi Frank," Lyssa addressed the security guard at the front desk. Frank looked like an aging linebacker.

"Evening Ms. Lyssa," he always addressed her.

"Frank, this is Alex. I work with him. My boss pays him to do things like jump in front of bullets and throw himself on live grenades so I don't get hurt. Can you call him a taxi please?"

"Sure Ms. Lyssa," Frank laughed and phoned for a taxi.

"Go get some sleep," Alex said to Lyssa.

"Ok."

She started to leave and came back. She hugged him.

"Thanks for not being a bastard," she whispered.

"Goodnight Lyssa," he chuckled.

"Goodnight Alex."

After she left, Frank hung up and turned to Alex, "The taxi will be here in a couple minutes."

"Thank you."

"You'd really take a bullet for her?" Frank asked.

"Who wouldn't?"

Frank laughed. "True."

"How long have you worked here Frank?"

"Seventeen years. Been on the five to one shift for two years. Pays extra and I got kids in college now."

Alex nodded. "Anyone strange been around lately?"

"Nope. Same people every day. Just the tenants and maybe their guests."

Alex pulled a business card out of his wallet. "Just in case someone unfamiliar comes around for Lyssa or if there's an emergency," he pushed it across the desk. "She's worth a lot to a lot of people."

Frank took the card. Alex was sure he'd probably throw it away but it was worth a shot.

"How long until the kids are out of college?"

"Three long years."

Alex chuckled. "You're a good man to work the five to one for them."

The taxi pulled up.

"Thanks for keeping watch here Frank," Alex shook his hand.

"And thanks for keeping watch out there," Frank smiled.

Alex left. Frank opened up the small card file they kept under the counter. Everything was digitized but he still liked to keep the paper handy in case the computers weren't working during an emergency. He flipped to WINFIELD, LYSSA - 303B - EMERGENCY CONTACTS.

"If Ms. Lyssa trusts you with her life, I think we can too."

Alex's card joined the other two that were already there. Bryan's and Chase's.

4

Martinelli's was an Italian restaurant opened in the late 80's by two brothers from Sicily. The atmosphere was bright and airy. The colorful cloth panels on the ceiling replicated the feeling of being under a canopy on the Italian countryside. The wine flowed freely and the patrons felt like family. Lyssa was quite happy to be out of the office.

"Have you ever eaten here before Lisa?"

"Lyssa," she patiently corrected her date. "And no I haven't. It's a very nice restaurant."

"My Aunt recommended it."

"Is she Italian?"

"No, she's Polish."

Lyssa waited, but no further explanation came for why Gerald's Polish Aunt recommended the Italian restaurant on which he decided to bring her on their third date.

"Did she recommend the combo platter too?"

"No. She hates Italian food."

By now none of this should have been a surprise. Their first two dates had been as frustratingly bizarre.

Lyssa decided to focus on the mural on the wall of an Italian vineyard, complete with grape pickers and donkeys pulling carts. She'd like to visit a real vineyard in Italy someday. Preferably with a more vivacious date. Or even just herself. Since that's kind of how it felt being on a date with Gerald.

Buzz buzz buzz…

"Is that your phone?" Gerald asked her, reaching for his own to be sure it wasn't him.

"Probably. Just ignore it."

"What if it's an emergency?"

"From whom?"

Gerald was stuck for an answer. Of course he had no idea who would call her as an emergency. Somewhere along the way he'd forgotten to ask about her family.

Buzz buzz buzz...

"Oh, for crying out loud," she mumbled, pulling it out of her purse. "I'll just turn it off and —"

The first buzzing was a missed call from Alex. The second was the text he sent.

Received another email. We need to talk.

"Forgive me Gerald. It's work. I'll just respond quickly."

"Be my guest."

I'll see you in the office Monday morning.

"There. Now we can —"

Buzz buzz buzz...

Her jaw clenched.

Now would be better.

I'm on a dinner date.

It's important.

So is dessert. And tonight I really want dessert. I deserve dessert!

She turned her phone off before waiting for the response.

"I'm sorry. He can be very demanding. He'll just have to learn that I'm not going to be at his beck and call."

"I can quite understand. You have strong work ethics but you don't want to be abused."

"Yes," she smiled, pleased he came to some realization about her personality that was spot-on.

"What do you do again?"

She swallowed back the exasperated sigh that had crawled up her throat and patiently explained her job to him. For the third time.

As she was explaining where she fell in the company hierarchy she noticed Alex walking in the door. She tried to convince herself that the quickening of her heartbeat was from the fact that he was probably going to interrupt her dinner date and had nothing to do with the faded jeans, black t-shirt and leather jacket he was wearing.

I managed to go the entire day without seeing him at work. Why did he have to show up now?

"Lyssa."

"Alex." She looked up, trying not to grumble as she greeted him, and failing miserably at it.

"I'm sorry to interrupt, but we have to talk."

"It can't wait?"

"No."

"Tomorrow. I'll come in tomorrow morning just to talk to you."

He stared at her. He was not going to go away.

"I'm in the middle of dinner."

He glanced over the table. He surmised everything about the date immediately.

"You're splitting a meal?"

"The combo platter is a lot of food," she patiently explained.

"I can see. It's probably a bargain per pound."

Lyssa was starting to glare.

"Best value in the city!" Gerald proudly stated. "Especially if you have the coupon."

Lyssa sighed. "Gerald, this is Alex. He works in the Security Department at Markison. We're working on a sensitive project right now and apparently something's happened that demands my immediate attention."

"Really? Sounds exciting."

Lyssa had never seen the accountant so animated before. This was the type of reaction she'd hoped for when she wore the sweetheart peek-a-boo red dress on their second date. Instead he'd looked like he was expecting lightning to strike him down whenever he even glanced at her cleavage. At least the guys that worked in valet parking had appreciated it when she walked by.

51

Not that they used the valet parking, of course.

Pay for that unnecessary expense?! Plus tipping??? The horrors!

"Please, have a seat," Gerald gestured.

"Oh, no. He doesn't really... oh dammit he is," she sighed heavily as Alex pulled over another chair from a nearby empty table. He removed his jacket and sat down.

"We have plenty of food," Gerald continued. "Breadstick?" He held up the basket.

"Thank you," Alex took one. "We got another email."

"Yay," she said, not particularly emotional about it either way.

"This time it mentioned the downfall of the 3200 M4," he referred to the most recent server they bought that was located in the main server room.

"So?"

"It mentioned Harley by name."

She shrugged, again not really caring.

"That's the department's nickname."

"Nickname for what?" Gerald asked, watching their conversation intently, as if it were a riveting episode of CSI.

"For the main programming server," Alex explained, apparently not concerned about Gerald hearing all this.

"We already expect the man stalking us has inside information," Lyssa continued. "And it is just a nickname. Knowing it doesn't give someone magical access to it."

"How do you know it's a man?" Gerald asked.

"The emails are unoriginal and tacky," Lyssa surmised. "Just like most men I know."

Apparently her explanation wasn't good enough because he looked to Alex for a better answer.

"There's a high-probability the threats are coming from a white American male. In his late 20's to mid-30's. Our beliefs stem from the verbiage and font choice used in the emails."

"What I said. They're boring."

"Doesn't mean they're any less real," he pointed out to her.

"And just because he knows the name of one of the servers doesn't mean I'm going to start freaking out. Which is probably what the emails were designed for in the first place."

Alex picked up Lyssa's extra fork and stabbed a couple ziti.

"Oh, just help yourself."

"I missed dinner," he muttered by way of explanation. "This is excellent." Looking back at the bar area, he yelled out, "Questo ziti è fantastico! Proprio come mamma!"

He received a rousing cheer and toasts from the elderly men sitting around the bar. For a quiet intimidating guy, Alex certainly knew how to charm people when necessary. Apparently tonight it was necessary to charm her date and the entire bar of an Italian restaurant.

Why me? Actually, I think the question here is why not me?

"We should get you a plate," Gerald looked around for the waiter.

"Here." Lyssa pushed her plate over to him. "I've lost my appetite."

As Alex proceeded to slice up a huge meatball, the bartender brought over aperitifs.

"I didn't order this." Gerald was suddenly concerned.

"It's on the house," the bartender explained.

Alex raised his glass. Lyssa followed suit. Gerald sniffed his first, then toasted with them.

"Salut."

Alex and Lyssa downed theirs in one shot. Gerald barely took a lick.

"Licorice," he grimaced. Detesting it, he set it back on the table.

"Well, don't want to waste it."

Lyssa picked up his glass and downed that too.

"Quite practical, my dear!"

Gerald was actually proud of her. Alex was proud too, but

only because it was a very strong drink.

While the guys continued to talk about the problem Lyssa also polished off her glass of wine. The waiter came over to see if she wanted a refill.

"Oh no. I wouldn't want to blow the budget," she said.

The waiter smiled at her understandingly. So many times he'd seen this. A cheap bastard on a date with a beautiful woman who was slowly losing her interest and her respect.

The introduction of the third wheel to the dinner date was new though. Usually when a second man showed up it was the boring, jilted husband looking for the handsome rogue his wife was cheating on him with and then a fight would ensue. This was completely backwards.

"Club soda and lime please," Alex ordered.

As Gerald jabbered on about some embezzlement case he'd helped the police with years ago, Lyssa noticed the edge of Alex's shirt sleeve was flipped up. She reached over and flipped it back down, then brushed it off to make sure it was flat over his firm bicep.

He glanced over at her and noticed she was just moving absent-mindedly. He couldn't tell if it was the liquor setting in or Gerald's story that was turning her into a zombie. Either way he kind of liked that she was relaxed enough around him to be this way.

Then he looked back at Gerald. He wasn't a bad looking guy. He was no Cary Grant, but he could be Cary Grant's accountant. He actually looked like a young Bob Hope, but with a much less pointed nose.

When Gerald started asking questions about Alex's investigation that's when Lyssa woke up.

"Ok," Lyssa tossed her napkin onto the table. "I think I've had enough fun for this evening. You boys enjoy your date."

She picked up her purse and stood.

"You're leaving before dessert?" Alex asked.

"Are you kidding? I'm not having a three-way with a piece of key lime pie."

"Not here," Gerald shook his head. "They don't have it. I hear the chocolate cake is good though. Really big slices."

"You were really talking about dessert, weren't you?" Alex suddenly realized. "I thought it was a euphemism."

"Goodbye Gerald. Alex," she said between grit teeth.

She walked away. Gerald turned to watch.

"She does have a lovely behind."

Alex was a bit surprised. He wasn't expecting that from the accountant who seemed almost oblivious to her presence.

"This is wrong," Alex admitted and set down his fork. "Let me fix this. Lyssa! Wait!"

Suddenly loud shots echoed through the restaurant and one of the windows near the door broke. Pains of glass shattered and fell to the floor. Lyssa's hand jerked back from the front door handle, reaching for her left shoulder. The pain in her face was obvious.

Alex sprang into action, bolting from his chair. Running to Lyssa, he carefully pulled her down to the floor on the far side of the bar, pulling her out of view of the front windows.

"Ow," she whimpered.

"Let me see," he carefully pulled her hand away.

Her shoulder and palm were pink. Bright pink.

"Paint?" he guessed.

"Gross," she muttered.

"It's on the windows too," the bartender nearby pointed out.

Shots that hit unbroken windows dribbled pink paint down the glass. The one that hit Lyssa must have come thru the front door when she opened it.

"Stay with her," Alex told the bartender and took off out the door.

"Wow," Gerald could only stare from the table.

Within ten minutes Alex was back with a paintball gun in hand. The owners of the restaurant were sitting in the bar area with Lyssa. Unlike earlier that evening, she was very relieved to see him walk through the door. She'd attempted to clean up. The pink paint was now a purple stain on her light blue dress.

Alex took a moment to catch his breath, then said, "Anyone know Tony P?"

He set the gun on the bar. Etched into the barrel was the name. It was obviously scratched in there by an amateur using a small knife.

The owners faces contorted to reveal that they did indeed know Tony P.

"That little sonuvabitch!"

The fatter and older of the two threw his napkin on the table with rage. The younger and thinner Martinelli brother started cursing in Italian.

"It was a local kid?" Lyssa asked Alex.

He nodded. "Quick little bastard too. I nearly had him at one point. I gave up when he ditched the gun."

"Should we call the police or something?" Gerald asked from his uncomfortable spot near Lyssa. "Someone could have gotten seriously hurt. Not to mention the property damage!"

"I think the brothers can handle this," Alex pointed out, knowing enough not to interfere with justice in an Italian neighborhood. And besides, it was a kid. Maybe fourteen or fifteen. He was going to catch enough hell from the brothers, his parents, and probably half the block.

Lyssa downed her gin and tonic, then handed the leather jacket draped across her lap back to Alex.

"Thanks Lyss," he said quietly, slipping it on.

"Thank you Frederico. Martino." Lyssa kissed each owner on the cheek.

"Please see that this flower gets home safely," Frederico asked of Alex.

"I will."

The waiter came out with a take-out bag.

"Thank you," Lyssa smiled at him. "You can give that to the big intimidating guy."

"Of course," he smiled back at her.

She'd been a wonderful, calm and understanding customer. He secretly wondered when she relayed this evening to her friends which part would be the worst. The cheap date, the frustrating interruption of the man she secretly but so obviously cared for, or getting hit by a paintball.

As Lyssa left Gerald followed right behind her. Alex turned to get the bag from the waiter, who said to him quickly and quietly, "She put back two drinks while you were gone. Just letting you know."

Alex nodded to him. "Got it. Thanks."

At the curb, Lyssa was hailing a cab. Gerald was trying to convince her not to.

"I can take you home Lisa."

She didn't bother to correct him this time. The booze was setting in along with the feeling of hopelessness for this situation.

"It'll save you money."

"I don't need to save my money Gerald. Especially since Frederico and Martino comped everything."

"Lyssa," Alex started. She looked over at him. "You ok?"

She nodded.

"Does it hurt?"

She shrugged. "It's not so bad."

"A little scary maybe?"

"It was just a paintball."

"Well, you must be braver than me then, because for a moment it wasn't and it scared the shit out of me."

"I'm fine," she gave him a little smile, making him smile back.

As much as she wanted to hate him, his heroics made up for

it. All the time he was gone chasing after the assailant she was a nervous wreck waiting for him to get back.

A taxi pulled up to the curb. Alex opened the door for her.

"Here's your food," Alex gestured to the bag after she'd seated herself.

She glanced up at him. "It's for you."

Alex handed the bag to Gerald to hold and leaned down to talk to the cabbie. He pulled out a twenty, at least ten more than the meter would read at the end of the ride, and handed it to him.

"Take her to Bay Front Apartments. Make sure she gets in safely."

"Yes sir," the cabbie nodded back to him.

"Thank you Al," he read the driver's name from the taxi license.

The cab pulled away from the curb.

"Gerald, let me give you a bit of advice," Alex turned to him, taking back the bag. "Next time let the lady order her dinner first. And let her order anything and everything she wants."

Alex propped the take-out bag in one hand and opened it with the other. Inside the Styrofoam container were noodles with roasted peppers, artichokes, and squid in a lemon-pepper-garlic sauce.

"Wow. That looks very rich," Gerald grimaced. Alex wasn't sure if he was referring to the detriment it would cause his stomach or wallet. Probably both.

Alex pulled out a squid ring and popped it into his mouth. He savored every bite. He offered some to Gerald, who took a pepper to be polite.

"Oh my," he was surprised.

"Yes. The lady knows her food. And she's worth every penny."

He bid Gerald goodnight and headed to his ride, which if it wasn't his Ninja motorcycle he would have taken Lyssa home himself. Along the way he pulled out his phone, scrolled through the contacts to find the name he'd only entered into it a couple days ago, and hit the Call button.

"Bay Front Apartments," a familiar voice answered soon on the other end.

"Is this Frank the hardest working security guard in the city?"

The deep bellowing laugh in response confirmed it. "I don't know about hardest, but I'm definitely working."

"This is Alex Dane. Lyssa Winfield will be arriving by taxi shortly and if you could be so kind as to meet her at the door it'd be most appreciated."

"Of course."

"She had a disappointing night and might need a steady arm to hold onto."

"I fully understand sir," he said with a sympathetic voice. This was the voice of a man who knew all too well how disappointing her nights could be. Alex wondered from how many shitty dates she stumbled thru his doors after.

"Thanks. I'd have done it myself, but she's none too happy with me right now too."

"I'm sure deep down that Ms. Lyssa appreciates you very much. It just wouldn't be right for her to show it."

Yes, this man understood a lot about their situation. Probably more than they did right now.

"I hope so Frank, because I have a feeling this is only the beginning."

5

Lyssa was sitting behind her desk when Alex tapped twice on the doorjamb. Looking up, she spied the handsome bodyguard resting against the doorway sporting a sexy smile. Despite the fact that he was damn near irresistible she wanted to slap the ego off his face.

"You look deep in thought."

"Someone's gotta work around here," she responded and turned her eyes back to the laptop monitor.

Alex walked over while taking off his jacket and tie, tossing them into one of the chairs.

"About Friday night..." he started.

"What about it?"

"Why?"

"Why what?"

"Gerald."

"He's a nice man."

"Boring."

"Perfect for me."

"Until this is over you can't see him anymore."

"Excuse me? I will see whomever I want."

He shook his head.

"And since when are you in charge of me?"

"Since our esteemed CEO, the brilliant Bryan Markison, made me your boss."

"He would never!"

He nodded, smirking like the devil himself. She stood to file the folder of papers she was done with.

"I would quit before I'd work for you."

"Admit it. You need me."

She closed the drawer and walked over to him, her arms folded in front of her chest in a show of defiance.

"I need no one."

"I would rather not be in this position, trust me. I liked my job. International spy for a millionaire. Now I'm stuck here. Babysitting you."

He reached up and brushed her hair from her neck, looking her over like he was inspecting cattle.

"At least I'm getting a little entertainment value out of you."

He pulled on her crossed arms with one finger and they magically fell to her sides. She tried to remain resolute in her stance which she could feel herself crumbling away under his long, hard gaze.

"Perhaps you can convince your rich buddy this is nothing more than a scare tactic and you can go back to Tahiti or Venice or whatever foreign land you'd prefer to be dragging your balls through."

He quickly wrapped his arm around her waist to her back and pulled her sharply against him.

"Why do that when I can have you right here?"

Reaching behind her, he swept his arm, wiping everything off the desk. The tablet, the laptop, the cellphone, the landline phone, the pager, the stapler, the chunky electric ten key calculator that was currently out of paper, the pencil holder cup, the paper clip receptacle, the sticky notes, the other cellphone. Even the cheap plastic Niagara Falls snow globe her Uncle Flannery gave her for Saint Patrick's Day thirteen years ago in which half the water had mysteriously evaporated.

"The Maid of the Mist!" she gasped as it went flying off the end of the desk with the rest of her office supplies.

With his other arm, he hoisted her up to sit on the edge of the desk.

"I will have you," he growled and kissed her forcefully.

He slipped off his shirt and it just seemed to float away on a mysterious breeze.

"Oh Alex," she panted, wrapping her legs around his waist. "You make me so hot down there."

"Oh yeah baby," he growled again, pushing himself against her. "Beg me. I want you to beg me."

"Take me Alex."

"Louder."

"Take me! Take me right here! I want to feel your beautiful love stick between my lady thighs!"

"Oh yeah! I got what you need and I'm coming for you... heathen sex goddess!"

"... and then I woke up."

"Holy Shiva," Val's jaw hung in shock.

"I know! It's like a really bad romance novel! I mean, whose shirt just floats away on a mysterious breeze? Even if the office is on the sixteenth floor it's not like the windows open. If they did the breeze wouldn't be mysterious. It would be gale force."

"You need to patent the term beautiful love stick."

"It's better than Game of Hearts."

"You should call it Heathen Sex Goddess!"

"Misleading, but it would definitely sell more games."

"And you've been dreaming this for how long?"

"Four nights. In a row. Ever since that hideous date with Gerald. And each night it gets longer and longer. At this rate he'll have me naked by next week and screaming his name by Arbor Day."

"When is Arbor Day?"

"I don't know. Does it really matter?"

Val pondered this briefly. "Nah. I wish I could have dreams like that!"

"I wish you would! I don't want them."

"You don't?"

"No. He's an ass."

"He is?"

"In my dreams."

"He's not in real life though?"

"No, not really. I mean, he was a little on date night, but… ok, I really don't have any idea what that was about."

"All those drinks you still didn't sleep with him?"

"No. Wait, you're still talking about Alex right?"

"Of course."

"No, I didn't."

"And Gerald?"

Lyssa reached over and lightly slapped Val's cheek.

"Ok, that's a no. But you're going to in your dreams, right? Still talking about Alex."

"Yeah. It looks like it."

"In your dreams, where he's an ass."

"Yes."

"Let me get this straight, the really nice, hot guy you crave in real life you're sleeping with only in your dreams where he's a douche."

She nodded.

"That's screwed up," Val drained her wine glass and poured another.

"The strangest thing about it all is the part that bothers me the most is that I don't have a filing cabinet in my office."

"That's the strangest part?"

"What do you think it all means?"

"Stop eating ice cream before bed."

Lyssa pondered this. "You're probably right."

"Here's to lady thighs!"

They toasted.

"You know, your stories are getting to be part of my weekly rotation. You're going to become my regular Tuesday night slot."

"I beat out the biter for your slot, great."

Val laughed. "So, have you told him about the dreams?"

"Alex? No! Are you crazy?"

"He might be flattered."

"I don't think so. He doesn't seem the type. Besides, I haven't even seen him since Friday night."

"I thought he was your bodyguard."

"No. That's a joke. Kind of. He's a bodyguard for the project, which means he follows me around sometimes. Mostly to meetings and stuff. I don't know what he's been up to this week. And I've been trying to secure the music for the game."

"I still think you should tell him."

"He already thinks I'm weird and pathetic. Why make it worse?"

"Why would he think that?"

"Because I'm weird and pathetic."

"Oh stop! You're not! You're just lonely... and picky... and... ok, Gerald was a little pathetic."

"Gah! You set me up with him!"

"I know. I was just trying to get rid of him. I didn't think it'd get past the first date."

"Get rid of him? Did you date him?!"

"Um, didn't I mention that?" She suddenly wished she hadn't brought up his name.

"Oh, my God! Did you sleep with him?"

"No! Well, wait a minute. Does a hand job count?"

Lyssa's eyes widened so much it was a wonder her eyeballs didn't fall out of their sockets.

Val laughed. "I'm kidding!"

"Did you?" she demanded.

"No! I was only kidding! Seriously, do you think he would have let me? Come on!"

"I guess not," she relented.

"Actually, I think he's gay."

"Great," Lyssa grumbled.

"The man would have to be to deny you in the red dress.

Hell, I wouldn't deny you in the red dress and I'm not a lesbian."

"Yet."

"True. Well, don't worry. Gerald is in the past. I'm sure you'll never have to see him again."

6

"Lisa—"

"Lyssa."

"Thank you for taking time out of your busy day to see me."

"That's no problem Gerald. I'm quite surprised you called to visit. I was pretty sure you had no idea where I worked."

"Of course I know where you work! You work with Alex."

"Oh yes. How could I forget."

"I won't take but a moment of your time. I just wanted to thank you for being a wonderful, beautiful, and patient woman. I know you were saving yourself for a stronger commitment."

"I was?"

"But I'm afraid I can't give you the type of future you're looking for."

"That's very likely true."

"Alex has made me think."

"Oh, fantastic."

"Alex is a man of action. He lives in the here and now and he doesn't wait for life to find him. He creates life!"

"You mean drama."

"I've decided I want to be like Alex."

"No you don't."

"I've successfully broken the lease on my apartment and sold my collection of rare Precious Moments figurines. Monty's always admired and wanted them. I marked the collection up ten percent and he paid it! A foolish move on his part, but if he can't be bothered to keep up with the market value prices, then—"

"Gerald!" she interrupted, her patience growing thin. "Why did you sell everything?"

"I've enrolled in Stanford."

She stared at him.

"I'm going back to school to be an archaeologist!"

"A what?"

"An archaeologist. It's what I've always wanted to be, but I was too afraid. Alex has taught me to not be afraid."

"But you're allergic to dirt."

"A minor technicality."

"You got a rash when you brought me flowers from Costco. And those were wrapped in plastic. And fifty percent off."

"I just need to build up my tolerance, that's all."

She stared at him blankly.

"You don't believe in me, do you?"

"It's just that you're kind of..."

She looked at Gerald and the little glimmer of excitement and hope in his eyes started to fade. This was the first time he'd shown any kind of emotional reaction to her. And it was going to be a disappointing one.

"You're kind of a nice guy and I hate to see you go," she smiled to him. "I have no doubt that you'll be a fantastic archaeologist."

"Really?"

"Of course! You're a natural-born digger."

"I am one helluva auditor," he grinned proudly.

She saw him to the door. To her dismay, Alex was standing at Marlene's desk. She hadn't seen him since the last time she was with Gerald.

His timing is impeccable.

"Alex!" Gerald burst out as soon as he spotted him. "I'm so glad to run into you. I want to thank you."

"What for?"

"For inspiring me."

Gerald explained his future plans to him quickly, which was completely futile since Alex already knew everything. He'd spent most of Saturday tailing Gerald and casing his apartment. He'd listened in on all his cellphone conversations with Monty and his landlord Phil. He went through his entire internet history, which was as boring as his apartment's stark-white walls. Alex figured he'd have at least one closet fetish, especially after his confession the night before about the view of Lyssa's buttocks. But he had none.

Just for fun Alex did a Google image search for "nice asses" while he was there. Even with the Safe Search set to Strict it still returned some nice photos. In his mind the computer thanked him for it.

Alex briefly wondered how pissed Lyssa would be if she knew he had spied on Gerald. It was possible the accountant was actually a criminal mastermind who was posing as a clueless, unassuming schmuck on his dates with Lyssa just to get information out of her.

But he wasn't. He was truly a schmuck.

"Take care of our girl for me." Gerald shook his hand.

"I'm trying to."

Lyssa swore he was snickering when he said it. Marlene definitely was.

"Goodbye Lisa."

Gerald kissed her politely on the cheek then left.

"Lisa?" Marlene looked up at her boss. "What the hell?"

"I have a conference call with Buffalo at two," Lyssa said to her. "Hold all calls and visitors."

"Ok, but what just—"

"I'm sure Alex will enjoy telling you all about it and then you can bring the entire building up to date. I'd be surprised if I didn't get an email by four from someone asking where they can find the goddamn coupon."

She stepped into her office, closed her door loudly, and snapped the lock.

"I would never," Marlene spit.

She looked up to find Alex staring at her accusingly.

"Not on purpose," she added sadly.

"Why does she date guys like Gerald anyway?"

"She once told me that dating assholes is worse. I can't argue with that."

"But what does she expect from him?"

She looked up at him. "I'm starting to think we're related."

Alex cocked his eyebrow at her. It was a disturbing thought.

Marlene pulled up an email for him to see.

From: Marlene B.
To: Lyssa W.
Subject: dinner
do you want to come for dinner friday?

From: Lyssa W.
To: Marlene B.
Subject: Re:dinner
I'm sorry, but I have a date with Gerald.

From: Marlene B.
To: Lyssa W.
Subject: Re:Re:dinner
ok but tommy will be crushed. he loves his aunt lyssie! why do you date gerald anyway. i know he's not an asshole but you said he's kind of boring. what do you expect from him that's any better.

From: Lyssa W.
To: Marlene B.
Subject: Re:Re:Re:dinner
If I'm lucky I'll get my own dessert. If I'm not lucky, well, Louie's Bakery is open until nine and they're used to seeing me by now. And goodnight kisses are heavily overrated. Probably. Either way, he's about the only thing in my life not work related. Nor does he give a shit about video games. He's <u>completely</u> unattached.

"Marlene?"

"Yeah?"

"We're just gonna pretend today didn't happen, ok?"

"Fine by me. I'd rather just forget it myself."

* * * * *

It was late, after nine, when Alex returned to Lyssa's office. He knew she was still there. He knew when she passed thru security. He knew when she logged into her computer. He even knew the GPS location of her phone. She wasn't going anywhere without him knowing about it.

So when he knocked on her door he was kind of surprised that she didn't answer. He carefully opened it in case she'd taken an impromptu nap on her sofa, but her office was empty.

Doing a quick sweep, he noticed her PC monitor was off, but her purse was sitting in the chair. She would be back, so he waited, passing the time by looking out the window over the business district at night.

It was only a couple minutes later when he heard footsteps enter the room and stop.

"Hello Alex."

"Hi Lyss," he turned to her. "This is kind of late even for you, isn't it?"

"I'm doing a little catch-up, that's all. It's quite normal."

He nodded. "About Friday night-- "

"I'd rather not talk about it," she interrupted quietly, praying this wasn't another dream.

"What I did was rude and unprofessional," he soldiered forth anyway, determined to say what he'd avoided for days. "I had no right to intrude like that. My only excuse is that I was concerned."

"You don't have to worry so much. The project will be fine."

"I know. My concern was for you."

She looked up at him, a little surprised.

"I take threats against your life very personal. Job hazard."

"You should know by now that my life is an endless stream of minor irritations and disappointments frequented by moments of brilliance that make Markison millions of dollars. That's all it is."

He stuffed his hands in his pockets. She loved the relaxed office look on him. The loose tie. The turned up shirt cuffs. The collar unbuttoned just enough to give her a glimpse of his undershirt.

"I'm sorry for what I added to it."

"You don't add to it. You do have an uncanny ability of pointing it out though. Make it a lot more obvious. My life seemed a lot less pathetic before you came along."

"That was never my intention. I'm sorry Lys--"

In a move that would have HR reaching for the pink slips, Lyssa put her fingers up to his lips to stop him. He closed his mouth and she pulled her hand away, letting it come to rest on his arm. His cotton dress shirt was cool to the touch.

"You don't have to apologize for that."

Alex reached up and brushed her hair from her neck. His fingers started to wrap around the nape, turning her face up to him, drawing her closer until—

I WANT TO FUCK YOU LIKE AN ANIMAL! I WANT TO FEEL YOU FROM THE INSIDE!

"Chase," Alex grumbled, backing up to take the ringing phone out of his pocket.

Lyssa laughed a little nervously and moved over to pick up her purse which put some much needed space between them at the moment.

"He picks his own ringtone, I swear," he assured her.

"Oh, I know. He puts it on mine too."

"Yeah," he answered, annoyed at having to do so. "No... No... Ok... Good luck."

He hung up and slipped the phone back into his pocket. He

took it out again.

"Where is that song again?" he mumbled, fighting with his phone.

"Let me."

Lyssa carefully took the phone from him and found the song immediately.

"Deleted," she announced, handing the phone back to him.

"For a while," he shook his head.

Tucking her purse up onto her shoulder, Lyssa walked out of her office. Alex followed, turning off the lights on his way by.

On the way to the elevator...

"I know he doesn't show it well, but Gerald does like you."

"How can you tell? You only met him briefly. Or is that one of your many secret agent talents?"

"It is, but he said you have a nice ass. Or as he put it, a lovely behind."

"You're lying!"

"I don't—"

"Lying! Kidding! Whatever!"

"I'm not though. That's what he said. He liked to watch you walk away."

"Well, he saw that enough."

She pushed the button to retrieve the elevator.

"Maybe that was his plan," Alex surmised. "Upsetting you so he could keep watching your curves swaying back and forth as you left."

"I don't think Gerald has a plan that doesn't involve a 401K or a spreadsheet."

Alex snorted. "Probably not."

The elevator arrived. Despite the fact that he was going back up to the penthouse suites, he rode with her to the parking garage.

"You don't have to keep following me."

"I know, but I happen to like watching your lovely behind also."

She looked up at him.

"You didn't hear that," he mumbled.

She giggled; he laughed.

The elevator stopped at E2 where she was parked in her designated space very near the elevator. Normally she wouldn't have one, but given the lateness of the hours she put in, security assigned her one. It was a small perk to the position that she didn't argue with. She hated the parking garage. It was kind of creepy. The sooner she could be in her car and out of there the better.

Except maybe tonight...

"I can't believe you drive a Civic," Alex commented as he walked her over to her little silver car.

"Why not?"

"This is the exact same car I drive when I'm working undercover. It's the most common car in the world and completely non-descript. I would have expected you to stand out from the crowd a little more. You strike me as a Porsche girl."

"I like Porsches. And Benzs. And Beemers. And Ferraris. But honestly, for as much time as I spend in my car, the Civic is perfect. It's quite comfy actually."

"True."

"I'm not really as high-maintenance as you might think. I just happen to buy what I like. I like my Coach wallet and my Michael Kors bags. My shoes today are from Marshalls and my underwear from Kohl's. Sometimes I happen to like the expensive things. Sometimes I don't.

"And before you assume, no, I didn't like Gerald the way you're thinking. He was just a guy that I could go to dinner with. Yes, he was clueless, but he was also harmless. Most importantly, he didn't have any expectations of me."

Alex shrugged. "He seemed nice enough."

"Do you know what my biggest problem with Gerald was?"

He shook his head.

"He liked you better."

Alex laughed.

"Thanks for walking me to my car." She pulled out her car keys.

"Do you forgive me?"

"Of course," she smiled.

"I owe you a very nice Italian dinner."

"I've always wanted to dine outside at Da Gianni Cacio e Pepe."

"I'm not familiar with it. Where is it?"

"Rome."

He chuckled.

"Do me a favor?" she asked.

"What's that?"

"If you want to see my lovely behind, just ask. You don't have to piss me off."

He leaned forward and kissed her lightly on the cheek, close to her mouth.

"Goodnight Lyssa."

"Goodnight Alex."

Blushing, she fumbled with her key fob to get in her car. Eventually she got the door open and climbed in. Alex started to meander back to the elevator, a smirk on his face he couldn't remove with a crowbar. He pushed the button to recall the elevator and took a moment to reflect on the past week.

He was fooling himself about last Friday night. He didn't go there out of concern over the email. He went there to see what kind of man she would date.

Gerald was a safe man. A man that wouldn't break her heart. A man that didn't expect anything more from her than a little dinner conversation.

Focus, Dane. Focus. There's a bigger mission at risk here.

No sooner had the words passed through his brain then he heard the crunching of wheels against the pavement behind him. He turned just in time to see the back of Lyssa's car get clipped by the front end of a '68 Impala.

And now it was coming straight at him.

"Oh shit."

At the last second Alex jumped up and landed on the hood as the car smashed into the wall and elevator doors. There was a horrifying screeching sound as the elevator, trying to reach its destination, was cut off by the inwardly damaged doors. This set off an alarm.

Ignoring the stinging from where his forehead hit the windshield, Alex pushed himself off the car. Lyssa was already out of hers and headed for him.

He held up his hand for her to stop. Surprisingly, she obeyed.

He knew they were in one of three possible situations. The driver was either just a terrible driver, dead at the wheel, or an assailant. Possibly the one that sent the emails. Readying himself, he yanked open the car door and was met with a fourth scenario he hadn't counted on.

There was no one in the car.

Alex's attention turned to where the car had come from. It was dark on the ramp that led to the deck above them. He would have crept up the side to surprise anyone up there, but he had to secure Lyssa's safety first.

"Get your purse," he said to her quietly.

While she retrieved it from the car, he stood vigilant, watching from all directions.

"Do you have your laptop or anything else from work?" he asked when she joined him.

"No."

"How about personal items?"

"Just my yoga gear in the trunk."

"Leave it."

Steering her towards the stairwell, he looked in first, then finding it clear, ushered her through the door. They hurried up the two flights to the ground level where they found security quite active.

"One of the elevators is reporting a malfunction," the night security manager said to Alex.

"I know. A car drove into it."

"A car did wha—" he paused. "You're injured Mr. Dane."

"It's nothing," he instinctively put his hand on his forehead and winced. He'd scraped it pretty good where it skidded over the edge of the windshield. "It looks like a runaway car in the parking garage. It hit the tail end of Lyssa's car then tried to run me over."

"Are you injured Ms. Winfield?"

"No," she shook her head.

The security manager ordered his men to secure the parking garage then he taped an Out Of Order sign to the front of the dysfunctional elevator.

"Are you sure you're ok?" Alex asked Lyssa as they sat on one of the lobby sofas.

"Yes. I didn't really hit anything. Just shook me up a bit."

Alex took out his phone and made a call.

"Where are you?... There was an accident in the parking garage. Lyssa's car was damaged... Yeah, everyone's fine... Thanks."

He hung up.

"Bill McLean is on his way. I work with him in security. I have to stay here so I'm gonna have him take you home."

"I can take a taxi," she offered.

"I'm not taking any chances tonight."

"You should do something about that," she pointed to his forehead.

He took her hand in his and rubbed the back of it. She may have said she was ok, but she was shaking.

"The fire department will be here soon. I'll get something from them to put on it. In the meantime... "

He slid down closer to her, wrapping his arm around her

shoulder to comfort her.

"Do you think it was him?" she asked quietly.

"I don't know. I don't really think it was a runaway car though."

That wasn't helping her nerves any.

"Bet you wish I was a lying bastard right now."

"No," she rested her head against his shoulder. "I wouldn't change you."

The alarm triggered a lot of things, including fire and police. The security manager greeted all of them.

"The camera's show there was no one in the elevator at the time of the accident," he reported. "Mr. Dane and Ms. Winfield were witnesses to the accident."

The police came over to collect some details. The EMT's followed, looking for someone to treat, and found Alex, who only needed some antibiotic cream and a Band-Aid.

Shortly after all that a large, brown-haired, clean-shaven man came rushing into the lobby.

"Jesus Dane. Did you try to stop the car with your face?"

"Pretty much."

Alex introduced Bill to Lyssa, then gave him an even shorter version of what happened.

"Can you take Lyssa home?" Alex asked him in the end.

"Of course."

"I have to stay here," he turned to Lyssa. "But if you need anything, call me."

"Ok."

She started to leave with Bill and looked back just before passing through the lobby doors. Alex gave her a smile and a little wave. She waved back.

"Don't worry," Bill said, noticing the exchange and worried look on her face. "We don't call him The Great Dane for nothing."

7

"Hey! Wonder Woman!"

"Yes, Hulk?" Lyssa replied without even having to look up to know it was Chase standing in her office door.

"Lunch?"

"I'm vaguely aware of it. It's a meal. Usually during the middle of the day."

"I take it that means you haven't had any."

"Your powers of deduction are improving."

"If you promise to stop being a little bitch, I'll treat you to some."

She raised her eyes to him.

"Pleeeeeeeeeeeeeeease!"

"Why?" she asked and went back to working.

"Because I want lunch and I don't want to eat alone with Marshall Spitzer."

"With who?"

"Mia Shistel."

She looked up at him finally, starting to get annoyed.

"My sister, ok?" he confessed. "I'm having lunch with my sister."

"Ha! Good luck!"

"Please come."

"No."

"Why not?" he whined.

"Because last time I went to lunch with you and Trixie I spent the entire afternoon fielding emails, texts and phone calls from everyone who saw us in the cafeteria wanting to know if I could fix them up with her."

"It'll be different this time around."

"How's that?"

"I made her promise to wear clothes."

"No. I'm still not going."

"I'll pay you."

"Not enough."

He sighed heavily. "You know, I didn't want to have to do this, but you leave me no choice."

She looked up at him, suspect. He pulled out his phone and showed her a photo on it. She gasped.

"A rare maroon leather Gucci purse. From 1970-something. I don't know exactly, but it's old and smelly and I know where it is."

"You blackmailer!"

"So let's try this again." He took a deep breath. "Lunch?" He wiggled the picture on the phone at her.

"I'd love to." She gave him a smile that bordered on evil.

"Great. And just to be nice, I won't even make you go to the cafeteria with us. We're going to eat upstairs."

"A slight improvement."

She closed up shop and grabbed her planner, tablet and purse. She still wouldn't leave her office without them.

"You're impossible sometimes," Chase sighed.

"Yep!" she proudly agreed.

When Chase said upstairs, he meant all the way to the very top, to the glass-enclosed pool patio on the roof.

"How is Alex doing today?" she asked.

"You can ask him yourself."

She noticed someone swimming in the pool and immediately deduced who it was.

"Doc ordered your boy to take the day off," Chase explained. "I thought having lunch up here would be a good way to help him behave for a change."

"I take it he doesn't follow doctor's orders often."

Chase snorted. "Try never."

Alex climbed out of the pool and Lyssa nearly fainted. He was wearing nothing but dark blue Speedos and a smile. His chest was chiseled and to her surprise he did have some chest hair. Not quite like Tom Selleck's manly chest full of curly goodness circa *Magnum PI*, but definitely more than none. It was very short though. She briefly wondered if he used his goatee trimmer on it.

"This is a surprise," he said, grabbing his towel from the nearby lounge chair. He was talking to Lyssa, but Chase responded.

"I told you we'd be up for lunch."

"At one. It's twelve-thirty. You're never early."

"I'm always on time. It's Trixie that's always late. That's why I told her noon. She thinks she's running a half-hour late. They just let her through security now, so she'll be up here in a couple minutes."

"Nice trunks," Lyssa picked on him.

He wrapped his towel around his waist. "I only wear them when I'm doing laps. They're not for the beach."

"I can't see you at a beach."

"Really? Get your suit and let's go."

"I don't have a suit," she was forced to admit.

"Ah, nudist. I should have known."

"No!" she playfully slapped him on the arm. He laughed at her. "Oh dammit. I was trying to get through the day without hitting anyone."

"You'll have to try again tomorrow."

"I guess so."

"Oh, my God!" a shrill voice echoed through the glass dome. "Is Alex smiling?!"

"Yes Trixie," Alex rolled his eyes. "It does happen occasionally."

As if Lyssa weren't already feeling overdressed in her blouse and slacks, Trixie came bouncing in wearing a very short spaghetti-strap sundress. In her hand was the rare, maroon leather Gucci purse. It was her photo that Chase had shown her.

"I told you I knew where it was," he smiled to her painfully, as if he were fully expecting her to kick him in the balls.

"God, I hate you so much," Lyssa smiled up at him, grabbing him by the cheeks like his grandmother used to do when he was a kid. But Lyssa's hurt more. A lot more.

Chase looked over at Alex, who was starting to glare. Now he had two people pissed at him.

"I'd hug you, but you're wet," Trixie curled up her nose at Alex.

He picked her up in his arms anyway, making her scream.

"I missed you Trix!" he laughed.

"You bastard!"

She slapped at him until he put her down. Lyssa barely contained her claws.

"This is not going well," Chase muttered just loud enough for Lyssa to hear. He rubbed his forehead in frustration.

"I'm going to get changed," Alex headed over to the changing rooms.

"Gross," Trixie fluffed out her dress, or what little of it there was, hoping to dry it off.

"Hey Trixie," Chase began. "You remember Lyssa, right?"

"Of course!" Trixie's face lit up again. "The only other person you know with good taste!" She held up her purse.

"Very nice," Lyssa noted with a smile that Chase couldn't tell was put on or not. In truth, it was a little of both.

"It was a birthday present from Bryan. Is he coming to lunch?"

"No," Chase answered. "He has a meeting with...um, someone. Don't remember who."

"It's always someone," Trixie pouted.

"Being a millionaire is hard work."

She huffed.

They sat around the lunch table as the private waitress came out to serve them.

Alex returned shortly in his grey/black warm-up suit that he often traveled in around the penthouse to-and-from the pool and workout center. The man looked good in everything.

They sat down to lunch.

"How are you feeling today?" Lyssa asked Alex.

"A little sore, but I'm okay. You?"

"Fine," she smiled.

"What happened?" Trixie asked, noticing the large Band-Aid on his forehead.

"Got hit by a car."

"Hit by a car?!" she squawked and it echoed painfully through the large room.

"Trix," Chase grimaced. "Dome. Loud."

"Sorry," she whispered.

Alex gave her a brief explanation of what happened. He conveniently left out the details of whom they suspected might have done it and why.

"Are you ok?" Trixie asked Lyssa.

She nodded. "It didn't hit me too bad. My little Civic is pretty durable."

"You drive a Civic?" Chase looked up, surprised by that.

"Yes."

"Huh," he pondered it.

"What?" she was starting to glare.

"Nothing," he threw up his hands in surrender. "Nothing at all."

"There's nothing wrong with a Civic."

"I didn't say there was!"

"I would have picked you for a Porsche," Trixie said, not realizing she really shouldn't have. Trixie doesn't realize a lot of things until it's too late.

Lyssa slowly looked over at the man snickering next to her. Alex showed no fear in his smirk.

"The Civic suits her perfectly," he said, hoping to save

himself from the pain of the slap that was brewing.

"Short and cute?" Trixie guessed.

"I'm not short," Lyssa pointed out, but imagined how someone who wore four inch hooker shoes might think she was. In their stocking feet Lyssa was actually two inches taller than Trixie.

"She's good on gas," Chase joked.

Without hesitation, Lyssa launched the cherry tomato off her fork. It bounced off his chest and landed in his lap.

"Dammit," he muttered. "There's vinegar and oil on my pants now."

Alex was still snickering. Lyssa reloaded her fork with more salad toppings, preparing to assault him as well.

"I meant it's silver and it sparkles," he quickly explained. "Like your eyes."

Lyssa pondered this, determined it was good, and ate the contents on her fork.

"The backend view is a little damaged though," he added like a smart ass.

She started to reach her fork back into the salad and he swapped the bowls, leaving her with his empty one.

"Hey," she whined.

She was about to argue, but her phone buzzed. Setting down her fork, she picked it up to reply to the text.

"You're not supposed to be working," Alex grumbled to her. "It's lunch."

"Not in L.A. it's not."

"You should still take an hour for yourself. It aids in your mental health."

"Mental health tips from the man that doesn't sleep!"

"I slept last night. A little."

"Did he?" Lyssa asked Chase.

"No."

Chase wasn't about to help his friend in this battle. He was afraid of ending up with Eggplant Rollatini or something equally as messy in his crotch. Alex flipped him off.

"Besides, you stole my food!" Lyssa added.

"I'm just saving you room for dessert," he smirked at her.

"I want the other tomato." She pointed down to the one remaining tomato in the bowl in front of him. He stabbed at it with the fork.

Chase pointed to his lap. "This one is still between my legs if you want to dive down and —" He got hit in the forehead with a second tomato. "Great, thanks. A matching pair."

"Yep," Alex gave him a strained smile.

"Serves you right," Lyssa stuck her tongue out at him.

Chase continued to mutter while he dabbed at the new stain with his napkin. Meanwhile, Alex held out the large kalamata olive to Lyssa instead. She picked it off his fork with her teeth and happily ate it. He winked to her quickly and bit into the next one himself. The exchange did not go by unnoticed by Trixie, who was surprisingly quiet about it. Her attention was quickly diverted anyway.

"You came!" Trixie squealed when she saw Bryan walking out onto the patio, causing everyone to cringe again. "Sorry."

"My meeting got over early," he gave Trixie a quick hug, then joined them at the round patio table.

"Will you please tell your software development production manager to stop working?" Alex asked their boss.

"Why would I do that?"

"It's lunchtime Bry-Bry," Trixie said as if it was the most obvious thing in the world.

Lyssa glanced up at the nickname.

"Don't ask," Alex whispered to her nonchalantly.

She went back to her phone instead.

"Stop," he put his hand over the phone.

"Why are you giving me such a hard time?" she sighed heavily.

"Because if you work, I have to work, and you work too

much."

"You love to work. That's all you do."

"That's not all he does," Trixie spoke up.

"Really?" Lyssa raised her eyebrow at her, not entirely sure if she wanted to know what Trixie knew.

"He does kung fu."

"Kendo," Alex corrected. "And that's really just for exercise."

"You have your art!"

He shrugged. "I don't do it much anymore. Too busy." It didn't appear he wanted to talk about it.

Lyssa snorted. "Where have I heard that excuse before?"

He glanced up her, ready to argue. She was staring at him like one of the zombies from the game. He chuckled. "Yeah, ok. I deserved that."

I'M GOING OFF THE RAILS ON A CRAZY TRAIN!

Lyssa snatched up her phone and walked away from the table.

"Hi Sharon!" she said as she answered the phone. Alex's eyes followed her. He obviously wasn't happy about her taking the call.

"Let her work," Bryan said after placing his lunch order with the waitress. "She likes it."

Alex sighed heavily.

"You should get some sleep. You look like shit."

He squinted at Bryan, who chuckled.

As Trixie told them all about her trip to Acapulco, Lyssa wandered around the pool's edge talking on the phone.

Five minutes later, she was back and just about bursting at the seams. She sat down, put her phone on the table, and picked up her fork to dig into the vegetable lasagne that had shown up by now.

"Well?" Chase asked.

She looked up. "What?"

"What was it?"

"Just a phone call."

"That wasn't just a phone call. You were happy. And bouncy. Very bouncy."

She shrugged. "Just a phone call."

"Even I have to admit that I'm a bit curious," Bryan said.

"I have to tell Patrick first. It's only right."

"Ok," he relented, understanding the power structure of a business. He didn't think Patrick would care if she bypassed her direct boss and told him, but he didn't want to put her in the position to worry about it. "Tell Patrick first."

"It's business stuff, isn't it?" Trixie asked.

"Yes."

"Oh," she was disappointed. She was hoping for a piece of gossip. Didn't even matter who it was about. She just loved gossip.

"Psst," Alex got Lyssa's attention.

He tapped his ear.

She shook her head.

He tugged on her sleeve.

She growled at him like an angry cat.

"Damn stubborn Leos," he mumbled.

"Ok," she gave in, "I suppose I trust you."

She whispered her secret to him.

"No kidding." His eyes widened. "Way to go."

"What is it?" Chase whispered loudly to him.

"No!" Lyssa clamped her hand over Alex's mouth.

"Oh come on! I can keep secrets too!" Chase whined like a little kid.

"You cannot! You're a total security leak!"

"You are," Bryan agreed.

"I won't tell. I promise. Give me a chance."

"I gave you a chance and you--ow!" she pulled her hand back. "Oh, my God! Did you just give me a hickey?!"

Alex was snickering at her.

"Can you even give people hickeys on the palms of their hands?" Chase asked.

"Yes," Trixie answered confidently.

Everyone stared at her.

"Ew!" "Gross!" "I'll take your word for it." "I need a tetanus shot."

Lyssa picked up her tablet and shot off a quick email to Patrick with the good news and a plea for him to tell Bryan as soon as possible. Not ten seconds later Bryan's phone buzzed. Normally he wouldn't so much as look at it during lunch let alone answer it, but given the situation...

"Yes Patrick... Uh huh... Yes... That would be because we're having lunch with some friends and she's presently sitting across from me... Ok... I will... Thank you for calling me and letting me know."

He hung up the phone, set it down, and went back to his pecan-encrusted pork chops.

"Well?" Chase asked him, getting more frustrated.

Bryan looked up at Lyssa and smiled. "You know, I didn't think you could impress me anymore than you already have, but you prove me just a little more wrong every single day. You," he pointed at her with his fork, "are destined to be my favorite."

Alex gave him a quick, sharp glance. Bryan ignored him by looking at his watch.

"I have another meeting."

He stood and walked around the table to pat Lyssa on the shoulder.

"Good job dear," he smiled down at her. It wasn't meant to be condescending. It was genuine praise from a man that wasn't surprised often. Today she'd amazed him.

He started to leave and came back.

"I don't trust this with you," he said to Chase as he grabbed his plate of food and left.

"Asshole," Chase mumbled after he was well out of

distance.

"Oh, my God! Is that the time? I have to go too," Trixie scrambled to grab her bag. "I'm meeting Pierre at Crossman's for a bra fitting."

"Seriously?"

"Yes! Getting the proper bra is a very serious thing. I'm sure Lyssa knows how it is."

"Of course!"

"Ok," Chase stood. "I'll see you out."

They left, leaving Lyssa and Alex alone on the patio.

"Do you really know how it is?"

"Nah. I have no clue. My bras come from the Vanity Fair Outlet."

Alex chuckled.

"I almost called you this morning," she started a little more quietly, "to see if you were still ok."

"Why didn't you?"

"I didn't want to bother you early in the morning."

"You never bother me."

She shrugged.

"You can call me anytime," he stressed. "I mean it. Anytime of the day or night."

"Ok."

He sat back after finishing off his broiled tilapia. Picking up his beer, he took a long swig before starting into the conversation they had to have.

"It was Avery's car."

"The cafeteria cook?"

"Yeah. He said it wouldn't start at the end of his shift so he hopped a ride home with his brother, who also works in the cafeteria. They'd planned to come back today to get it. I guess it's not the first time it's died in the parking garage so he didn't really think much of leaving it there."

"Do you believe him?"

"I do, but the fact of the matter is that he left the car in 36D."

"He's sure?"

"Yeah, because he made a joke out of it. It's his girlfriend's bra size."

"Am I the only woman around here with normal-sized tits?" Lyssa mumbled.

Alex realized he wasn't meant to answer that, which is good because no answer would have been correct. So he ignored the question and continued.

"There's no way the car could slip out of gear and travel from that spot to the ramp. Not on its own."

"Any clue as to who did it?"

He shook his head. She tried not to let this information upset her.

"Did the investigation keep you up all night?"

He gave a hard sigh. "Most of it. I couldn't sleep anyway."

"Why?"

"It might have had something to do with one of my co-workers being in peril. I was a little hyped."

"I was hardly in peril."

"You were in a car that was struck by another car. You could have been."

"It's just a fender bender. Another annoyance. Like the paintball incident."

"I think your tolerance of the situation is what makes me the most worried."

He picked at the corner of the Band-Aid on his forehead.

"Stop," she warned.

"It's irritating me," he mumbled.

"Alex!" She lightly smacked his hand away from his forehead.

"Ow," he said more out of reflex than from pain.

"You would never let me get away with that," she smiled and carefully pulled the Band-Aid off.

"True, but I never got to perform triage on you either."

"I didn't get hurt last night."

"No, but over a week ago you were standing in the middle of your office giving me a hard time about my concern for your pain and suffering."

"Ok. Next time I have an allergic reaction to my underwear I'll let you apply the Benadryl ointment," she teased.

"You'll probably never stray from your cotton undies again now," he smirked.

"I just won't wear any at all."

He groaned and his smile, as well as the front of his pants, grew a little wider.

She carefully cleaned off the wound. Like most things in life, it wasn't as bad as she remembered. It certainly didn't warrant another Band-Aid. She noticed a scar on the right-side of his chin. It seemed so obvious now but she'd never noticed it before.

"I was in a road race in Bahrain and I hit a camel," he explained when he noticed her inspecting it.

"Ouch."

He shrugged. "I got lucky. The Lamborghini I was driving was completely wrecked."

"When did this happen?"

"Three years ago."

"Well, that's way too late to kiss it and make it better."

"Yeah, but..." he pointed to his forehead.

She put her hands over his ears and tilted his head forward, kissing the middle of his forehead, being careful not to actually touch his wound.

Bent forward over her chest, Alex breathed deeply.

"Lavender," he moaned.

"Another essential oil," she sat back.

"What's this one for?"

"It's supposed to relieve nervous tension and promote sleep."

He gestured for her to come close again, which she did. Positioning his face further into her neck, he breathed deeply, taking in her essence.

"It's working," he announced and let his head fall to her shoulder.

She could hear the smile in his voice as he exhaled, relaxing even more.

"This is much nicer than the hood of an Impala," he mumbled.

Alex blessed the gods that his eyes were open at that very moment because while the sound of her giggle made him smile, the sight of her beautiful breasts jiggling ever so slightly inside the top of her blouse made him the happiest man on Earth.

"Wow."

Lyssa turned her head to find Chase walking back out to the patio.

"Shh," she hushed him. "I think he's finally falling asleep."

"There's a better way to get a man to do that, you know," Chase smirked.

Alex sat back up, throwing Chase a side-eye to let him know the intrusion wasn't appreciated.

"Is that all you think about Chase?" Lyssa rolled her eyes.

"Yeah, pretty much," he admitted. "I get bored in-house. I want to go to Miami. Or Honolulu. Or even Portland at this point."

"No one goes anywhere until Lyssa is no longer under threat," Alex stressed.

"And the rest of the project too," Chase added just to be an ass.

"Of course," Alex grumbled.

"Make Alex go to bed please," Lyssa begged as she spooned the remains of her meal into a to-go container.

"She's right," Chase honestly agreed.

"Maybe," he stood and stretched. "Yoga tonight?"

"I can't. Jay, Chris and Simon are coming over tonight for

dinner. We get together once a month to go over the workload schedule and discuss whatever issues or concerns they have."

"You're cooking?"

"Sort of. June Cleaver is cooking Angel Alfredo for us."

"June Cleaver?"

"My crock pot! She cooks all day for me while I'm at work."

They laughed.

"You can come over too if you want, but only if you promise to get some sleep first. You are a cranky bitch when you're tired."

"I've been nice this time."

"I suppose," she smirked.

"I'm probably going to be busy tonight. There's still a lot to review."

"Ok. Oh! Whatever you do, don't tell Marlene about tonight's dinner. She uses it as an excuse to escape her family. I love her, but it's hard to get anything done when she just wants to drink and gossip."

"I won't tell her," Alex agreed.

Lyssa pointed at Chase in warning.

"I will do one better and avoid her at all cost."

"What's on the schedule tomorrow?" she asked as she picked up her items from the table.

Alex shrugged. Either he didn't know or didn't remember. Either way it didn't appear he cared.

"Well, I'm going to need help tomorrow with Austin so get lots of rest. I'm going to abuse the crap out of you."

"Sure," Alex smirked. "I was going to see you first thing in the morning anyway to apologize."

"What for?"

"Don't know yet, but I've had to apologize more in the week I've known you than the rest of my life combined. I'm sure I'll figure out what I did wrong tomorrow."

She gave him a quick hug and turned to leave, but he held onto her waist, pulling her back close to him.

"I meant it," he stressed. "Call anytime."

She nodded to him in understanding. He let her hand slip away. After giving Chase a cute little wave, Lyssa left the patio area.

It was a full minute after she was gone because Chase spoke.

"You make the damn cutest couple."

"Piss off."

"It got kind of cozy too, didn't it?"

"I suppose. For me."

"For anyone. Especially with her. She kids and jokes and slaps and occasionally gives hugs if she's super happy, but that was borderline harassment."

"By HR standards, I'm pretty sure it was over the border."

"Lyssa doesn't live by the same standards as HR. She's more of a reality-based creature. And the reality of it is you two are close. Very, very close. The kind of close that we'd start an office pool for. Pick your when, where and how for a dollar. Closest without going over wins the pot."

"Pick the how?"

"Missionary, doggy, reverse cowgirl —"

"Ok!" he loudly interrupted. "I get it now."

"Actually, no you don't," Chase joked.

"Maybe if I weren't so damn tired..." he mumbled.

"Who are you kidding? If you weren't so damn tired you wouldn't have been cuddling up to her at all. You'd have been in Great Dane mode. Protecting the damsel in distress from being abused by anyone, including yourself."

Alex looked up at his friend. He was right.

"You better be careful," Chase quietly warned.

"Maybe for once I don't want to be."

"You say that now, but tomorrow you'll be back to your normal self and you'll be pissed you let yourself go today. And that'll be your apology. She'll pretend she understands, but you're really gonna break her heart."

"How do you know her so well?"

Chase looked at him like he was a moron. "It's obvious dude."

Alex shrugged it off.

"For Christ's sake get some sleep. You're gonna need it for Austin tomorrow."

"Ok. Ok. Ok."

Alex started to walk off.

"Wait a minute!" Chase shouted back. "What was the good news Lyssa got?!"

"Can't hear you! I'm going to bed! Goodnight!"

"Assholes."

* * * * *

"Are you freaking kidding me?!"

"No."

"You got the Prince of Darkness?!"

"Yes."

"He's gonna record a song just for our game?!"

"Yes."

"He's coming here to record our song?!"

"No."

"Oh."

"He's coming here to preview the game then he'll record the song at his home recording studio."

"Still. Wow!"

"Are you going to hyperventilate?"

"I might."

Simon laid back on the couch.

"This is huge," Chris finally commented. "How did you do it again? You just called him?"

"I called Sharon."

"Oh sure, that makes sense," he rolled his eyes.

"Everyone knows he and his kids were huge fans of the first

game. They played online all the time. They racked up more hours than ninety-percent of our game base, including the beta testers. So I called Sharon and told her about the sequel and she said she'd talk to him about it. He wants to see what we've got for the sequel and then he'll record a song for it. Hopefully. I mean, there's always the chance he'll change his mind, but right now he's very excited about it. He may even bring the kids with him."

"Crazy awesome," Chris grinned.

"And this is happening when?" Jay asked.

"Probably in a month. Maybe mid-May, if we're lucky."

"So we've got some time."

"Oh yeah. Some. It'll go by quickly though."

"Yeah. Not too quickly, I hope."

Jay had been kind of quiet all night. Quiet all week, actually.

"Do you have concerns that the game won't be ready in time for them to beta test?"

"No. Not really."

"Then what's up?"

"Nothing. It's all great."

Jay could tell from the look on her face that she knew he was a terrible bluffer.

"There's been rumors," Chris said, taking the pressure off him to speak.

"Rumors?"

"That someone tried to kill you."

"No! Who said that?"

"Everyone."

"We know about the car in the parking garage." Simon sat back up.

"It was an accident."

"Bullshit," Chris coughed.

"Ok. Probably not, but it wasn't anything to worry about. I just got my fender banged up a little. The car will be back from the shop tomorrow."

"And what if next time he speeds through a red light and runs you down on your way to Meemah's Deli?" Jay grew more animated.

"It'll probably hurt."

"I'm not kidding."

"I know. But what do you expect me to do? Lock myself in a small room until the world goes away?"

Jay had no answer to that.

"And we don't even know I was the target. It could have been Alex. He's probably got his fair share of enemies."

"Is he really a secret agent?" Simon asked.

"I don't know," Lyssa pondered. "He certainly looks like one."

"Boing," Chris pointed his fingers at her, mimicking erect nipples.

"Ha ha," she tossed a napkin at him. It didn't go far.

"He's got creepy eyes," Simon shuddered.

"They aren't creepy!"

"So defensive!"

She wadded up another napkin and threw it at Simon. It didn't go any further than the first one.

"I'm surprised he's not here," Jay said, collecting the dirty dishes before Lyssa decided to use them as projectile weapons.

"He said he has to review more of the accident data."

"So they're not buying it's an accident either."

"He takes nothing for granted."

"Good."

"Alex is a pro. I'm not worried about anything happening."

"God, you are gonzo for him," Chris mumbled.

"Shut it," she warned. Chris just laughed at her.

"I don't blame you. The guy's ripped."

Jay came back and stared down at Chris with a funny look.

"Oh come on! Tell me if you didn't have a vagina that you wouldn't throw it at him."

Jay pondered the idea for a moment. "Yeah, probably," he admitted.

They got more drinks and sat back to discuss the business on the night's agenda.

An hour later they were just getting done when the door intercom chimed.

"Ms. Lyssa, this is Frank from downstairs."

"Hi Frank."

"There's a Marlene Arezzo here. She says she's a guest but she's not on the list."

Everyone groaned.

"Let her up Frank."

"Are you sure? She's kind of hostile."

They could hear Marlene squawking in the background.

"Hostile? I haven't even laid a finger on you yet. A finger, by the way, that you would be lucky to get laid by! Oh, wait a minute. That's not right."

"No it's not!"

"Ok!" Lyssa interrupted, sensing that Frank was starting to freak out a little. "You definitely better let her up before she gets herself arrested."

A few minutes later...

"The nerve of that overgrown ape," Marlene came in complaining, "trying to keep me out."

"That's his job Marlene."

"He damn well knows who I am."

"What are you doing here?"

"Can't I just stop by to say hi!"

Lyssa stared at her.

"They were having a sale on avocados and I know you love avocados. So I brought you some. See?" She held up the grocery store bag. "I was only thinking of you."

"Asparagus."

"Wha??"

"I love asparagus **and artichokes**. Not avocados."

"Damn. I didn't even buy the right thing?"

"No, but I'll take them anyway." She swiped the bag from Marlene's hand. "Alex loves avocados in his salad."

The guys snickered.

"Shut it!" Lyssa warned.

She slipped off into the kitchen to put away the avocados and get Marlene a drink.

"How did you know about tonight?" Lyssa asked her.

"I didn't."

"I'm not buying your story about produce being on sale."

"Fine. But I didn't know you were all here. I **just thought** Alex might be here."

"You're looking for Alex?" she got a little snippy.

"Arning-Way. Oss-Bay Ealous-Jay," Chris said.

"What the hell is wrong with you?" Marlene **crinkled up her** nose at him. "Are you drunk?"

"I am not jealous." Lyssa forced herself to calm down.

"I should be so lucky that you would be jealous of me and Alex! That would mean I have a chance!"

"You have a guy!"

"Who left me!"

"You kicked him out!"

"I... Oh yeah."

"Why aren't you home?"

"My sister's babysitting because it's supposed to be my **date** night with Jerry, but he never showed up."

"Wait a minute. Isn't **date night** on Fridays?"

"Yes."

"It's Thursday Marlene."

"Oh!" she suddenly realized Lyssa was right. "Oh shit. I gotta work tomorrow. I thought it was gonna be Saturday."

Everyone laughed.

"Wait a minute," Lyssa interrupted, "if it's Thursday, who's staying with the kids?"

Marlene's eye flew open. She pulled out her phone. "Michael! Are you home?... Oh, thank God. Can you keep watching your brothers and sisters for me? I'm kind of delayed... Yeah, working late for the boss again."

"Excuse me?" Lyssa blurted out.

"Ok... Ok... Oh, he is?... Well, that's good... I'll be home in a little while... Love you baby boy. Bye."

She hung up.

"Jerry's with the kids. Apparently he came back. And I'm here." She looked around the room. "Why are you all here? Are you all looking for Alex too?"

"It's the monthly project manager meeting," Simon answered.

"Oh. That's good. Why wasn't I invited?" she turned to Lyssa.

"Because you got drunk at the last one and didn't keep notes."

"Oh yeah. So, is Alex here or not?"

"No he's not!"

"Sorry. Jeez."

Lyssa took a deep breath. This was going to be a long night.

"I need a drink," she said and returned to the kitchen while her guests proceeded to argue about some reality TV show she didn't watch.

She decided to take a moment to make a phone call.

"What's wrong?" Alex immediately answered the phone.

"Well, hello to you too sunshine," Lyssa rolled her eyes.

"Sorry. Hello. What's wrong?"

"Nothing. You said I could call any time."

"I know, but I didn't expect you to unless something went wrong."

"So you didn't mean it?"

"Oh, I meant it. I just didn't think you really would."

"Is this a bad time?"

"No."

"Did you get any sleep?"

"Yes."

His reply didn't really convince her. "Alexander Dane! You were supposed to get sleep!" she said loud enough that her company overheard.

"I know. I did. For a couple hours."

"It's obviously not enough."

"No," he sighed. "I had a lot to do tonight. I'm turning in right now."

"Really?"

"Really. You actually caught me undressing for bed."

"I'm not sure I believe you. Pics or it's not true."

Alex laughed. "I'm afraid I can't accommodate your request. Unlike Chase, I don't have a mirror over the bed."

"TMI!"

He laughed again.

"Ok. I only called to ask if you found out anything more."

"Not really," he confessed.

"Just so you know, most of the project staff knows what happened and they've guessed at a lot more."

"How?"

"A lot of people knew about the parking garage incident. Oh, and there's this really hot mysterious security guy that spends a lot of time around my office. He's kinda out of the ordinary. Especially the part where he's around *my* office."

He laughed. "Gotcha."

"My people are dorks, but they're really smart dorks."

"We're lucky for that."

"Yeah. Well, I just wanted to check in with you. See if there's anything new."

"No. Sorry."

"You're not supposed to apologize until tomorrow

morning."

"Um, sorry?"

She giggled. "Ok sweetie. Sleep tight."

"I will now."

"Bye."

She hung up and came back out into the living room area, sitting on the couch and setting her phone on the table. Everyone was silent and staring.

"What?"

"We thought you were talking to Alex," Chris said.

"I was."

"You call him sweetie?"

"Apparently I do. Because I did. Hmm..."

She pondered it, then decided not to overthink that too much.

I call a lot of people sweetie. Right?

"And you're worried I'll drink too much," Marlene snickered.

* * * * *

In Markison Tower's suite 152H security specialist Alexander Dane set his phone back in its holster on the nightstand. He'd wrenched it out of the cradle when it rang and almost broke it in the process.

He felt bad lying to Lyssa. He told her he didn't lie. But there was no way he was going to tell her he'd been asleep when she rang. It was only nine o'clock, after all. Hardly late. Especially when she'd still been working at this time the previous night.

No, there was no way he was telling her. She needed to feel comfortable enough to call him at any time. It was important. Her trust meant everything to his success in the mission.

For both their sakes, he was grateful nothing was wrong. He was barely able to keep his eyes awake during the call. He would never have been able to physically get to her if she needed help. He could barely lift a finger now.

Then why in God's name was he pitching a tent large enough to hold a rock concert under?

That would be one helluva picture to send her.

He rolled over so he wouldn't have to see the peaked terrain on the bed's horizon. Pulling his pillow firmly under his head, he shut his eyes, confident Lyssa would be safe for the night.

Did she call me sweetie?

8

At 12:45 Alex was waiting patiently in Lyssa's office. She'd emailed him earlier that morning asking if he'd attend a meeting with her at one pm. The meeting with Austin was expected to be quite trying and she was looking for someone to go with her as moral support. Or as she put it in the email...

Someone to keep me from jumping over the table and stabbing that pig in the throat with my stylus.

How could he say no?

At 12:55 she came rushing into the office.

"Every meeting I've been in today has run late," she explained as she hurried. "I hate that."

He simply nodded in response.

"So disorganized and inconsiderate."

He could sense just how much she hated it and wisely kept his mouth shut.

"I haven't even had any lunch and now I have to run off to the next one. No time to do this formally."

She opened her closet door and rummaged through the contents on the top shelf. Pulling out a bottle of Southern Comfort, she took a swig, then offered him the bottle.

"No, thank you."

He found this not only odd but extremely disconcerting. She didn't strike him as a closet alcoholic. Or the type to be this frazzled by work-related incidents. If anything she was normally happy-go-lucky and confident in business matters. It was the personal stuff that irritated her and threw her into a tailspin. Like interrupted dates and impromptu yoga visits. She wasn't even this upset when her car was hit in the employee parking garage.

She took yet another hit from the bottle, then tapped a bit of the booze on her neck and chest as if it were perfume, recapped the bottle and put it back in the closet. She ended the routine by straightening her blouse and skirt.

"Alright, let's go meet with Austin."

She grabbed her usual meeting accoutrements --- tablet, planner, phone --- and headed out the door. Alex was right behind her.

Walking to the elevator she received words of encouragement from her fellow employees...

"Good luck boss!" "Hang tough Lyss!" "Make us proud!"

While waiting for the elevator Alex decided he needed more details.

"So, who is Austin?"

"Oh, you don't know? I thought for sure Chase would have told you. You're fortunate to have been spared the honor and privilege of meeting them thus far."

She stabbed at the elevator button impatiently three more times before continuing.

"Austin Gametronics. A small hardware firm owned and operated by one Mr. Robert Larrity. Or Big Bob, as he likes to be referred to by people who have never actually seen his penis."

"And you have?"

"No, but every time he tells someone to call him Big Bob his fifth wife rolls her eyes. It's women's universal code for, 'Yeah, he's not.' Actually, she might be the sixth wife. I lost count. He gets a new one every few months. I had the pleasure of meeting Valerie? Veronica? Betty? Whatever, I met Mrs. Larrity six months ago when we visited Gametronics offices in Austin to be personally insulted on their home-turf."

"Why are we working with this company?"

"About a year ago Gametronics contacted us about a new gaming system they're developing called Vortex. Something to rival the Wii and Kinect. Gametronics is looking for a company to partner with that will make video games for it. Bryan asked Chase and I to review it. That was how I met Chase actually."

"How is the Vortex anyway?"

"Oh, it's crap. But we still meet with them every couple months to review how it's going. Chase manages to get himself out of the meetings every time. Apparently I'm not that bright."

"How insulting are they?"

"Not-So-Big Bob likes to thinks of himself as old fashioned. He believes a woman's place is in the home. Cooking, cleaning, bearing children, and attending to her husband's needs. He firmly believes that is what women want too. That we're only truly happy being breeders and housewives."

"So, he's a chauvinistic jackass."

"Yeah, pretty much. He doesn't like my presence at the meetings or my involvement in the project *at all*," she stressed. "His way of coping with it is to make jokes at my expense. Oh, and don't be surprised if he calls you a Middle Eastern terrorist."

"I was born in Charleston, South Carolina."

"Doesn't matter. Everyone with dark hair and a tan is a terrorist."

"Bryan forces you to endure this?"

She shook her head. "I have a choice, but I'm a Markison girl. Occasionally I take one for the team. Admittedly it's getting more and more difficult to put up with him."

"If you were my girl I wouldn't allow it."

"I didn't mean Markison as in Bryan. I meant the company."

"I know what you meant. I still wouldn't."

She looked up at him. He stared straight ahead, serious. She smiled to herself, then looked back down. It was good to have Alex in her corner.

"As annoying as he is I kind of like throwing it in his face that he can't proceed without my cooperation," she admitted. "It really pisses him off."

"Is that why you're wearing a very short skirt and nearly

see-thru blouse?"

"Is it see-thru? I had no idea," she lied badly.

Alex smirked at her.

"It's not too see-thru is it?" she asked, suddenly concerned she may have gone too far.

"No," he lied badly back at her.

She giggled. The blouse was so see-through that he could see the flower pattern on her bra move when she laughed. It looked like a rose bush in an earthquake. He nonchalantly tugged on the front of his trousers.

The elevator doors opened to the conference room floor. It was one of the business floors. Bryan didn't allow Austin access to the penthouse floors. He didn't really like dealing with them either, much less want them on the floors that his office was on.

"Ready?" Alex asked when they reached the conference room doors.

She nodded.

He opened both doors with the same flair the Queen's guards might use for her own entrance. Once she passed through he closed them again.

"Dr. Winfield!"

"Hello Mr. Larrity." She didn't bother correcting him since he got a kick out of calling her that after the first time she pointed out she didn't like it.

"Ah ah ah. Call me Big Bob."

She just smiled back in response. She couldn't address him as Big Bob without throwing up in her mouth, so she stopped doing it months ago.

In addition to the fat stereotypical Texan, present around the table were two more representatives from the Austin-based gaming company and three from Markison Industries. Representing the home-team were Bryan, his business assistant Barbara, and Patrick.

"Thank you for coming Lyssa."

Bryan stood when he addressed her and all men followed

suit. They remained standing until Lyssa sat down. Alex took his position just behind her right shoulder. He could have sat, but he chose not to. He preferred to be standing and intimidating. It must have worked because no one questioned his decision.

Bryan introduced everyone else in the room, then Patrick took over.

The meeting seemed to go well... at first. But then the insults came slowly.

"Whatever happened to that strapping lad Chase? He's a man's man... "

"Boston women are certainly assertive... "

"I wish I had an assistant as pretty as you... "

Why Bryan ever allowed these things to happen no one really understood. It's not like they really needed Larrity's company. If anything, they were doing Larrity a favor.

Lyssa was calm and cool. She showed no stress on her face. In her lap she held her planner. She adored the little thing. It was a standard-size small planner with a worn leather cover. She could get refills for it from any office supply store whenever it ran out.

Today she scribbled a question in it then passed it back to Alex along with the pen.

Can I harass you for business purposes?

He jotted down his two-word answer and passed the planner back to her.

Please do.

She read the answer, closed the planner, and set it on the tablet.

Lyssa figured she could probably sit through this if she had one more drink in her but she failed to bring her flask. It was one final fatal remark by Larrity that finally pushed her over the edge...

"Markison, you're lucky no man has swiped this filly from you. If she were mine, I'd put her to work making me lots of brilliant little baby boys."

"You know what? You're right," Lyssa stood. "I really

should have a brood of children instead of working here and making you men oodles and oodles of money."

"What?" they suddenly became attentive and nervous.

"I quit."

She picked up her security badge and tossed it to Patrick.

"Um, you're quitting?" Larrity questioned.

"Sure, why not? It's what you've been telling me to do for over a year now. I think I'll go home, cook some dinner, and wait for my stud to get home."

"Your stud?"

Lyssa walked around the chair and slid quite easily into Alex's arm.

"I'll get him a beer, massage his feet, make him forget all about his long day at work." She smiled up at him. "I might even bake a cake too."

He nodded to her, quite liking that idea.

"But what about the new design?!" Larrity squawked.

"What new design?"

"The new game console design! The one we're working on! The one you have all the specs for!"

She giggled. "I'm just a girl. What do I know about that?" She looked up at Alex again, mindlessly playing with his tie. "What kind of cake would you like dear?"

"Carrot," he replied.

"With cream cheese frosting?"

He nodded.

"Anything for the future baby-daddy."

She smiled sweetly, brushing her fingers over his jaw to his chin. He smiled down at her.

"You don't need to quit your job Lyssa," Bryan finally spoke up.

"Right! You can keep your job and still have babies!" Larrity said, misinterpreting what Bryan meant.

"I can?" she pondered. "Well, why not?"

She suddenly grabbed Alex by his jacket lapels and with surprising strength tossed him back onto the table. Climbing over him, she straddled his groin. She pulled his tie apart with ease and flipped it out from his shirt collar, tossing it at a delightfully surprised Barbara.

"What are you doing?" Patrick asked, trying to remain calm.

"Making babies at work, of course."

She began to unbutton Alex's shirt.

"I don't think he meant at work specifically."

"Really? Eek!" she squeaked as Alex reached under her skirt and ripped off her light pink cotton panties. He held them to his nose, sniffing them briefly, then flung them behind his head.

"Aren't you going to do something about this?" Larrity said to Bryan.

"Don't look at me. It was your idea."

"Vile, perverted Yankees!" he declared and stood.

"Actually, this is Red Sox territory," Patrick pointed out.

Larrity and his people stormed out of the room.

"They can keep their stupid games and their whore and her terrorist pimp," he grumbled on the way out.

"Ha! I told you you're a terrorist." Lyssa giggled as she leaned over Alex.

He was just about to manhandle Lyssa's breasts when a gentle but commanding voice stopped him.

"Ok. I get the point."

They both looked over at Bryan.

"You're sick of their bullshit."

"Yes, but more importantly, Alex's got a point now too."

"A pretty big one," he mumbled to her.

Lyssa nodded wildly with a huge grin.

Bryan rolled his eyes and sighed heavily.

"I'll cancel the contract."

She squinted at him in distrust.

"If you're lying to me--"

"I'm not," he assured her.

"I have Sir Richard on speed dial."

"I know."

"He likes me."

"Of course he does."

"Offered me a spot on the next space launch."

"He did?"

Bryan was momentarily taken by surprise. That was something he did not know. There wasn't a lot going on inside his company he did not know. Especially when it involved other millionaires and billionaires.

"I promise you."

She considered him for a moment longer, then sat up. Holding her hand out, Patrick placed the security badge in her palm. She carefully climbed off Alex, who proceeded to push himself off the table, grab her panties from where they landed next to Bryan's laptop, and retrieve his tie from the blushing young assistant whom he heard had a bit of a crush on him. He turned and Lyssa straightened his collar and jacket for him.

"Well played Lyssa," Patrick said with a tone that insinuated he wasn't happy about it though.

"Who's playing?" she said with a sudden seriousness that left them speechless.

Lyssa picked up her tablet and planner, then left the room. With a stern jaw and fierce look in his eyes, Alex nodded to his associates and followed her out.

"Well, that didn't go well," Patrick sighed heavily.

"I'm surprised it lasted as long as it did."

"You are?"

"I expected her to snap months ago."

"Why did you keep going anyway?"

"I honestly liked the Vortex."

"So make your own."

"Market's already flooded with systems. But if they released it and we put out games formatted for the Vortex and the other systems, then it wouldn't be a total loss for us even if the Vortex bombed."

"Sometimes it's just not worth it."

"I was also waiting for his head to explode when he figured out I was Jewish."

He noticed Barbara staring at him with a scowl.

"I know. I'm an ass."

"As long as you know it," she mumbled, picked up her laptop, and left.

"Not well at all," Patrick sighed and left Bryan alone in the conference room.

"I know. I know... "

Lyssa and Alex traveled in silence to the elevator. As they waited for the elevator, Alex heard Lyssa sniffle.

"Are you ok?" he asked quietly.

"I don't like being the bad guy."

"It's not a bad thing to defend yourself. If anything, Bryan should be ashamed he let it get this far."

"Apparently it isn't enough to be the best. You have to be a bitch too."

The elevator arrived and they entered. Alex pushed the button for her floor.

"You're not a bitch. If anything, you let them off easy. I'm pretty sure anyone else might have hit them with harassment charges."

"Instead I created some more. I'm sorry for involving you like that."

"I kept praying, 'Please God, don't make me have sex with this beautiful woman for business purposes. It's been a long time, but I couldn't possibly do it and *not* personally enjoy it.' Yeah, it was horrible."

She looked up to find him smirking down at her.

"Bastard."

She was trying not to giggle and mostly failing.

"Come on." He gave her a quick side-hug. "I'll treat you to a late lunch in the cafeteria."

"You eat in the cafeteria?"

"Nothing deflates a semi faster than lukewarm mixed veggies from a can."

"Gross. Oh wait! It's not grilled cheese day is it?"

"No."

"Thank God. I don't have any underwear on. I'd have to eat nude."

"That's not helping the deflation rate any," Alex mumbled. "Neither is this."

He pulled her torn panties out of his pocket. They were irreparable.

"You didn't really smell them, did you?" she asked quietly.

His smirk grew more devilish. Her eyes widened instantly, making him laugh.

"I can take those..."

She started to reach for them, but he immediately pulled his hand away and tucked the panties back into his front pants' pocket.

"Souvenir?" she asked.

"War trophy."

"Ew," she shivered.

He laughed again and escorted her off the elevator as the doors opened.

Meanwhile, a certain CEO who was shamelessly monitoring the security video in private elevator number two smiled.

"Good boy Alex. Good boy..."

9

Saturday morning arrived and it still really bothered Lyssa that she'd assaulted her hunky bodyguard to make a point. Albeit a very valid point. After the incident, they'd had a wonderful lunch during which he tried to assuage her fears of pending insanity. He even told her a couple embarrassing stories of his own from college to make up for it. He'd made her laugh again.

Even though it was the weekend, Lyssa figured Alex would be at Markison Industries. All members of Bryan's personal security staff had living quarters there as it wasn't exactly a Monday to Friday kind of job.

Dressed in jeans, sandals, a perky bra that Marlene once commented made her boobs bounce when she walked, and a blouse cut low enough to show it all off, she hiked back to her place of employment. Instead of using her pass to access the employee elevators, she stopped at the guard's station.

"Yes Ms. Winfield," the guard greeted her. "What can I do for you today?"

"Can you buzz up and see if Alex Dane is in please?"

"Certainly ma'am."

He phoned and waited... and waited... and waited.

"No answer ma'am."

"Oh, well. I'll just--"

"Hey Lyssie Baby!"

Jay and Chase had just exited the elevator.

"I'll just ask them. Thank you."

She gave the guard her usual cute smile and wave, then crossed to her co-workers.

"It's off hours. I can call you Lyssie Baby off hours, right?"

Jay asked.

"No, but I'll grant you a full pardon today since I'm in a good mood."

"Yes!" he cheered.

"What's going on?"

"We just finished installing some more security software on the servers," Chase explained. "Got that done and we're headed to O'Malley's to catch the game. What are you doing here?"

"I came to see if Alex was around."

"He's at the studio today."

"Studio?"

"His art studio."

"Oh!"

"He's got the weekend off so he's hiding there."

"I tried calling him, but got his voicemail."

"He never answers the phone when he's in artist mode. It could be taped to his head and he wouldn't hear it. But I can give you the address if you want to go see him."

"Well, I don't want to bother him."

"Oh no! He'd love for you to visit."

"He would?"

"Then he can show you his artwork. He hates to admit it, but he loves an audience."

"Really?" she asked, still suspect.

"Trust me," he pulled out his wallet and handed her Alex's artist business card.

"Ok. Thanks," she smiled, waved and left.

"Damn she's cute," Chase muttered.

"Wasn't that the jiggly bra?"

"Yup."

"And was she carrying a cake?"

Chase nodded. "Lucky bastard."

"Speaking of lucky, where's your sister Trixie today? She is one fine woman. No offense."

"None taken. She's a total ho. She went to Alex's today too. In fact, he's..."

He stopped and looked up as realization hit them.

"Ah crap."

"How's it going?"

"Um, not too good. Sorry Trixie. It's been a while."

"Are my boobs too big?"

"No good can come from answering that question."

"I mean it. I think I might need to get them switched out."

"You make it sound like an oil change."

"More like detailing. Do you think I'm too used up?"

Alex stared at her.

"I've been with so many men. I'm afraid I might be getting old though. Might need to nip-tuck the cooch."

He was staring even wider now.

"Sorry. I made it weird, didn't I?"

"It was already weird."

"You're just supposed to see me as a piece of art."

"I was until you asked me to judge how you look sexually."

"Then judge me as a piece of art."

"Ok, then I can tell you that after having seen you nude a good dozen times—"

"When?!"

"At the pool."

"I always wear a suit!"

"You know it's not covering a damn thing."

"Well…"

"Not to mention all the times you streaked through the house."

"That was years ago!"

"Sufficed to say I'm not as impressed as I used to be. But I believe this recent discovery comes more from the fact that I'm desensitized to your body parts than from the state that they're in."

"Jeez. I wish I hadn't ask."

"Me too."

The door to the studio suddenly burst open and two men came running in. Alex remained surprisingly calm and just watched the scene unfold.

"Grab that ho!" Jay pointed to the blond who was currently stretched out on a day bed in the buff.

"What are you doing?!" she shouted as Chase threw a nearby painting tarp over her and hoisted her up over his shoulder. "Put me down!"

"Hush up woman!" he smacked her in the ass. "We don't have time. Taxi's waiting. Speaking of which," Chase pointed to Alex, "you owe me. I had to give the cabbie a fifty to break every traffic law in the city to get here ASAP. And check your damn phone once in a while," he grumbled as he left with Trixie still fussing to be put down.

"Seriously bro?!" Jay scooped up her clothes and purse from the nearby chair. "Why the hell I gotta carry the purse?!"

He left as quickly as the others.

"What the hell?" Alex mumbled to himself. Nothing about these people should have really phased him anymore, which was why he silently stood by they kidnapped his nude model.

Alex glanced over at his phone. He really hated his phone. Never once in his life had he gotten anything good out of it. Every call was about work. Every text led to something he didn't want to do. Even the photos of possible hook-ups he was constantly sent were just a distraction seeing as there was no woman on the face of the planet that was a friend of Chase's that he wanted to date.

He flipped thru a number of telemarketing texts until he got to the new one Chase had sent him just ten minutes prior to their interruption.

DUDE! HIDE TRIX! U GOT COMPANY ON WAY! LAST THING SHE WANTS TO SEE IS HER NAKED ASS!

"Hello?"

He looked up to see Lyssa walking into his studio.

"Hi Lyss," he smiled, a lot happier to see her than he was willing to admit to himself.

"I'm sorry for showing up unannounced, but Chase and Jay assured me it was ok."

"Of course it is."

She walked up to him and held up the circular Tupperware container she was carrying.

"The carrot cake I promised you."

"With cream cheese frosting?"

She nodded; he chuckled. Taking the container, he looked down into her pretty eyes. Lyssa could feel her knees weakening under his gaze. She forced herself to turn away.

"This is a wonderful studio," she said, trying to focus on the artwork around her.

"Would you like a tour?"

"If I'm not interrupting."

"Not at all. Then after we could have cake and coffee."

He set the cake container down on a nearby table and turned back to find her staring at his sketch pad, and more importantly, the half-finished sketch of the reclining nude model that was in his studio not five minutes ago.

"Ha!" he blurted out, feeling like he'd been caught in the act of doing something that looked bad but was completely innocent, which it was until Trixie brought up the state of her private parts. "Don't judge my work by that. It's crap."

She shrugged, not a good judge of artwork anyway

"My friend Andre has an art gallery in Rockport. He's hosting a nude exhibit this weekend and called on local artists to contribute. He asked me but I haven't sketched a nude in years. Not my specialty then and it's definitely not now."

"The daybed looks right," she gestured between the actual daybed and the picture, trying to be helpful. "Are you sketching a naked woman from memory?"

She tried not to be jealous of whoever the source of the sketch was. He was an artist. It was just art to him. It was probably the way he looked at her too. Just a bunch of lines and colors.

"What memory?" he scoffed. "Our CEO cock-blocked me, remember?"

"Are you saying that's supposed to be my backside?"

"No!" he immediately refuted. "It's obviously not. Way too big. Not that you're scrawny. Not by any means. Just about right really. You know… ah, fuck it."

He tore the page off and crumpled it up, tossing it into a nearby trashcan. She giggled.

"Can I have a do-over?" he asked with a sigh that was definitely directed towards himself.

"Sure," she tried to hide her giggling.

"Let me show you around my studio."

He took her around, pointing out his favorite pieces, trying to explain what they meant to him. While there were some portrait sketches and a couple sculptures, he preferred Impressionist style painting. And his favorite theme was the cityscape at sunrise.

"It's wonderful," she smiled up at him. "This is a lot more than just dabbling. This is fantastic."

He was pleased that she showed real interest in his hobby. Sometimes Alex wished he weren't so good at his job because he could read people instantly. He knew when someone was just being polite about his artwork and they were actually unemotional about it. But her eyes were full of life as he spoke. She genuinely cared.

Before he started boring her with long winded explanations he grabbed the cake container and they went upstairs to the small studio apartment that he stayed in when he wasn't needed at Markison Industries.

It was one large room with a galley kitchen and a small dining room table that seated four. In the middle of the room was his bed. A California king with a fluffy burgundy comforter that he was suddenly grateful he made that morning. The bed was flanked by two large oak nightstands, but only one of them had items on it. An alarm clock. A lamp. A box of tissues. A Kindle. Along the back wall were three doors. She guessed that two of them led to closets and one the bathroom.

Walking around the kitchen island, Alex put the cake on the counter and grabbed two plates and forks.

"If you make me cut this I'll butcher it."

She joined him behind the counter where he handed her a knife.

"Thank you."

As she proceeded to remove the cake top, he slid his arm under hers and swiped his finger thru the side of the cake.

"Hey," she glanced back at him as he sucked the frosting from his finger. He winked at her.

"Tasty."

As she sliced carefully into the side of the circular cake, he slid his hand back around her waist to her stomach. As he watched over her shoulder, he pushed himself up tight to her back. His other hand caressed her arm.

Please don't be a dream, she silently begged.

"I can't stop thinking about you," he confessed in a soft, deep voice.

Pushing his face into her hair, his lips found her ear so he could whisper...

"Please let me finish what we started yesterday."

The linen pants he wore when he was working in his studio left nothing to the imagination. She pressed back against him just enough to feel his erection against her tailbone. She set the knife on the counter and raised her arm, sliding her hand up to his head, running her fingers thru his hair as he kissed her ear, her jaw, her neck.

His hand slid up her stomach to her breast. She fit perfectly in his palm. Looking down at the unfondled orb, he could see the erect nipple thru the thin fabric of her bra and blouse. It pleased him to know that his touch could so openly affect her. He rubbed his hand over her cupped breast just enough to feel the other erect nipple against his palm.

She took another deep, sharp breath and put her hand over his. It wasn't to stop him or pull him away, but to encourage him to continue.

"Lyssa," he whispered again, begging. "I need you... now... please."

"Yes," she whispered, trying to not sound as desperate for him as she felt and knowing she was failing miserably. She wanted this man badly. She didn't care if he destroyed all her clothes to get to her.

Turning in his arms to face him, she stood on tiptoes to press her lips to his. Their kiss started gentle, but turned passionate quickly.

He picked her up easily in his arms and carried her over to the spacious bed. Originally bought to occupy his above-average height, he was glad he'd have the extra-large space to explore his lover. A fabric canvas for mastering the art of making love to this woman.

He forced his thoughts to slow down. First he needed to get her undressed.

Her blouse was easy enough to unbutton. He paused for a moment to view her breasts in their lacy bra covering.

Looking up into her eyes, he smirked just slightly, making her blush.

"Heavenly."

Enveloping her in his arms again, he kissed her forehead, her cheek, her neck all while trying to unclasp her bra. It was proving to be a much more difficult task than it should have been. If he didn't think it would kill the mood completely, he would have just violently ripped the damn thing apart. As it was, she started to giggle at his fumbling.

"They don't teach this stuff in art school," he chuckled along with her.

"Allow me."

Reaching behind her back with one hand, she easily unclasped it with one flip.

"Thank you," he smiled down at her.

She continued with the chore of undressing. Slipping off her sandals. Unbuttoning her jeans. Sliding out of both her pants and panties at the same time.

He would have thanked her again, but he was stunned silent at the sight of her nakedness.

"So beautiful," he finally exhaled.

It was a simple matter for him to disrobe. Slip off his shirt, push down his pants. Done.

Lyssa's eyes trailed down his muscular chest to his tight abs and finally to his groin. Just like his height, his member was slightly larger than average when fully erect. To her complete delight, what little pubic hair he had was the same silky black color as the hair on his head.

He was the most gorgeous man she'd ever seen in her life.

With a twinkle in her eyes, Lyssa slowly slid back onto the bed and he crawled after her. A beast stalking his lovely prey.

Poised over her, Alex kissed her lightly on the lips before lowering himself. Allowing his skin to slowly merge with hers, pushing her carefully into the plush bedding. As his hips came to rest on hers, he came to a sudden realization. This time he didn't bother to hide his disappointment.

"Ah damn."

"What's wrong?" She brushed her fingers lightly over his cheek.

"I've never entertained anyone here. I never really expected to."

She thought she knew where this was headed but waited for him to confirm it.

"I don't have any condoms," he was embarrassed to admit.

"I have no medical conditions that necessitate one."

"Neither do I."

"And I can't get pregnant," she said quietly, as embarrassed as him now.

"Oh good. Neither can I," he said, hoping to make her at ease again. It must have worked because she smacked him on his backside. He twitched in surprise.

"Smart ass," she laughed lightly.

"I also know that some women don't appreciate the... um... aftermath."

He tried to be as sensitive as he could without saying 'mess' as that insinuated an accident was made. And this was no accident.

She smiled up at him, full of joy at his sensitivity towards her.

"I'm as concerned about my body being soiled as you are about these sheets."

The corner of his lip curled up in that way that always made her weak. The devilish look in his eyes made her heart race. The sudden deepness in his voice made her legs quiver.

"I look forward to breaking both of you in."

He resumed the task at hand with great passion, kissing her long and hard. Her fingers pushed thru his hair as his tongue crossed into her mouth and lightly danced across hers.

As his hands explored her soft, sensuous curves, her leg brushed up against his. As much as he wanted to just plunge into her loveliness, he forced himself to wait. He had a much more important duty to perform at this point and he was looking forward to it.

Rolling off to her side, he took a moment to look her over. His fingers traced an invisible line from her neck, down between her breasts, to her little patch of neatly trimmed pubic hair.

He noticed her hand was resting just above her hip. It was awkward enough that it caught his attention. She was covering something. He slid down and kissed her belly lightly in several different places. Eventually he made his way over to her hand. Carefully pushing it aside, he revealed the tiny scar. It was only an inch long, but it was a mile long to her.

Being in security, he'd had access to her personnel file. He'd read about the incident in London seven years prior. The terrorist attack in the Tube that caused the accident.

But it wasn't a topic for today. Or even tomorrow. Someday... maybe.

He lightly kissed the site of the wound; making her tremble for a brief moment, then put her hand back over the scar.

Sliding back up to her face, he brushed the back of his fingers over her cheek, down to her shoulder.

"I would never hurt you. Not intentionally. Promise me if I do you'll tell me."

"I promise."

As he kissed her, he ran his hand back down her chest, over her belly. This time he didn't stop on her abdomen. He slid his fingers thru her hair and wrapped them down over her pelvis. He pressed his index and middle fingers to her mounds and found them swollen and moist. Slipping his fingers carefully into her, she gasped.

She was very wet and very ready for him.

He drew her wetness up to her clitoris, stimulating her with the same two fingers.

She gasped again with pleasure and whispered his name delicately.

"Alex... "

He continued to gently rub her clitoris while occasionally slipping his fingers back into her vagina. Her moaning and panting increased with each stroke.

"Are your breasts sensitive?" he asked.

She had been enjoying herself so much her brain refused to comprehend the words.

"What?" she looked up, vaguely aware he spoke.

"Can I taste your nipples?" he rephrased his question to get right to the point.

"Yes."

He slid down to her chest. Running his tongue lightly over her right nipple, he noticed she arched her back up against him, pushing her breast harder onto his lips.

Soon she would make a new noise. A breathy squeak.

"Right there," she panted. "Don't stop. Please don't stop."

He didn't really have any intentions of stopping, but she'd slapped him on the forehead.

"I just meant get off my tit."

His fingers resumed their happy task of stimulating her clitoris.

"Sorry."

"Don't apologize."

She placed her hands on either side of his head and pulled him forward, kissing him roughly. She let him go so she could scream louder this time.

"Alex! Yes!"

Her hands grabbed the bed sheets and pillows in a death grip.

This was the most intense orgasm he'd ever had the pleasure of being a part of.

Then her back arched more and she quieted completely. She didn't even breathe. This was "la petite mort." The French phrase meaning "little death." Indeed, the only sign of life from her was her hand wrapped tightly around his bicep.

Just as he was starting to think she was going to never start breathing again she gasped for air finally and relaxed into the bed. As she calmed, she closed her legs and pulled on his wrist to free his hand from her. She drew his arm around her waist. Kissing him on the lips, she looked at him quite seriously.

"I want to feel you. In me. Now."

That was one command he would never argue with.

Climbing back up on top of her, she brought her knees up on either side of him and raised her pelvis to meet him. He was being delicate about it and she could sense this.

"All of you Alex," she whispered.

He pushed himself as deep into her as he could. She bit her lip, trying to suppress her screams of ecstasy.

"You are so warm. And so tight," he confessed.

As Alex slowly pushed in and out of her, he soon realized that this wasn't going to last long. As much as he wanted to enjoy being inside of her for hours... forever!... he knew he only had minutes. Two, maybe.

"Lyssa, you feel so good. I can't..." he trailed off, dropping his head, not even sure how to tell her.

"Can't what sweetheart?" she ran her hands over his face, kissing his forehead.

"I can't last... I'm gonna come... soon... tell me where."

She said nothing but wrapped one leg around his buttocks tightly, holding him close and looking into his eyes.

And that pushed him right over the edge. He thrust fast and hard. She clawed at his back. Not enough to break the skin, but enough for him to know that she was there and that she was enjoying him.

"Oh God," he groaned as he exploded inside of her. She could feel him ejaculate, each throb making her whimper.

Too soon it was over. He lay almost lifeless on top of her. His forehead resting on hers as they tried to calm their breath.

"My Lyssa," he whispered, kissing each of her eyes. "I'm so sorry."

"You're not supposed to apologize," she gently reminded him.

"I didn't mean to come so quickly. It's just been a long time. And you feel so wonderful."

Giving him a gentle kiss, she smiled up at him. "You were perfect. You still are."

He finally got up the strength to push himself off of her. She rolled to her side and curled up on his chest while he wrapped his arm around her, holding her close.

"I'm still gonna say I'm sorry though," he kissed the side of her head.

"Then I'm gonna have to apologize for slapping you."

"Not a problem. Now I know the cease-and-detit sign."

She giggled and he chuckled with her.

"Then I'm sorry for being so loud."

"Oh, that I like."

"That's good, because I don't think I could stop that if I wanted to. I'd probably explode."

She relaxed into his side, loving how well they fit together, except…

"Ok, I gotta clean up now. Bathroom?"

He pointed to the far door on the right. "Use whatever you like. There's all kinds of stuff in the cupboards. Help yourself."

While she cleaned herself up in the bathroom, he took the opportunity to wipe down himself and the bed. Or he tried.

"I will gladly sleep in the wet spot," he mumbled to himself and moved over a foot. "California king and I manage to nail it right where you can't avoid it. Good one Dane."

She came out soon and curled back up on his chest. She looked up and kissed him quickly, then snuggled back in.

"Thank you," she said quietly.

"My pleasure and honor," he smiled as he fell asleep.

* * * * *

Alex wasn't sure how long he'd been out. He hadn't checked the clock before he fell asleep but he was guessing about twenty minutes. Somewhere in that time Lyssa had rolled over and now he was spooned up behind her. He was surprised that none of that had woken him up.

But what shocked him even more, and slightly terrified him, was that someone had managed to come into the studio and up the stairs to his apartment. And that someone was standing in the middle of the room looking at him.

"What the hell are you doing in my apartment?"

"Staring."

"No shit."

"You told me to stop by."

"The studio, Andre. The studio."

"You weren't there. So I checked up here."

"Understandable, I suppose, but why are you still here?"

"I was trying to figure out if it was really you."

"Of course it's me. It's my apartment."

"I thought so but there's a woman in your bed, so I thought maybe you moved or were subletting."

"You're an ass."

Lyssa finally giggled. She'd woken up early enough in the conversation to know what was going on.

"Oh, my God," Andre gasped. "What an adorable little thing."

"Hi," she waved to his effeminate friend with the tips of her fingers.

"I love her," he whispered loudly, not really trying to hide it from anyone.

"Alright," Alex sighed. "Go back down to the studio. I'll be there in a minute."

"Okie dokie," he practically skipped out.

"I hate my friends," Alex mumbled.

Turning Lyssa over onto her back, Alex kissed her tenderly.

"I'll be back in a couple minutes."

"Ok," she smiled up at him.

He rolled her over onto her side again, gave her a light smack in the ass, causing her to squeak, then slipped out of bed. Lyssa was giggling the entire time he redressed.

"Harlot," he winked to her just before leaving.

Downstairs Alex found Andre looking over his new work.

"I like it. A lot."

"Thanks. I don't have a nude sketch for you. I probably never will."

"Couldn't do it?"

He shook his head.

"Was that your model?"

"No," he scoffed.

"Hooker?"

Alex glared at him.

"Sorry. Just asking. I mean, it is you."

"I told you I was picky."

"No, you said you weren't looking. There's a difference."

"Yeah, and I wasn't. She just sorta found her way into my life."

"You mean bed."

"That too," he rolled his eyes, irritated by Andre constantly correcting him. Even if he was right.

"Honestly, I thought you were just refusing to come out of the closet."

"You wish."

"You know me!"

"I do," he grumbled.

The second most common insinuation people made about Alex's character was that he must be gay. Good looking, single guy. Definitely gay. This was far more annoying than the number one insinuation that he wore contacts.

"This one meets your high standards?"

"If you mean she's sweet, smart and sexy, then yes."

"Congratulations. If I were so patient I could afford to be pickier myself."

"Problems with David?"

"Always. I don't wanna talk about it," he brushed the

depressing conversation away. "I'm curious; did you even try to sketch one for the exhibit?"

"Oddly enough. Yes."

Alex pulled the sketch he'd crumpled up earlier out of the trash. Opening it, he showed his friend, who shrugged.

"Not bad."

"Not good either."

"So sketch the naked chick in your bed."

"I can't."

"Why not?"

"Because the sight of her naked drives me insane and I can't sketch with a raging hard-on."

Andre laughed. "Yeah, ok."

"No offense Andre, can I have my apartment keys back."

"Of course. I'm just glad to hear you've finally got a piece of tail."

"It's not like that."

"I'm sure it's not with you, but I'm just especially glad you're getting some. If you got anymore uptight I thought I was going to have to do you myself."

"No!"

Andre laughed again. "Ok. I gotta go. I have to stop by Jacobson's Art Store to pick up my latest shipment of crap I don't really need."

As he was leaving he shouted back, "Have fun tapping it!"

He laughed once more before disappearing completely down the stairs.

"Ass," Alex mumbled to himself.

"Sweetie?"

Lyssa was crossing the room to him, fully-clothed. It was just like she was arriving again, sans cake carrier.

"I was just about to come back up. I swear."

"I believe you, however I have to go. I promised Janice I'd help her pick out paint for her living room today. She's redecorating and has no sense of color whatsoever."

She reached up to hug him and he wrapped his arms around her waist, picking her up off the floor.

"Thanks for ending my dry spell," he said.

"Thanks for picking me."

He set her feet back on the floor and looked down at her. "I didn't really have a choice."

"You didn't?"

"You bewitched me."

"I didn't bewitch you. I threw you on a table. The giant boner's your problem."

"And you're my solution," he smirked.

She reached up and kissed him. "Goodbye handsome."

"Bye Babe."

Lyssa reluctantly slipped from Alex's arms and forced herself to walk away. At the door she looked back and gave him a little wave to go with her little smile. He nodded back with his own smile.

Once the sound of her footsteps on the stairs had died away, he gave a huge sigh.

"I can't think about this right now. I need a nap."

* * * * *

"I really appreciate you meeting me down here on a Saturday to help me do this. I know you normally work on Saturdays, so taking the time off to do this is really nice of you. My mother-in-law was supposed to take the kids today so I could shop without having to constantly look after them --- Joshua! Put that down! --- but she went to Portsmouth to visit her sister. I guess she tripped while gardening yesterday and twisted her ankle and --- Mary! Sit back down in your seat! You can't get out yet. --- and it's swollen. My mother-in-law took her up some lunch and she's going to stay there for the weekend since it hurts her to --- Joshua! Stop touching that! It's not yours! --- walk around. It's really nice of her. She's always doing stuff like that, but I had so hoped to have a day - -- Eat the Goldfish in your tray, Mary. --- where I can get this done without the kids. As you can see --- Don't interrupt Mommy while she's talking, Joshua. --- it's going to be difficult to get this done with the kids here. I wasn't very good at this without them, and with them --- I'll take you to the bathroom in a minute, Mary. --- It's almost impossible. So again, I'm really appreciative of any help you can give me."

Janice finally stopped talking and smiled tiredly at Lyssa.

"I slept with my bodyguard."

Janice stopped pushing the stroller and stared at her friend.

"This morning," Lyssa confessed further.

For once in the woman's life, she had nothing to say except...

"Holy shit."

"Mommy! You swore!" Joshua was quick to point out.

"You would too if you knew what I knew."

"It just kind of... "

"Happened?"

Lyssa nodded. "It wasn't entirely a surprise though. We've been working our way towards it. Rather quickly too."

"You mean the S-E-X?" she spelled out.

"Pizza?" Mary looked up at her Mommy.

"No Mary! Pizza is P-I-Z-Z-A. Duh." Joshua stuck his tongue out at this sister.

"Stop it. Right. Now," Janice warned her young son.

"Oh, well, the whole thing was..." Lyssa searched for the right word for it. "Very satisfying. I mean, he just looks at me and I wanna explode, so anything above and beyond that is frosting on the cake," she smirked at her little inside joke.

"I bet Iron Man can look at you and make you explode! He's cool!"

"How was it?" Janice asked quietly, trying to ignore her

son's outburst.

"Amazing."

"Really?"

"He's beautiful and hung like an Adonis."

"Wow."

"What's an Adonis, Mommy?"

"A rare and beautiful thing. Now stop eavesdropping."

"What's eavesdropping, Mommy?"

"He's at the age where everything is a question," she explained to Lyssa.

"That's eavesdropping?"

"Eavesdropping is when little boys listen to Mommy's conversations with her friend when they're not supposed to."

"What else am I supposed to listen to? We're in Lowe's."

Lyssa snorted. She couldn't help it.

"I guess he does have a point," Janice frowned.

They'd arrived at the paint section. Janice pulled out a magazine from one of the many bags she seemed to always have with her. Some on her arm, some hanging from the stroller. Flipping it open to the paper-clipped page, she handed it to Lyssa.

"Do you think that'll work in my house?"

"No," Lyssa said bluntly.

"Ah shit," she mumbled, then looked around quickly to find that Joshua was too busy acting out a battle scene from one of the Iron Man movies to notice she swore again.

"I like this room for your house." Lyssa pointed to a picture on a different page.

"Really? I thought it was too bold."

"You need bold. You live in a giant box."

"It might be easier to just move."

"Maybe."

"So," Janice looked around her again for nosey neighbors, "Who is it, anyway?"

"Oh, I thought you knew."

"No."

"I kind of blurted out to Patrick one day that I was interested in Alex Dane and –"

Janice gasped loudly, making her stop.

"What? What's wrong?" Lyssa panicked.

"He is so hot. I am soooo jealous."

"You are?"

"We went to Bryan Markison's house… pfft, house… it's a freakin' mansion… anyway, he hosted a barbeque last summer. We shipped the kids to my mothers and spent the entire weekend there. It was fantastic! I tell Patrick all the time that it was the best vacation we ever took. Anyway, Alex happened to be in town and stopped by. That man in a pair of swimming trunks is the finest thing I've ever seen. And I could kiss whoever taught him to trim his mustache and beard, because it's always perfect. Just the right length. Somewhere between respectable and nasty in the sack."

Lyssa was wide-eyed staring at her at this point. Normally Janice's rambling made her want to jam a pair of scissors into her ears. This was not normal.

"I think that was the last time Patrick got serviced orally too. And all because of that man. Well, and the other hot guys in the pool. That security department is supah fine!" Janice started slipping into ghetto speak, which she usually only did when she was drunk. "But Alex? Mmm-mmm-mmm-MMM! I was under the impression he was slippin' it to that blond bimbo with the fake yabbos."

"Blond bimbo?"

"Oh, what the hell is her name? The horny blond guy's sister. Jesus. Is it hot in here?" She started fanning herself with her shirt collar.

"Do you mean Chase and Trixie?"

"Yes! She's a damn ho. Nice enough to me, but still… RAWR!"

She cat clawed at Lyssa's face, making her lean back

momentarily.

"I'm pretty sure you could take her. You're a solid girl," Janice laughed, poking at Lyssa's hips.

"Yeah, ok, thanks for the vote of confidence. Maybe we should just get the paint," Lyssa looked back at the wall.

What was supposed to have been an exciting story she needed to share with a friend was turning out to be more information than she wanted. Lyssa was starting to wish she never said anything.

"I say we cutta bitch."

"Janice!"

"Sorry," she bolted upright. "Sorry. That was bad. Kind of lost myself for a moment."

"Not in Lowe's please."

"Right." She looked around to verify no one was still watching. Thankfully they weren't.

"What makes you think that about Alex and Trixie?"

"Oh, she was kind of hanging all over him. Or maybe that was me. But she was never far away. I assumed it, I guess. But he's your guy now right?"

Lyssa shrugged. "I don't know what it is now."

"I'm sorry sweetie. I shouldn't have said anything."

She shrugged again. "I'd have found out eventually. Better now than later."

"I'm sure it's nothing. Ignore me. I was drunk that day anyway, so what do I know!"

"It's alright Janice."

Lyssa continued to look for paint swatches that matched the photo in the magazine.

"I didn't mean to ruin it for you," Janice started to tear up.

"Janice. It's fine."

"We don't talk for months and you finally tell me the best news I've heard in years and I screwed it all up," she was practically bawling now.

"Stop!" Lyssa pleaded. "Oh, my God! Please stop!"

"You were so happy and I didn't even get to ask you if the carpet matched the drapes."

"It does. Unless you meant the actual flooring. It was hardwood and the drapes were white sheers with cranberry scarf valances. Very simple, but tastefully done."

"I meant the forest around the mighty oak trunk."

"Oh! Yeah. It does."

"What size was the bed?"

"Huge king size. Might be a Cali king. Not sure. I didn't stop to ask."

"Does he put out guest towels and those little decorative soaps?"

"Um, I don't know. He wasn't really expecting me, but he doesn't seem the type. The bathroom was clean though," Lyssa shrugged.

"I'm sorry. I've just been so emotional lately," she wiped her eyes.

"Are you pregnant again?" Lyssa asked quietly.

"No. Quite the opposite this week. And --- Joshua! You do not climb up the shelves! Get over here! --- And it's just been terrible. The cramps and bloating and mood swings. You know how it is. Oh, actually..." she started blubbering. "I'm sorry! I did it again! I can't do anything right today!"

"No, quite alright. Believe me. I'm kind of happy the baby-making factory's shut down. Especially after today."

"Yeah... I should probably look into... some solutions... like that too... Joshua!"

"What?" He was standing right behind her.

"Oh. Stay here and watch your sister so I can pick out paint, ok?"

"Sure Mom."

Janice finally calmed enough to start looking at the swatches Lyssa picked out.

Until…

"You stink. Mom! I think Mary shit her pants!"

"Joshua!!!!!"

"You said it first!!!!!"

10

Lyssa had nothing on her schedule for the last day of the weekend. Normally on Saturday she worked from home and spent Sunday housecleaning, doing what little grocery shopping she needed to do, and staring into the case at Marc Jacobs convincing herself she didn't need a $300 watch. Hell, she didn't even wear a watch. But the things were just so damn sparkly!

Today she didn't care. She didn't want to go anywhere or do anything. She didn't want to buy anything. Nothing was going to cheer her up. She was filled with self-doubt before, and after the paint-excursion-from-hell with Janice it'd just gotten worse.

Janice is a crazy hormonal woman.

Lyssa was trying to convince herself that her crazy hormonal issues were far different. Janice was trying to remember what happened at a barbeque she was admittedly drunk at over a year ago. Lyssa was just trying to get laid without the emotional baggage that often comes with sleeping with a super hot guy that's probably got women all over the world and a blond bimbo right in the same building they both worked in.

Yeah, this isn't working.

After an hour of staring at her email, trying to convince herself that she was 'organizing it' and not waiting for something new from someone-special-who-shall-not-be-named-because-that's-not-what-we're-doing, Lyssa set about cleaning up the spare bedroom. For years it'd just been a place to throw things. Things she didn't want to deal with. It was currently filled with extra purses, extra shoes, and junk that most people drag around with them wherever they go.

"The past," she stared at the boxes furthest across the room.

"Forget it. Let's focus on the shoes. Oooooo! Shoes!"

After she'd organized everything that didn't have a negative emotion attached to it, she took a break to make some lunch.

She'd just opened the refrigerator door when her door buzzed. Peeking out the peephole she recognized Henry the daytime security guard from the front desk.

"Hi Henry," she opened the door. "Ooo!" her eyes lit up at the sight of the large bouquet of flowers in his hands.

"These just arrived for you Ms. Winfield," he handed them out to her.

"Thank you Henry!" she took them from him.

"You're very welcome Ma'am."

Henry gave her a smile and a nod then closed the door for her as her hands were full.

Lyssa was squealing with delight. She rarely got flowers. She didn't actually care for them. Probably because she rarely got them. These were a beautiful arrangement of wildflowers.

"Please say you're from Alex," she prayed as she set the vase on the table.

Slipping the small card from its envelope, she gasped.

It was a tiny cartoon drawing of a man and a woman. The bearded man was kissing the smiling, shy woman on the cheek. There were three little hearts over their heads. Written on the back was, "Thank you for the cake. It's almost as sweet as the baker. Alex."

"Oh," she choked up, tears of joy swelling in her eyes.

Not only had he sent the flowers, he'd obviously picked them out himself and filled out the card. She recognized his signature from the drawing he did of the bridge in her planner. It was definitely him.

After she'd read it about a hundred times, she put it back in its holder amongst the flowers. She took a moment to compose herself, then sent a text.

Thank you for the flowers. They're lovely and the drawing is adorable.

To her surprise, he called back almost immediately.

"Hello Alex," she answered the phone.

"You did say you baked the cake, right? God, please tell me you were the baker."

"Yes," she giggled. "I was."

"Thank the lord. After I wrote that I thought maybe you bought it from Fat Lou's bakery. The idea of sleeping with him gives me nightmares."

She giggled again. There was just no stopping it at this point.

"I gotta go. I was on my way to my cousin's house to help him repair his bike and I pulled over to call you."

"You repair bikes too? You have way too many talents."

"Actually, we never repair anything. Ron just wants to sit in his garage and drink beer without his wife Shirley nagging at him, which she won't if I'm there."

"Ok. Have fun. Ride carefully please."

"Always."

"I'll see you tomorrow."

"I hope so. Bye Lyss."

"Bye Alex."

She would carry a smile with her for the majority of the day. Whenever her mind started to nag at her, giving her reasons to doubt him, she'd go look at the flowers and the little cartoon and she'd smile again.

But come Monday morning she'd be back at work and she wouldn't have the flowers to look at and the doubt would settle back in again. And this time it would take some answers.

11

"Chase?" Lyssa stood in his office doorway. "Can we talk?"

"Sure," he looked up from his desk with a smile. He was always happy to see her.

She entered and closed the door. This was serious. She never closed the door.

"What's up, sweetcheeks?" he asked. "Wait a minute. How did you get up here anyway?"

"I blackmailed Patrick into letting me up onto this floor."

"Ok," he nodded, content with that answer.

"Is it true that your sister and Alex were together?"

"Did he tell you?" he was disappointed.

"No. Someone else suggested it to me."

"Ah hell. I mean, what was the point of pulling her naked ass out of his studio if someone was gonna tell you she was there."

"Wait. Wha???"

"Saturday. The nude thing. Whatever you call it."

"She was the nude model?"

"Yeah, that's it."

"Really?" she said with a cocked eyebrow and he realized he might be up shit-crick now.

"Um, yeah. That's what you were talking about, right?"

"No."

"Ah, crap."

"I was talking about them sleeping together."

"Whoa!" he stood up so fast from his chair that he knocked it over. "What the fuck!"

"Didn't they have a relationship?"

"No! Did they? When?"

"Well I was under the impression it was last year, but apparently it was this past weekend?"

"No! That was just a nude sitting for that sketch he promised Andre! Wait. So, no one told you about that then?"

She shook her head.

"Ah, supercrap. I blew it."

He walked around the desk to address her.

"She was there before you arrived. She was doing Alex a favor so he didn't have to hire a nude model. He hates the damn things but he promised Andre he'd do a sketch, or whatever it is he does. Paint? Bah! Anyway, Andre is one of the few artist friends he kept from college so he didn't want to let him down.

"The problem is I didn't remember that until I sent you over there, so Jay and I raced over to the studio --- literally --- and we kidnapped her so you'd never know. I mean, it's hard to pick up a new girl if you have a naked one hanging around already. I don't think Alex was unhappy about it either because he didn't lift a finger to try and stop us."

Chase chuckled as he remember the incident.

Lyssa suddenly grabbed Chase by the front of his shirt and with a surprising amount of strength, pushed him up violently against the door and held him there.

"Jesus Lyss!"

"If you're lying to me—"

"I'm not!"

"I swear to every god, in every religion, on this planet, and all the other ones too, that if you're lying to me I'll flatten your balls with my car!"

"Redrum! Peanut butter! Terminix!"

"What?!"

"I forgot the safe word!"

Lyssa let him go. "You're an ass."

Chase laughed. "I'm sorry Lyss, but you're starting to go mental on me."

She glared at him.

"But," he straightened up quickly, "I have no doubt that it's for a very, very important reason. I'm just a bit confused right now. Please don't hurt me. Again."

Lyssa turned and sat down in one of the guest chairs. Chase sat in the opposite, bent over, his arms resting on his knees.

"Tell me what happened."

She shook her head.

"Lyss, I know I come off as a pompous, self-centered tool, but I promise that I can be a very nice guy too. You can tell me and I'll try to help you and I won't say a thing to anyone."

She shook her head again.

He pulled his chair closer and put his hand on her knee. "I'm sorry. Being funny and acting like a jackass is kind of my thing. But when I'm serious it's the real deal. Hence why I freaked there for a minute when you suggested that they might have..." He shuddered. "But I can be serious now. I promise. I'll even—"

"Shut up," she said quietly.

"Ok," he simply replied and sat back in his chair, waiting patiently.

"Alex and I..." she trailed off.

"Relocated your relationship from the office to the bedroom?" he gently suggested. "Or whatever room you might have—"

"Yes!"

"Ok."

"You didn't know?" she glanced up at him.

He shook his head. "I guessed that might be the case, but he hasn't said anything to me about it. In fact, that's the entire reason why I suspected it in the first place. On Sundays we normally do laps at the pool, then catch a game on TV, sit around and bullshit, catch up on each other's lives, jobs.

"But he didn't really talk much yesterday. He did his laps, then left. Said he had a lot of work to do at the studio. It was odd. I mean, Alex isn't a huge talker anyway, but it's not like him to avoid me. Unless there's something he didn't want me to know. Considering the previous morning's events, I guessed something either went really wrong, or really right, with you. And it was the latter?"

She nodded. Chase couldn't help smiling.

"As far as Trixie's concerned, she's as much a sister to Alex as she is me. The fact that we had different parents is a minor technicality. We all grew up in the same house with the same adopted parents, so—"

"You did?" she was shocked.

"Yeah, you didn't know?"

She shook her head.

"Alex, me and my sister were all orphaned as children. My sister and I were very young. Alex was ten when his parents were killed in a car accident. But we all ended up in the same foster house. We were lucky. Our foster parents were great. Eventually they adopted all six of us."

"Six? I had no idea."

"Yeah. We all stayed in the same house until college. Most everyone is scattered around the world now, but if you think about it, Alex and I are pretty much still in the same house. It's just a high-rise office building now. Sure, we have apartments off-campus, but it's still the same house."

"I didn't know any of that."

"It's not a secret. We don't talk about it a lot, because we're security guys. It's what we do. Only leak out the information you have to. Crap like that. Especially Alex. He still broods about the past occasionally. Lets it follow him around like a dark cloud. It's taken him a long time, but I'm glad he finally gave in to you."

"Long time? We haven't even known each other two weeks!"

"I mean, 'you' as in happiness. He doesn't enter into these things too lightly. And he's never, ever, with Trixie. I promise you.

Even if they weren't siblings by circumstance she is not his type. Never has, never will be. I was starting to think he didn't have a type."

She wiped her eyes quickly and let out a deep sigh of relief.

"By the way, who suggested Alex and Trixie..." he shuddered again, still not able to say it.

"Oh, well... " she hemmed and hawed.

"I won't say anything, I promise," he crossed his heart.

"Janice Kelty."

"Ha!" he blurted out laughing. "It's the summer pool party thing, isn't it?"

Lyssa nodded.

"Oh, my God. Janice was so hammered. Have you seen her drunk?"

Lyssa nodded again with a smirk.

"One of the funniest things I have ever seen. She gets her black on."

"Yes!" Lyssa laughed. "Totally ghetto."

"It was awesome! She kept mumbling to me about how much of a ho Trixie was. Accused Alex of being her pimp. And to make matters worse, Trixie had just broken up with some poor schmuck from HR so she was hanging by Alex just in case the guy showed up. He wasn't even invited! And the last I heard HR guys weren't the type of people to raid a pool party to seek revenge on an overrated slutbag. It would kinda be against their religion."

"That's kind of harsh about your sister."

He shrugged. "I love Trix but she is a bit of a slut. And I gave up caring about who, what, or where she was banging a long time ago. She's all grown up now and that's her choice. I got enough of my own problems without adding hers to the list."

"I guess I overreacted."

"You didn't know. Hell, if I didn't know I might have wondered too. I think it's kind of nice Alex has a girl who cares enough about him to threaten my life."

They stood and Lyssa hugged him.

"Thanks Chase."

"Anything for my brother's girl."

"I don't know if that's what I am actually. We haven't discussed anything above and beyond Saturday."

"Don't worry," he stressed. "I won't say anything. I promise."

"Thanks," she smiled.

"And if you need someone to talk to, I'm here."

He gave her a fist bump and she left. Or she tried to. As she was reaching for the door it swung open at an alarming rate and hit her squarely in the face.

"Jesus!" Chase shouted and caught Lyssa as she stumbled back while grabbing her nose.

"Oh, my God. Are you ok?"

It was Trixie.

"Are you kidding me?" Lyssa said, but it came out, *Ahd oo kidda me.*

"I'm so sorry," Trixie apologized, looking quite mortified. "You've got..." Trixie pointed.

Lyssa looked down and there was blood flowing down the front of her shirt. Trixie turned pale and slipped to the floor, passed out cold.

"This is not good," Chase said.

"You take care of her. I can take care of myself," That came out as, *Oo take cahr uv er. I ca take cahr uv mysef.*

He caught enough of it to understand, especially when Lyssa went directly into his office bathroom. She lowered her hand and noticed blood dripping from her nose.

"Dammit." And it came out as, *Dammit.*

"Hey. Trixie. Stupid ho. Wake up," Chase nudged at her. "Jesus. What a clusterfuck. Hey Lyss! I got a great name for the game! Mutation 2: The Clusterfuck!"

He heard her laugh for a moment, then swear again.

"Sorry!"

By the time she left Chase's office Trixie was still passed out on the floor but Lyssa's bleeding had stopped. Mostly. As she stood waiting for the elevator Lyssa devised a plan in her head. A plan that would get her to her office without being seen.

The door opened and she stepped in, promptly planting the heel of her favorite pumps perfectly in the crack between the elevator and floor. As she proceeded to step forward the heel snapped off the shoe. She stumbled and landed on her knee.

"Ow," she whined.

Standing, she looked back and saw the heel, still stuck in the crevice, being repeatedly smashed by the elevator doors which were trying to close. She wedged herself between the doors and yanked the heel out.

Grateful the hallway was still devoid of people, she stepped into the elevator and pushed the button for her floor.

"Dammit," she mumbled again when the elevator doors reopened.

She was so preoccupied with her broken shoe that she completely forgot the plan was to go to the nearly-vacant floor below theirs and take the stairs up a flight, where it entered the programming floor much closer to her office.

Limping from the loss of the heel and bruised knee, her white blouse covered with dried blood stains, and still holding an ice pack over her nose, Lyssa set about traveling the entire length of the floor.

"Hey boss," Kenny stepped out from his desk at that precise moment. "Oh."

She just waved to him and continuing on.

"Boss? You ok?"

Word spread thru the department faster than a bird flu epidemic. By the time she reached Marlene's desk everyone was standing and staring. Heads popped out of every office door.

Taking a deep breath, she turned to address them.

"No one says a damn thing! Understood?!"

"Yes ma'am," they replied in unison and quickly went back to work.

Looking back at Marlene, Lyssa said quite calmly, "I will be in the conference room. Please hold my calls."

"Yes ma'am," she replied quietly.

And she promptly stepped into the women's room. As soon as the door was closed, Marlene picked up her phone and dialed the three digit extension she'd written on a sticky note that was tucked under her keyboard. She often dreamed of using it but never in a million years did she think she'd actually have to.

When Alex arrived he found Lyssa leaning over the same sink as the first time he invaded the women's room.

"Lyssa?"

"I'm fine," she automatically replied, able to recognize his voice by now.

"I heard a rumor that you got into a fight."

"Ha. Ha." She stood up straight and looked at him. He was a bit stunned. Marlene wasn't kidding. She looked like she'd been in a bar brawl.

"Did you at least win?"

She would have glared at him but her face hurt. So she picked up the heel from the sink basin and flung it towards him. It was a pretty good shot for not even looking at him, but he dodged left and it just missed him. He picked it up off the floor.

"Well," Lyssa pondered. "I *was* the only one standing when I left the room."

"I don't doubt it."

"I was talking to Chase and went to leave just as Trixie was coming in his office. I caught the door with my face. She saw the blood and passed out."

"Wuss," he mumbled.

"Chase was still trying to revive her when I left."

"Are you ok?" he asked, actually quite concerned about her.

"I don't think it's broken."

She looked in the mirror.

"Jesus. I look like one of the zombies from the game."

Alex snorted. He shouldn't have, but she was right.

"Um," he tried to cover it up, knowing that was futile. "Your shoe?" he looked down at the heel in his hand.

"Oh, that broke when I went to get in the elevator."

"Maybe you can get it fixed."

She took one last look in the mirror to make sure that her face wasn't a complete mess. Satisfied that it was as good as it was going to get, she walked over to him and took the heel, tossing it into the trash.

"I have two more of the same exact pairs at home."

She continued to walk past him and out the door. The department was prairie dogging to take a peak over cubicle walls and beyond doorways to see what she looked like now.

"Put me in the game and I swear I'll return from the dead to feast on the flesh of your grandchildren!"

Alex had to physically cover his mouth to keep from laughing. He managed to maintain his composure as he followed her into her office and closed the door.

"It's karma. That's what it is," Lyssa mumbled as she kicked off what remained of the shoes into the trash can. "This is my punishment for listening to Janice Kelty."

"Janice Kelty? Is that the Janice you were helping paint her living room?"

"Yeah." She rifled through her office closet for clean clothes.

"She once asked me to put my stump in her trunk at a barbeque."

"Ha!" she blurted out from somewhere deep in the closet.

"She's a bit crazy when she drinks."

"I know!"

"I've been told she's quite a lovely woman when she isn't

148

drinking."

"Or suffering from PMS!"

"So what did she say?"

Lyssa pulled out a clean blouse and draped it over the chair. "Nothing. It was just girl talk."

"Uh huh," he obviously didn't believe her.

She suddenly pulled her blouse off over her head, tossing it into the trash, hoping the sight of her standing before him in her brassiere would distract him enough that he'd drop this conversation.

It kinda did, except…

"Babe, you're… um…" he pointed to her cleavage.

She smirked at him, then looked down to access her boobage herself. "Dammit! It soaked through to my bra too?!"

She dove back into the closet while Alex locked the door to prevent anyone from walking in while his lover was traipsing around her office half-dressed.

"Honey, if she said something that upset you…especially about me —"

"No!"

"I didn't do anything with her."

"I know!"

"Did she say —"

"No! She didn't!"

Lyssa came out of the closet and flung her blood-stained bra at him. He caught it clumsily.

"There, now you have your own to practice with."

One arm was barely covering her breasts while in the other hand she held a clean bra. He was smirking. He couldn't help it.

Tossing the clean bra into the chair, Lyssa sauntered over to him and wrapped her arms around his neck, pressing her chest up against his.

"You shouldn't tease me like this," he groaned.

He tossed the bloody bra in his hand aside, not really giving a damn where it landed, then slid his hands around to her backside, pulling her closer, kissing her.

As they kissed, he slowly inched up her skirt so he could feel her soft, cotton-covered asscheeks against the palms of his hand. He'd just slipped his fingers under the elastic band when...

"Ow!" she backed away, putting her hand to her nose again.

"Sorry Babe. I didn't mean to... ah shit."

He grabbed the blood-stained shirt back out of the trash and wadded it up, pressing it up to her face. Her nose was bleeding again.

"Oh," she whimpered. He couldn't see it, but he could sense her lip was quivering.

"Don't cry. It'll be fine," he said gently. "I'm sure the swelling will go down."

"My nose is swollen?"

"No."

He glanced down at the bulge in his pants. She started whimpering again.

"It was a joke Babe," he assured her as he put the ice pack on the back of her neck. "I mean, it will. But... ah shit."

He gave up trying to talk to her and decided he best get her back into clothing. For both their sakes. She slipped on the bra, but couldn't latch it with one hand so he had to.

"This demonic device was forged in Mordor," Alex grumbled as he tried to clasp the clean bra, which made Lyssa giggle. He was at least grateful for that.

He eventually managed. Then he buttoned up her blouse. The closer he got to the top of her cleavage, the more he smiled.

"I should thank you," he said in his sexy, deep voice.

"What for?" she asked, not really feeling sexy or a need to fake it.

"For the first time in my life I understand how Chase feels. You're in pain and I'm having impure thoughts."

"Sorry."

"Don't be. At least the semi will keep me awake during the conference call with L.A."

"Ha ha," she snickered. "You have to talk to L.A."

"Laugh it up. As soon as you're feeling better, I'm gonna be back to defile these."

He cupped her breasts up in his hands and kissed the overflowing cleavage. One delicate kiss per globe.

She gasped, then slapped him on the head. He backed up, chuckling.

"Not now," she muttered.

Alex's phone buzzed. He pulled it out of his pocket and glanced at the text message.

"Gotta go Babe. L.A.'s had their coffee and wants to talk now."

He tucked the phone back into his pocket then stood. Bending over, he kissed her lightly on the forehead.

"Be a good girl," he smiled down at her.

"Uh huh," she mumbled.

He left her office, closing the door behind him. She imagined he would tell Marlene that she would be ok and to not let anyone bother her, but check on her at lunch to make sure she hadn't decided to take a nap and drowned in a pool of her own nose blood.

Ew.

When Alex arrived to his meeting he found Chase already there.

"Bryan's on his way. He's trying to get off the phone with Austria, or Belgium, or one of those European countries that talks too loud into the conference phone."

Alex nodded in response.

"How's your girl?" Chase smirked at him.

"Are we that obvious?"

"Oh yeah. And besides, you have some blood on your shirt. Looks like her color."

He looked down and sure enough there was a couple splatters. He grabbed a tissue and dabbed at it. Finding it already dried, he gave up and threw the tissue away. It wasn't enough to warrant changing into a clean shirt at this point.

"Lyssa's a little rough but she'll be ok. How's the wuss?"

"When I left she was sitting up and breathing. Man, how did our sister turn out to be such a pussy when it comes to blood? Especially having grown up with us. One of us was always broken and bleeding at any given point in time."

Alex chuckled. "True."

"That reminds me, Mom and Dad's anniversary is next month. I was thinking we should go down and surprise them. It's been almost six months since anyone last visited. We could take them out on one of those dinners on the cruise boats that they like."

"Sounds good."

Chase wasn't going to say anything, but it was killing him.

"Maybe you could take Lyssa," he suggested.

"Chase," Alex took a deep breath. "It's only been a few days. Give it some time, ok?"

"Ok."

After another minute...

"Can I at least tell Ma you threw yourself into the dating pool and caught a mermaid? Pleeeeeeeease."

"Chase!"

"Yeah, sorry."

Another minute...

"You know the doctor said Mom's sugar was high again. She needs to lose a few pounds. Maybe our visiting will be good encouragement for her to eat healthier. You know how if she thinks someone's going to visit she'll perk up and start exercising again."

"Fine! You can tell her!"

"Yes!" he cheered.

"You can't keep a secret for shit."

"I can! Just not this one."

"How the hell did you get a job in security?"

"I can't help it! I like that little squealing noise Ma makes when she thinks one of us is close to getting married. It's usually for Lincoln or Patty or Sheila. She kinda gave up on us years ago."

"They raised over a dozen foster kids and not one of us is leading a so-called normal life."

"I know. When she hears it's you, I bet the squealing will be off the chart. I'm talking dog hearing frequency."

Bryan walked into the conference room and closed the door.

"Sorry I'm late. Finland would not shut up."

"Finland!" Chase snapped. "That was it."

"Alex," Bryan nodded to him in greeting. "How's my favorite production manager?"

"How did you hear?" Chase asked before Alex could answer.

"I hear everything."

"The wuss," Alex said.

"Of course," Bryan chuckled. "Trixie came to me in tears. Something about she almost killed one of my employees and she thought she should turn herself into HR."

Everyone chuckled.

"The rest of it I got from Marlene."

"She called you too?" both Chase and Alex said, causing them to look at each other.

"I called her," he confessed. "I wanted to confirm it was Lyssa she attacked. She told me Alex was attending to the victim."

"Lyssa will be fine," Alex reported. "It's just bleeding, not broken."

"Good. I see she gave you a little souvenir for the road too."

Alex glanced down at the front of his pants. Despite what he'd told Lyssa, his semi was long gone. It didn't even last through the elevator ride.

"I think he was referring to the blood," Chase muttered.

"Ah shit," Alex sighed, rubbing his forehead.

Bryan laughed. He didn't laugh often. When he did it was almost always in conjunction with something his best friends had done.

"Bryan, I can explain—"

"Please don't Alex," he interrupted him. "You don't owe me any explanations. I know Lyssa well. She's a beautiful and entertaining woman. And quite brilliant to boot."

"She is."

"I know you don't need my blessing, but rest assured you have it. I'm well aware of how hard you both work and I'm happy you've found each other. As long as it doesn't affect your work too badly, of course. Just please, for God's sake, have fun."

"Thank you," Alex simply replied.

"Now, I think we've left the L.A. office waiting long enough to understand that they don't tell me when to phone them."

They all sat and the call began. Alex barely listened to it. He was distracted by the morning's events. He'd woken up that morning, determined to do his job as if nothing had happened that weekend. She was an after-hours pleasure. That's all.

Yeah, right. 'That's all' my ass. You almost boned her in her office.

When Marlene phoned him that Lyssa looked like she'd been in a fight or hit by a car, he bolted out of his office. Then when he saw her everything stopped. His heart, his breathing, his brain. All completely seized up. It was for only a split second and when he got his senses back he was filled with rage. The sight of her bleeding and battered angered him. He wanted to know who did it and he wanted them to suffer. Badly.

He didn't show that though. His years in security had trained him to never show it.

As soon as he found out it was an accident the rage subsided and he could focus on making his girl smile again.

But now Bryan's words ran thru this head.

"As long as it doesn't affect your work too badly..."

Ah shit.

* * * * *

"You don't have to stay here."

"I know."

"I'll be fine."

"I know."

"You're not really gonna defile my tits tonight, are you?"

Alex chuckled. "No. I prefer to wait until you're well enough to enjoy it."

"Ok. Sorry."

"Hey, if I'm not allowed to apologize, neither are you."

"Oh. Ok. Sorry."

After the long day at work, which only lasted until six-thirty, Lyssa decided she wanted to go home and stay there for the night. She still had a terrible headache from the accident that morning and she just wanted to lay on her couch and watch hockey.

Having been understandably turned down in his proposal to take her to dinner and shopping, Alex followed along shortly with Thai take-out.

"I love Thai!"

The best three words he heard all day long and they came from his once-again happy and twinkling girl, who did indeed truly love Thai. Almost as much as she loved the four-inch black glittery Buddha statue he gave her.

"He's so cute! Thank you!"

She leaned over and hugged him tightly when he gave it to her.

"It's just a cheap trinket I picked up at the Thai restaurant. They have the weirdest stuff for sale at the counter. I thought he could protect you from getting hit in the face with doors."

"Do they have one to avoid getting hit in the face with cars?"

Alex laughed. "I don't know."

After dinner he convinced her to take some aspirin, then

they sat on the sofa together, legs stretched out over the coffee table, her resting on his chest.

He swore under his breath when his phone buzzed.

"I better get this," he said when he pulled it out of his pocket and saw who it was. "Hey Trix... Yes... Yes she is... Let me check." He held the phone to his chest. "Can you talk to Trixie?"

"Sure," Lyssa sat up, taking the phone. "Hi Trixie."

Alex snickered as he could hear Trix sobbing for Lyssa's forgiveness over the phone.

"Trixie, stop. It's ok. It was just an accident... I know, but it was still an accident... No, Alex isn't going to kick your ass."

"I might," he mumbled.

Lyssa slapped his leg, making him almost snort out his beer.

"Everything's fine. It's not broken. Just a little sore... Ok... We can do that anytime. You don't even have to beat me up first... Ok... Bye."

She handed him back the phone.

"Do what anytime?" he asked. "Or don't I want to know."

"Trixie wants to treat me to lunch in the tearoom. What were you thinking?"

"Getting your butt cracks measured for thongs or something."

"Ha ha," she smacked his leg again, then curled back up on his chest.

After a minute...

"You know, speaking of butts, there's something I should tell you."

"What?" she looked up at him.

"Um, that nude sketch I threw out Saturday morning? It was Trixie. She was the model. She was there before you visited. It wasn't really working out though. She kept asking me if her various body parts needed to be repaired."

"Repaired?"

"If her boobs were saggy, stuff that I don't really want to

think about. She's my sister, for Christ's sake. She's a sweet girl, but a little on the vain side. I guess when your whole life is spent trying to keep rich guys interested in you what else do you have to worry about?"

"Is she some kind of prostitute?"

"Not by trade. Mostly by hobby."

"Huh?"

"Trixie's likes having boyfriends. Some have money. Some don't. She works as an administrative assistant for Bryan's personal lawyer so she doesn't necessarily need money. Well, maybe if she's thinking about another boob job."

"Should I get a boob job?" she looked down her shirt.

"No!" he quickly refuted.

"Everyone seems to have massive jugs, except Val, but she's a yogini. They would probably just get in her way. She's got enough guys as it is without them."

"I love your breasts. They are perfect. Do not ever change them."

"Ok," she chuckled. "Thanks for telling me about Trixie."

"I didn't want you to find out and think I was hiding it. Well, I was at the time. It's kinda hard to say, 'Hey, you just missed my naked sister, but come look at her fat ass I sketched'."

"Did she see the sketch?"

"If she did I'd have been dead when you found me. The death certificate would have read, 'Strangled by an Anna Nicole Smith impersonator'."

"Oh, my God! That's mean."

"Come on! She looks a little like her."

"Maybe a smaller, less colorful version of her."

"When she gets her hair cut short she looks like Chase in drag."

Lyssa started laughing and couldn't stop, which got Alex laughing.

"You're so mean!"

"I know. Besides, they're my twin siblings. I'm supposed to be mean to 'em."

"I didn't know they were twins."

"You didn't? I assumed Chase told you. I assume he tells you everything. He probably calls you from the bathroom to tell sweetcheeks he's taking a crap."

"Ew! No! Actually, now that you mention it, I do know he likes to take his morning constitutional at 9:45."

"See? It's just wrong that you know that."

"How did you know he calls me sweetcheeks?"

"He told me one time," he said, taking a swig of his beer before continuing. "Months ago. He said your ass is so sweet that he calls you sweetcheeks."

She sat up and kissed him gently on the cheek. "He may think that, but only you know that."

He looked at her. She was smiling to him. He set down his beer so he could wrap his hand around her neck, pulling her close to kiss her, rubbing his thumb over her jaw.

"I know Babe," he smiled to her and let her settle back on his chest.

And that was the way Lyssa's fifty-two hours of self-doubt and paranoia ended. She had nothing to worry about the whole time. And she discovered that her lover was jealous of his best friend!

"How's the nose?"

"Not too bad," she yawned. "I'm tired though."

"It was a long day."

He didn't have to wait long after that for the nighttime aspirin he gave her to kick in. Soon she was asleep, lightly purring on his chest.

He carefully scooped her up in his arms to carry her to the bedroom. Setting her down carefully, he was reminded of the last time he carried her to bed. This time he'd leave her clothes on and just drape a thin blanket over her.

He gently pushed her hair aside to kiss her forehead.

"Goodnight Babe."

She mumbled something. It sounded like I love you, but he figured he was probably mistaken.

Before leaving, he stopped at her PC. It was on. It was always on.

Pulling the thumb drive from his pocket, he plugged it into the tower. The drive had one program on it. He double-clicked the executable file's icon and a second later it was installed. He removed the thumb drive containing the spyware program they'd specifically designed themselves.

He felt bad for doing this to her, but it was pertinent to the mission. He'd only use it in the event of an emergency. He didn't actually want to know her computer activity. And hopefully she'd never find out it was on there. But if she did, he hoped she would understand.

Few of them ever did though.

12

The next morning Alex stopped round Lyssa's office early to get her for yet another meeting. As they waited patiently for the elevator to arrive, he sipped at the cup of coffee she'd brought him.

"This is fantastic," he commented.

"It's from The Bean."

"The what?"

"The Bean. It's the corner coffee shop on the same block as my apartment building."

"Hmm. Excellent."

"Thanks for taking care of me last night," Lyssa said to Alex quietly as they walked down the hallway. "I was a bit of a deranged lunatic yesterday."

"I wouldn't say that."

"What would you say?"

"A discombobulated genius."

"You would?"

"Anything else might get me slapped, and while it's an entertaining thought, we have a meeting to attend."

As they entered the elevator...

"You're not going to slap me anyway?"

"No."

"Why not?"

"I'm trying to remain focused and professional."

"Really? In those shoes?"

She looked down at the bright red three-and-a-half inch heels on her feet.

"What's wrong with them?"

"They're screaming for attention."

"They're screaming these are the colors my toes will be after wearing them all day long. Especially if I have to walk to too many meetings."

She looked up at him.

"Or the color of your cheeks," she pointed out.

He rubbed his face, trying to hide the blushing smile, and doing a terrible job of it.

"Don't bother. I can hear your loins screaming for attention."

"Meeting. We have a meeting."

"With who, anyway?"

"The security team and HR."

"Sounds hideous."

"It's serious. Very serious."

"Really?" She was finally growing as concerned as she should be.

"We need to review who might be trying to scare you."

"Oh. I guess that is serious."

When they arrived in the Security Center Conference Room, which was actually just an empty office, present already were Chase, Bill, and Morgan Taylor from the Security Department, and Mitchell Howards the director of HR. Bill led the meeting today.

"Can you think of anyone who might want to sabotage this project?"

Lyssa had pondered this question over and over again in her head many, many times. She'd had this discussion with numerous people, including Jay and Marlene. Everyone wanted to know who it was, but no one had any idea.

"No clue. I don't even think our competitors are that worried about us. We're not a huge drain on the market. It's not like we can compete or put any kind of dent in the business that Blizzard or EA Games is doing.

"And as far as disgruntled employees go, there's only a few that I can think of that left a little less than happy. They've all gone on to other things. People don't usually seek revenge when they're life gets better after leaving. They move on."

"Ok. Who are the few employees that you're thinking of though?"

"Patricia Johnson was the department assistant two years ago. She was fired for doing nothing but reading emails all day long. But I heard she got pregnant shortly after she left and moved to Arizona with her boyfriend. She had a serious attention deficit problem. She probably doesn't even remember she worked here, much less that we fired her.

"Stephen Brooks was an interesting guy. If you called him Steve he would go ballistic. A little touchy. He quit though to take care of his aging mother. His wife still works in the building as an auditor for one of the accounting firms. I don't remember which one. Stephen would have the knowledge, but since he quit it doesn't make sense that he would want revenge. Hell, I'd re-hire him if he came back.

"Pete Harris used to intern in the Graphic Arts Department last year. He was a young guy. Got fired for sexually harassing someone on the janitorial staff. He died of an accidental drug overdose though."

"Accidental?"

"Yeah. Took too many sleeping pills. They were pretty sure it was an accident, anyway. I suppose it could be someone who blames us and wants to avenge his death. Although from what the police told me he didn't have any family or friends. In fact, he was dead for a week before one of his flat mates found him."

"Good grief," Chase mumbled.

"We actually checked out all those leads. And you're right," Bill confirmed. "No one seems to care about what happened to Pete Harris. His apartment buddies have been through at least a dozen roommates since then.

"Stephen is indeed a stay-home husband caring for his terminally ill mother. He said he's actually much happier to be at home. His wife is on a leave of absence currently. She had carpal tunnel surgery. Goes to PT a lot. Her co-workers said they've gotten emails from her and she's doing good. I guess the job along with worrying about his mother was a strain on their marriage, but things are better now.

"Patricia moved to Arizona, then New Mexico, and now she's in Colorado. She still has an attention deficit problem. When I called she put the phone down to pick up the fussy baby and she never came back to the phone."

"Oh, well, that's all I can think of," Lyssa shrugged.

"Is there anyone on a personal level that you think might be a threat?"

She shook her head. "If you knew my life, which I have a feeling you might, you'd know I don't really have a personal level. It's all pretty much here at Markison."

"No exes with a vendetta?" Mitchell asked.

"No. I might have a vendetta with an ex, but... no. No one hates me. That I know of."

"Ok. If you think of anyone... anyone whatsoever... please don't hesitate to let us know."

"I assure you that it will be handled discreetly," Morgan stressed.

With the meeting wrapped up, Lyssa and Alex found themselves traveling back down the same hallway.

"I have a few leads to follow-up on tonight," Alex started.

"You should probably double-check Stephen. That guy was really weird."

"All programmers are weird."

"That's true. Have you ever thought that maybe it's someone who's still in-house?"

He nodded. "As unlikely a possibility as it seems, we are considering that too."

"Plenty of people hate their jobs and would love their companies to fail because they don't have the balls to quit."

"Exactly."

"I can't imagine anyone in my department or anyone on the project wanting to sabotage it. For one, they all seem pretty easygoing. But secondly, they put a lot of work into this and the idea that any one of them would want to ruin it all a few months before the release is unthinkable. But maybe someone from a different Markison department who knows about this project might."

He nodded again. "We're looking into all that too."

"Ok."

"What are you doing tonight?"

"I'm thinking about going to Val's for a Tai Chi massage. She owes me."

"Then home?"

"Yes, why? Stopping by?"

"Probably not. I have a feeling I'm going to be very late. I just like to know where you are."

"Are you stalking me?"

He snorted, then wiped the smile away. "That shouldn't be funny."

"But it is!"

At the next juncture Alex stopped.

"I have to go to my office and make a few phone calls."

After checking the hall quickly that it was empty, he gave her a quick kiss.

"Behave yourself."

"Only 'cause you asked."

She winked and bounced away down the hallway, a wiggle in her step. A wiggle she knew his eyes were following all the way down the hallway. A wiggle that was killing her feet.

Totally worth it!

* * * * *

Val screamed when Lyssa entered the yoga studio. She

didn't even have to tell her. She just knew from the look on her friends face.

"Ow."

"Oh, my God! You did it! It's about time!"

"Um, thanks?"

"I want all the details."

"No!"

"Come on. I tell you everything. Well, everything I think you can handle."

"And thank you so much for at least filtering some of it out."

"So. When?"

"Last Saturday. Morning. Mostly."

"Where?"

"His art studio."

"In the studio?" Val was enthralled with the details.

"He has an apartment over the studio."

"How romantic! Who instigated?"

"It was mutual. He started it, but I'm the one that took the cake there."

"Cake? What kind?"

"Carrot."

"With cream cheese frosting, right?"

"Of course!"

"Sorry. Proceed."

"It was a joke for something that happened the day before."

"Ooo! I want to hear about the joke too!"

Lyssa sighed. "Ok, but you have to rub my feet too. They are killing me."

"Sure."

She started from the beginning. She told her friend all about Austin, attacking Alex on the table, and what details she felt she could share about their tryst. She even told her about Janice's misconception of his relationship with Trixie and the accident with the door.

"Wow. You are a busy girl."

"I know."

"No wonder you don't get laid much. Look at what you've had to go through!"

"And he was easy."

"Easy?"

"He's Bryan's James Bond! He's probably used to having all kinds of women throwing themselves at him. Catching them can't be all that difficult for him anymore. He's probably got women all over the world. One in every country. Or every airport, at least."

"You don't really think that, do you?"

Lyssa shrugged.

"Well, did you talk about it?"

"No. I wasn't quite sure how to ask him what number girlfriend I am."

Val thought retrospectively. "I don't know. I still can't see it."

"You only met him once."

"He just doesn't strike me as the kind of guy with secrets like that. He's got too many professional secrets – dangerous secrets – to have secrets with women."

Lyssa rolled her eyes. Val was a yogini with an open view of the world. She thought nothing of sharing her bed with four different guys a week. That was fine for her, but it worried Lyssa that she might be Miss Saturday Morning.

"Well, he's a great guy and really good at his job. I do know that much."

"I think you're too worried about it. You're looking for something to go wrong. Just lay back and relax and enjoy yourself."

"I'm trying."

After a moment…

"Wait a minute," Lyssa looked up. "Were you talking about this massage or sex?"

"Both. Now quit fussing."

Val smacked her on the bottom to get her to lie down again.

* * * * *

Lyssa didn't really think Alex had women all over the world. She didn't really think she was the girl in this port. His Boston Harbor slut.

Can you be a slut after only one tryst? How many one-night stands do you have to have before you can be labeled a slut?

The question bothered her all the way from the yoga studio back home. So in true nerd fashion, she sat down at her home PC and asked Google.

After reading through a hilarious article by Cracked.com about one-night stands, she found other more serious articles on the topics of women's sexuality and promiscuity. The answer was quite simple.

She wasn't a slut.

They had a relationship above and beyond sex. It was a perfect mixture of business and pleasure. This fact was substantiated mostly by the fact that he sent flowers. Sluts don't get flowers.

She glanced up at the vase of flowers on the nearby table. They were still fresh and lovely. Crossing to the card, she pulled it out and read it for the 1,492nd time. She slipped the card into her wallet. It was safely encased in a plastic sleeve between her American Express Gold and AAA card. Now she could see it wherever she went.

"Kinda pathetic," she feared, but made no attempts to remove it from the wallet.

Sluts also didn't get to have conversations with their lovers. Nor did they watch hockey games with them or get tucked in after a long day at work. They got screwed. And that was about it.

Sitting back down at her computer, Lyssa decided to Google other items of similar interest.

How to be a Bond girl.
What does James Bond like in his women.
How to act like a porn star in bed.

Something about this seemed wrong. It wasn't that she was googling these things, it was that she couldn't imagine he'd care. He was dark and mysterious. He was a world traveler. He worked dangerously.

But when she tossed him on the conference room table, he'd torn off her underwear and kept it! That wasn't the act of a guy who slept around. That was the act of a dork. She imagined later that night he'd pulled them out and tormented Chase with them.

"I got Lyssa's undies! I got Lyssa's undies! Booyah!"

Dorks liked girls because they were girls. They were completely appreciative of the female form. Dorks didn't want to sleep with a Bond girl. They wanted to have tickle-fights and watch Monty Python in bed. Anything physical was a blessing from the gods!

It's no wonder Lyssa preferred to hang out with dorks. They were fun and easy to please.

Oh, my God. I'm a dork.

Despite her reasonable argument that she wasn't a slut and he wasn't James Bond, she still googled...

Tips for giving a great blow job.

"Just in case..."

13

"Hi Alex!"

Lyssa had spent three solid minutes outside his office preparing and she still sounded like a hyperactive high school cheerleader when he answered the door.

Alex glanced up and down the hallway. Satisfied that no one was there, he pulled her in quickly and closed the door.

"What are you doing here?" he inquired far more seriously than she would have expected.

"I'm fine. Nice to see you too," she said despite his question.

He sighed heavily. "Sorry. You just took me by surprise."

"Apparently."

"I just..." he calmed himself again. "I wasn't expecting you to show up here. How did you get up here anyway?"

"I murdered a couple of guards and stole a janitor's uniform."

Alex wanted to get pissed, but the way she said it made him smirk. He knew he deserved her attitude at this point.

"Am I interrupting something?" she asked with an insinuation that didn't go unnoticed. Her quick look past him into his office confirmed she meant it.

"No," he stressed. "You're my only something. You know that."

She shrugged.

"I told you it'd been a while. I'm not Chase."

She shrugged again.

"Who do you think I am?" he asked, honestly wondering what she thought of him right now.

"James Bond."

"No. No no no. I'm sorry to inform you, but I'm not that guy either."

"I'm not entirely disappointed by that news. He was a bit of a lush."

"So what are you doing up here then?" he smirked.

"I had a lunch meeting with Patrick, Jay, Simon, and a prospective contractor."

"Was it Gerhardt again?"

"No. It was a woman actually. And before you start having wild fantasies about that, let me assure you that she was definitely not interested in my legs. I was supposed to meet with Patrick afterwards but he got an emergency phone call. I told him I'd pass the time until he got done by torturing you. I'd say it's been a success so far."

His face fell as the realization hit him. She was up there on business. Not for him. And he was interrogating her.

"Did you really think I infiltrated Markison Industries penthouse quarters for a quickie?"

"Maybe," he muttered.

She cocked her head at him. She wasn't there yet, but he knew she was well on her way to achieving 'the glare'. The head tilt was step one.

"A man can daydream," he offered as a suggestion.

"You don't strike me as the type of man that daydreams," she crossed her arms. Step two.

"I didn't think so, but obviously you've affected me in ways that are above and beyond my control."

He reached up and brushed his finger over her cheek, tickling her, making her smile and blush against her will. He couldn't help but smile back.

"Occasionally I forget that it's not a bad thing and that there are some good surprises in life."

"Would you like a do-over?" she asked.

He nodded, dropping his hand.

She went back out into the hallway, closed the door, and

knocked on it. This time Alex opened the door, prepared to be more receptive to her surprise visit.

"Hi Alex!"

"Lyssa! What a pleasant surprise. Please come in."

She entered and he closed the door.

"I was just finishing up a —"

She'd pushed him up against the door and kissed him. Hard. Pressing her hips into him. Rubbing her leg up and down his own.

"Lyssa, I don't think —"

"Good. Because thinking hasn't really worked well for you so far today. And we don't want to waste any more time."

Despite his brain's feeble protests, his hands proceeded to actively roam her curves, cupping her ass, pull her closer to him, while she was unbuckling his belt.

"Oh," she suddenly stopped and looked up at him. "Is there video surveillance in here?" she whispered.

"No," he whispered back.

With one smooth pull, she flipped his belt out and tossed it halfway across the room. This just spurred him on more as he unbuttoned her blouse to get to her heavenly breasts, hoisting them up towards him, sinking his face into her cleavage. She smelled of Jasmine. How he loved that Jasmine!

He was so entranced with her scent that he failed to notice she was forging forth in her campaign of undressing him. Before he could stop her, she had his pants down around his ankles.

"Lyss —"

"Shhh… "

The sexy little smirk on her lips caused him to just stop and watch as she crouched down in front of him. She slowly peeled down his briefs to reveal his stiff member. She wrapped one hand around his erect penis and the other around his leg to steady herself. She kissed the tip in greeting. While she looked up at him, smiling, her tongue crossed over her teeth, just enough to lick the very end.

His eyes narrowed and his breath quickened with anticipation.

"You're so big," she whispered, still smiling at him.

She licked the length of his shaft, from base to tip.

He groaned and rested his head back against the door as she tantalized him. With one hand gripping the door handle, the other held his shirt back out of her way.

Sliding her lips over the head of his penis, she sucked on it lightly.

"Yes baby. Yes," he whispered, encouraging her on.

In most videos she'd seen, the woman spit on the man's cock to lubricate it. Lyssa cringed at the thought of doing it. She thought sound was a mood killer. Instead she decided to try and take as much of him in her mouth as she could.

It wasn't going to be much. He was huge. And gagging wasn't much more appealing.

She did her best and what she couldn't reach she licked with her tongue. Judging from his groaning, it was doing the trick.

Wet enough, she stroked his cock with her hand while teasing and sucking the head.

She brought him to ecstasy quickly. Just as he was peaking, voices could be heard right outside his door. A couple of employees having a work conversation.

Lyssa stopped. She didn't recognize the voices, but they worried her.

"Oh Babe," he whispered, looking down at her. "I'm so close."

She smiled at him and continued to pleasure him orally.

"Close. Very close."

Thankfully the voices outside the door moved along, none the wiser.

"That's a warning Babe. If you don't want it--"

"I do," she smiled up at him again, then once again took as

much of him in her mouth as she could.

He put his hand on her head, trying not to press too hard or hurt her, but he lost himself in the pleasure. She didn't mind. In fact, she liked it since she knew he was enjoying.

"Oh God."

He groaned and banged his head against the door as he exploded in her mouth.

"Oh fuck. Yes."

After his eruption, he had just enough energy left to look down at her. He was about to point out the office bathroom to her so she could spit him out when he noticed she was smiling up at him, still stroking his cock and licking up any residual semen that came out the end like he was an ice cream cone. That's when the few brain cells in his head that were actively functioned screamed in unison.

She swallowed!

Now he understood why some men cried after sex.

I am the luckiest bastard on the planet!

He continued to lean against the door, still moaning, still enjoying her tongue. As his breathing slowed and he grew quiet, she cleaned him up. It was a chore she was more than happy to perform.

Satisfied he was truly done, she pulled up his briefs and pants again, zipping them up just enough to make sure they wouldn't fall back down. He pulled her close, wrapping his arms around her, holding her against his chest.

"I can't feel my feet," he confessed.

She giggled. "Good."

"I'm still confused. You did come visit me for this? Or not," he said.

"I didn't but I couldn't resist the chance to make your daydreams come true."

"You put my daydreams to shame Babe."

He pulled her even closer, nuzzling his head against hers.

"I'm probably going to regret asking this, but as a man I'm required to, how in the hell did you do that?"

She looked confused.

"I haven't been treated like that often in my life, but even I know that that is special. You are amazing."

"The truth is that you inspire me."

"I inspire you?"

"I used to be a nice girl, but you make me want to be very naughty. As for the technique, chalk it up to research and girl talk."

"Research?"

"Google is a girl's best friend."

He held her in his arms for a few more minutes before her phone buzzed, interrupting their quiet lovers' embrace.

They silently finished properly dressing before she checked the phone.

"Patrick's detained longer than expected. And Sally's looking for me. I better go see her," she sighed heavily, not really wanting to go.

He put his hand on her jaw and turned her head up to him so he could kiss her. He could taste himself on her lips. Prior to today's encounter he would have found that to be unappealing but he was surprised to find it kind of exciting. Knowing that every time she licked her lips she'd be reminded of him.

"I owe you one," he said.

"I don't keep score."

"Perhaps not, but I bet you daydream too."

He was surprised that she started to blush. She kissed him tenderly.

"Goodbye Alex," she said quietly, then left.

After a minute or two, Alex kicked off his shoes, and stretched out on the sofa. Never in his career at Markison had Alex napped in his office. Then again, never in his entire life had he had a nooner up against the door.

This woman definitely had a serious effect on him. His life

GAME OF HEARTS

seemed rigidly charted and quite serious before she arrived. Now it'd taken a 180. He had no idea what the day was going to turn out to be like because of her.

It wasn't supposed to be like this. What scared him was that he'd spent half the morning trying to decide what to do about this situation. And when he'd finally come to the conclusion that he had to end it, he'd spent the other half trying to figure out how to do that.

Now he couldn't remember why he was going to let her go in the first place. And more importantly, he didn't care.

"Thank you Babe," he mumbled to himself just before nodding off.

14

The next day Alex caught up with Lyssa outside her office going through a small stack of mail.

"Hey," she smiled at him. "How did last night go?"

"Quiet. You?"

"Same."

Alex had texted her late in the afternoon the previous day to tell her he was helping Bill with a job that night and wouldn't be around. If she had an emergency she should contact Chase. As usual, she had none.

He noticed the administrative assistant's desk oddly empty.

"No Marlene?"

"This morning's meeting ran long so she's taking a late lunch. She should be back in about a half-hour. Is there anything I can help you with sir?" she bobbled her head like a ding-dong.

It broke his professional demeanor immediately. He wiped the smile from his face.

"We have to talk."

"Sounds serious."

He shrugged. "Have you had lunch?"

"No, but I have a conference call in ten minutes so I don't really have time."

She dropped the pile of mail, unimpressed with the findings, and went back into her office. Alex dutifully followed, closing the door behind him.

"You should still eat though."

"I have a stash of protein bars in my desk just for such emergencies."

"Good."

She stood behind the desk and opened the bottom drawer, pulling out several flavors.

"Chocolate peanut butter?" she offered.

"No thank you."

"How about oatmeal raisin? It tastes like the offspring between a day-old danish and an asbestos shingle."

"Yummy, but I think I'll pass."

She tossed the chocolate peanut butter one on her desktop and the rest went back into the drawer which she closed with one kick.

"So, what's up today?" she asked as they sat on the couch.

"We're still sifting through the pile of suspects."

"Suspects?"

"Everyone that is or has ever worked here."

"Wow."

"Even you, my dear."

"That sounds like a lot of fun."

"It's a riot. Especially when Chase decides it's more fun to organize them by how they would rank in a Miss Universe pageant."

"Ooo! Where did I place?"

"Eleventh."

"Eleventh?" She was hurt. "Not even in the top ten?"

"Not after he told me what he wanted to do to the top ten."

"Ew."

"Mostly. You are officially off his radar."

"You mean I wasn't before?"

"Yes, but only unofficially."

"Why unofficially?"

"Because you told him no every time."

"How does it get to be official?"

"I told him no. Once."

"Ah. Well, thank you for that."

He nodded.

"That isn't what you wanted to talk about, is it?" she urged.

He shook his head slowly.

"What is it then?"

He took a deep breath, but said nothing.

"Just say it Alex," she said quietly, expecting him to hit her with something she didn't want to hear.

"I'm still trying to find the right words."

"You don't want me to suck on your cock in the office anymore. It's ok. I get it."

"No, that's not it."

"Just so you're aware, I checked and the employee handbook says one employee cannot give sexual favors to another employee on the *business* floors of the building. Your office is on the penthouse floors and they don't count as business floors."

"I did not know that," he said, honestly surprised by that information.

"So if you thought I was trying to lure you into some kind of sex trap to blackmail you, or if you fear losing your job, I assure you it was not my intention at all. You have nothing to worry about from me anymore."

"That's unfortunate, because I added access to the penthouse floors to your security privileges."

Lyssa's eyes widened slightly.

"You can come and go as you please. Whenever you want."

Her voice became suddenly small and almost childlike. "I can?"

"It wasn't an easy decision for me to make. But trying to deny this from happening is tiring the hell out of me. You aren't supposed to get under my skin like this. I still need to work. Besides," he paused to smile at her, "I'd be a fool to pretend I'm not the luckiest guy in the world to have your attention."

"So, you weren't going to tell me we're through?"

He shook his head with a smile.

"Then what was so hard for you to say?"

"I wasn't sure how to ask you to be my girlfriend." He made a face at the final word. "It sounds so high school."

"You shorten it."

He thought for a moment, then nodded in favor of her suggestion. "Be my girl?"

"Officially?"

He chuckled and nodded.

"I would love to," she started to blush.

"I spend the majority of my day trying to figure people out. I'm usually pretty good at it. But I don't want to do the same thing for you. I don't want to see you as a suspect. I want to enjoy you just as you are."

"Oh, that's so sweet," she cooed, sliding over to hug him. "Who knew you could be so cuddly and warm?"

"Tell anyone and I'll deny it. I have a reputation to maintain."

Her desk phone beeped.

"Give me a second to get this," she said, and stood, walking over to her desk, and hitting the speakerphone button.

"Hi, this is Lyssa."

"This is Jack. We're still waiting for Mark and Christie."

"Ok. I need two minutes to finish up a meeting in my office then you will have my undivided attention for at least forty-five minutes."

"No problem. I'll wait."

She muted the phone and Alex stood to get a hug goodbye from her.

"I'm sorry I kind of went a little mental on you there," she apologized as she stood in his arms. "Your girl might be a little nervous. And paranoid."

He smiled down at her. "All better now that it's official?"

"Definitely."

They kissed tenderly and she let him slip from her arms.

"Oh, I almost forgot," Alex turned back as he put his hand

on the doorknob. "Andre called and asked if I could come to the gallery tonight. He bought some new metal display and it got delivered today. He needs a big muscular guy to help assemble it."

"I bet he does," she grumbled.

He chuckled.

"Do you want me to come along with you? To keep the Gay at bay?"

"No. It's not necessary. Go to yoga. I'll call when I'm back in the city."

"Ok."

He leaned back for another quick kiss, then patted her behind, making her jump slightly.

"Be a good girl," he winked to her then left.

She smiled to herself, then sat back down to prepare for the meeting. It was futile though. She would never be able to concentrate on this one.

I have a boyfriend... I have a boyfriend...

* * * * *

Alex was driving back from Rockport when his car stereo notified him of an incoming call. The display showed the name as LCW.

Lyssa Catherine Winfield.

Without hesitation he tapped a button on his dashboard to take the call.

"Is this business or personal?" he asked, debating how naughty he should be when addressing her. He was feeling kind of frisky tonight.

"Someone broke into my apartment," his girlfriend's scared, little voice informed him.

He switched back to bodyguard mode.

"You need to leave the apartment immediately," he stressed strongly.

"I'm standing in the hallway."

"Good, but you need to leave more. Go back downstairs, out the front door and walk down to The Bean."

"The coffee shop?"

"Yes. You need to go and go now."

"Ok."

"I want you to get yourself something to drink and order my usual too."

"Ok."

"Are you going?"

"I'm in the elevator."

"Good girl. Stay on the phone with me until you get there."

"They went through everything Alex." He could hear the tears in her voice.

"Probably Babe. I'm on my way. Twenty minutes," he said as he pressed down on the accelerator. "Maybe sooner."

"Should I call the police?"

"I'll handle it."

She paused. "Um, the lobby's empty."

"That's ok. Just wave to Frank at the security desk and keep going."

"Frank's not here. No one's here. It's completely empty."

That was not good. Not good at all. He tried to keep the panic out of his voice.

"Don't worry about it. He's probably fixing the parking garage gate. That thing is always getting stuck."

"Probably."

"You just keep walking Babe."

"I am. But why am I going to The Bean?"

The truth was that she was without protection and needed to be someplace public. Someplace with other people. He couldn't tell her that though. She was scared, and scared people weren't easy to motivate to action.

"Because when I get there I'm gonna want some coffee."

He was giving her an errand. Something else to focus on.

"Ok," she complied, trusting him completely in this situation. This was his job.

"You know me Babe. Order something I'll like and pick out a place to sit. I'll be there soon."

"Ok."

"I can be there in fifteen minutes," he glanced at the speedometer. It just hit triple-digits.

"Really?"

"Yeah."

"Then slow down before you get a ticket."

"I gotta see my babe," he chuckled.

"You're gonna see the back of a squad car. Or worse. Please slow down."

"Ok," he said and backed off a little. But only a very little.

"I have to hang up now."

"Why? What's wrong?"

"The girl at the counter is looking at me funny."

"You're at The Bean?"

"Yes."

"You'll stay there, right?"

"Yes."

"Promise?"

"Oh, my God. Yes Alex. Bye."

As soon as she hung up, he punched another button on his console.

"Chase. We've got an emergency..."

True to his word, Alex was at the corner coffee shop in fifteen minutes. Adrenaline was making his heart race. He wanted to run in shouting her name, grab her in his arms and drive her far, far away to where no one could find her. But that wasn't exactly subtle or practical.

As calmly as he could he walked in, glanced over at the

booths, and spotted his girl with two cups of coffee.

"Alex!" she jumped up and hugged him, clasping him tightly around the neck.

So much for subtle.

"It's ok," he reassured her. "I'm here."

He set her back down in the booth and sat opposite.

"Chase is at your place with the police," he explained.

"Already?"

"When Bryan Markison's goons call in for assistance people jump."

"What do we do now?"

"We just sit here. A uniform will be by shortly to get your statement. Then you go home with me."

"But my place--"

"Can wait until tomorrow."

She nodded, then sniffled.

"It's gonna be ok Babe," he said quietly and reached over, putting a reassuring hand on her arm.

She sat back and opened her purse, which was tucked securely in her lap. She pulled out a small object wrapped in a cloth. Setting it on the table, she pulled away the corners of the cloth to reveal her Buddha statue. Whether by mistake or on purpose, it had been broken by the intruder and the head was now separated from the body.

"I found it on the floor," she barely squeaked out.

"Oh," he mumbled, not even quite sure what to say. Tears slid down her cheeks. "It's just an inexpensive trinket."

"It's not."

"Babe, you have probably ten grand alone in purses up there and you're worried about this?"

"I don't care about the purses. Or any of the other crap I bought. I care about this. This came from you."

"I'll get you another."

"I don't want another! I want this one!"

"Then I'll fix it. Ok Babe?"

He slid into the booth next to her and wrapped his arm around her, letting her head rest on his shoulder.

"I'll fix all of this. I promise."

"How?"

"I don't know just yet, but trust me, I will."

"I trust you."

He wiped the tears from her cheeks.

"This is all I have," she mumbled.

"What do you mean?"

"I have a job, a broken Buddha, and you. Everything else is just stuff."

"Don't forget Marlene and Jay and Val. You have them too."

"And Chase."

"Yeah, I'd rather you not have him," he mumbled, making her laugh.

Alex settled further into the booth, letting her relax into his hold. A couple minutes passed by in silence until his phone buzzed.

"Yeah," he answered it and listened. "Can they come down to The Bean?... Ok."

He hung up, setting his phone back on the table.

"A couple of investigators are going to come down in a few minutes to ask you some questions. You ok with that?"

"Sure."

"I gotta hit the head. I'll be right back."

She sat up, letting Alex slip out of the booth.

Lyssa'd had a wonderful night at yoga. Val had celebrated when she'd said her and Alex were officially a couple now. She'd dedicated her yoga practice that night to Marlene, sending thoughts of peace and love to her, Jerry, and the kids. It had been a good night.

Until she got home.

That first vision of the torn-up apartment when she opened the door was still fresh in her mind. She knew she had to leave immediately. Not only would Alex be upset if she stayed, but it might hamper the investigation. She only traveled far enough into her home to find the broken Buddha on the floor next to the TV set. Then she went back out to the hallway to call her boyfriend for his help.

Thank God I have Alex and Chase to be strong for me when I can't.

Lyssa had always been a self-reliant woman. But even she wanted a shoulder to cry on once in a while. Like tonight.

I can't believe that bastard went through my things.

She gasped with a sudden realization.

She reached into her purse and pulled out her phone. She stabbed at the contacts looking for a certain name.

"Pick up - pick up - pick up - Chase! Are you still in my apartment?" she whispered frantically at him.

"Yes."

"You have to get something from the bedroom for me."

"I can't just take something —"

"Chase, you have to get *something from the bedroom,*" she stressed, "before they find it."

"Oh!" he suddenly realized what she probably meant. "You mean a playtoy?"

"Yes," she groaned.

"Ok. Where is it?"

"The nightstand on the left side of the bed. It's all in a satin bag."

"All? How many toys do you have?"

"I don't know. Three, maybe."

"Christ. No wonder... oops."

"Oops. What oops?"

"The drawer is missing."

"Missing?!"

"It's upside-down, on the floor, like everything else," he groaned as he bent over and picked it up. "Empty."

She whined loudly.

"Oh wait. Is it a black bag with a pink heart on it?"

"Yes!"

"It got knocked under the bed... I think I... can grab it... yeah. There. Got it."

"Just throw the whole bag out."

"Throw it out? Just because you have a well-hung man now is no reason to throw it out."

"I'm not using it again after that creep's been through my whole apartment! It's been ruined!"

"Ok. Ok. Oops."

"Oops. What oops now?"

"I must have hit a button or something when I picked it up. It's... um... moving."

"Oh, my God." She put her hand to her head.

"Maybe if I keep hitting buttons... ok, that theory isn't working. How many buttons are on this thing?"

"Chase... "

"Crap, it's getting worse."

"Chase, just stop... "

"Jesus! What the hell is in this bag?"

"Don't open it!"

"I am fairly scared right now. It's not gonna attack me, is it?"

"Just take it down the hall to the garbage shoot and throw it away," she grumbled.

"Uh yeah?!" she could hear him yelling off the phone. "No, it's nothing! Just my portable razor! I forgot to shave this morning! I'll just go to the lobby bathroom with this! Don't want to contaminate the crime scene!"

Lyssa sunk further down into the seat.

"Alright, I'm out with the goods. Where's the garbage shoot?"

"There's a door just past the elevators."

"Ah! Ok. Bombs away! Wow. This hollow, metal garbage shoot makes a great echo. I can hear it rumbling all the way to the

186

bottom. Shit, that's loud."

"Shoot me, please," Lyssa mumbled.

"Ooo! Sorry Frank! Didn't mean to hit you in the head!"

"What?!"

Chase laughed. "I'm kidding. He's not there."

"You ass."

"It did make one helluva racket though. But it's gone now."

"Thank you Chase."

"Sure thing kiddo."

"If you could not tell anyone about this..."

"Oh hell no. You think I want to tell people I was attacked by your sex toys? Especially since I'm pretty sure I lost the battle."

"I owe you."

"Not a problem sweetcheeks."

She hung up and put her phone back just as Alex and two uniformed police officers came over to the table.

15

The next morning Lyssa woke up alone in Alex's bed. She tried to recall how she got there.

There was a break-in and on her bodyguard's orders she went to The Bean. After Boston's finest showed up to ask her a few questions, Alex brought her back to his studio apartment. Chase had argued feebly that they should consider bunking down in the penthouse suites at Markison, but Alex quickly reminded him that he could protect her just as well no matter what bed they were in, so it might as well be the huge comfortable one.

Slipping out of bed, she threw on a t-shirt that was draped over a nearby chair. It was Alex's and it smelled like him.

"Ew."

Despite what television advertising would have women believe, not all clothing worn by men smells fantastic. Especially after a very long day and a frantic drive to save the girl. So she took the shirt off, tossed it back into the chair, and pulled a clean shirt out of his drawer.

"Ah," she sighed, much happier with the smell of his laundry detergent.

Shuffling around the corner to the kitchen nook, she found a note.

Lyss, Gone to get breakfast. Back soon. Stay! Alex.

"Stay," she grumbled to herself. "Like I'm some kind of — ah! He fixed Buddha!"

Sure enough, the note had been perched up against the repaired Buddha statue. This was definitely the same Buddha and not a new one. She could see the fracture line on his neck and a couple spots where the glue had seeped out.

"I love him!"

"That was for me right? And not the fat guy on the counter."

Lyssa turned to find Alex walking in. He had grocery bags in one hand and a carrier with two Green Mountain coffee cups in the other. He crossed to the island and set both down. She waited until his hands were free to hug him.

"How ya doin' gorgeous?" he asked.

"Better. Thank you."

"Don't tell anyone I left you alone for a little while this morning. Ok?"

She looked up at him.

"I figured you were safe enough. If anyone broke in and caught you before your morning coffee you'd murder 'em."

"I would," she smiled. "Good thing you came back packing."

She slid her hand down to his groin.

"No," he held her out at arm's distance. "We eat first."

"We do?"

"I missed dinner last night and I'm starving. You work your womanly wiles on me and I'll probably end up napping thru breakfast. And lunch too."

She giggled and it only made it worse for him to walk away from her.

"Nice shirt, by the way," he noted.

"I stole it from this really hot guy."

He groaned, turned her around, playfully smacked her behind (something he so obviously loved to do), then grabbed the grocery bags and retreated to behind the kitchen counter. Lyssa sat at the island with her Buddha and coffee while he cooked.

"I only know how to cook a few things. A killer Greek omelet happens to be one of them."

"Yummy," she smiled.

He looked up and winked at her with a faint smile. There were times when his girlfriend's carefree attitude worried him. Like when she thought nothing of walking nine blocks to Armand's All-Night Deli to get a gelato at two in the morning.

"The cool air's good for the circulation and I work off the gelato walking home," she'd told him at the time.

But today he was grateful for it. Whereas most people would be freaking out about having their apartment broken into, his girl was running around his studio in nothing but a t-shirt and a glimmer in her eyes.

"Coffee," she sighed peacefully and hugged the cup with her cheek.

"Hey! I'm just in time for breakfast!"

"Oh, it's you," Lyssa scowled back at Chase, who had entered carrying a four-pack of coffee. This one from McDonald's.

"Good morning to you too, Sunshine," he sat next to her at the island.

"I gotta take back my apartment keys from you people," Alex glanced up at his friend.

"What key? I broke in."

"Your security kinda sucks," Lyssa commented.

"Until you I've never had to worry about my own."

"Liar. Liar. Pants. On fire," she calmly taunted, making him laugh.

"What pants?" Chase looked down at her.

"Ugh," she sighed and slipped off the stool, holding the shirt as low over her behind as she could. "I have to steal more clothes."

"Try the third drawer. That might have something that will fit your curves."

As soon as she was gone...

"She's awful chipper. Did you give her a protein shake this morning?" Chase asked, hinting heavily that a certain sexual act had been performed.

"No, that was lunch Wednesday."

Chase damn near spit out his coffee. "You got a nooner? You bastard."

"Mention it and I'll neuter you," he threatened him with the large Ginsu knife in his hand.

"No prob," he held up his hands. "I like joking about it, but I really wouldn't want to have a serious conversation with Lyssa about what she's doing with your wang."

"You'd cry."

"Yeah, ok. Forget I brought it up."

"Any word?" he asked, turning the conversation to something more serious.

"No. They didn't find any prints at the apartment other than the people she mentioned. You, Marlene, Patrick and Janice, Jay, Simon, the yoga teacher there... um... "

"Val."

"Yeah. The usual crew."

"I never made it up there. Was the damage that bad?"

Chase nodded. "Went thru everything. Even the silverware drawer was turned over."

"Shit," he grumbled, growing angrier by the second.

"Have you discussed what you're going to do about — "

Lyssa screeched and came flying out of the bedroom. "It's Friday!"

"Yeah," they stared at her.

"I have to go to work!"

"No." "Not today."

"Is it some holiday I forgot about? Because I have done that before. July 4th in 2008 was on a Friday and I showed up for work."

"That's kind of pathetic," Chase pointed out.

"I prefer to think of myself as dedicated," she sat back on the stool.

"I thought you were putting on pants."

"I did, kind of."

She slid off the stool and pulled up the t-shirt to show off her covered rear end.

"Ha!" Chase laughed.

Alex shook his head in amazement. She was wearing his Speedos.

"I couldn't get anything else over my fat ass."

"Your ass is not fat," Alex stressed. "It's perfectly plump."

She glared at him. Apparently 'plump' was not a girl-friendly term.

"Besides," Chase pointed out, "it's probably your hips, not your ass that's preventing — ow."

She'd smacked him upside the head. "Shut up Chase."

"Shutting up."

"You're obviously not going to work today Lyss," Alex started, being delicate but stern about it.

She pouted.

"I'm sure they've all heard by now what happened, so you might want to send out an email letting them know you're ok. Marlene has already called me three times."

"Me twice," Chase added.

"But she's never going to believe us until you call her. Maybe after you eat you can give her a buzz," he suggested.

"Ok," she agreed. Marlene was probably making everyone crazy right now.

"They didn't find any clues Babe," Alex said regretfully.

Her pout turned from put-on to real.

"We'll find him. I promise."

"I know."

"Meanwhile," Chase piped up, "we're gonna get a little crew together and help you clean up your place."

"A crew?"

"Hi everyone!" a very chipper blond bounced into the room.

"Can everyone in the city just walk in here?" Lyssa whispered to Alex as he set an omelet in front of her.

"Note to self," he kept his head low, "change the keycode on the garage door."

"Are you ok honey?" Trixie set down the Dunkin' Donuts

Box O' Joe she was carrying and gave Lyssa a hug.

"I'm fine."

"Oh, my God, what an awful week you're having? First I try to break your face and then someone else breaks into your home."

Lyssa shrugged it off.

"What are you wearing?" she asked, finding the t-shirt awkward.

"Alex's shirt."

"She's got on his Speedos too," Chase added.

"Oh," Trixie suddenly smirked. "Uber sexy."

"Uber convenient," Lyssa corrected.

"What's for breakfast?" Trixie sat on the last stool at the island.

Alex muttered expletives under his breath while dragging the omelet ingredients back out of the fridge.

When they arrived at Lyssa's apartment, they found the door padlocked and the police tape still in place. Alex removed the tape while Chase dug the key out of his pocket. Upon Lyssa's request, it had been given to him by the police the previous night after apartment maintenance installed the padlock.

The plan was simple. They would split into pairs and tackle two rooms at a time. Lyssa and Alex started with the kitchen. Chase and Trixie went for the living room.

Lyssa had one simple rule.

If it's broken, throw it out. No matter what.

The kitchen was simple enough. Most items were just pulled from cupboards and tipped over. In fact, very little was broken.

"Probably didn't want to risk making that much noise," Alex surmised.

They did find one disturbing thing though.

"Where's my knives?"

"What's that?" Alex walked over to his mumbling girlfriend.

"I have a butcher's block but no knives in it. And the ones

from the drawer are all gone too."

"That's a little creepy."

Chase overheard the conversation and walked over to them.

"I know where they are."

"You do?"

He nodded slowly and turned around, starting to point across the room.

"Don't open that!"

But it was too late. Trixie was already standing in the spare bedroom doorway. She gave a gut-wrenching, high-pitched scream.

Chase hurried over to her but to his surprise Trixie pushed him aside to grab Lyssa. Hugging her, she smothered her in her massive chest.

"Uh, Trix, I can't breathe."

At least Lyssa was trying to say that but it was completely muffled by the bosom that was currently engulfing her face.

"Don't look baby. Don't look," Trixie held her tight.

"Loosen up there, chesty," Chase tugged on her arm.

Alex stepped past them to look in the room.

"Holy shit," he commented at the sight before him.

Lyssa gasped for air when she finally broke free of Trixie's hold.

"I'll be fine," she stressed and stepped out of her arms' reach.

Alex faced her while blocking the doorway.

"It's kind of a mess in there Babe," he said gently, rubbing her arm.

He was cushioning her for the blow. She knew it and while she understood why he felt the need to do it, she didn't necessarily like it. She liked to think she was a stronger woman than that. When she wanted that sympathetic shoulder she would ask for it herself.

"It's just stuff in there. I told you that."

He turned aside to let her thru the door.

It was a purse and shoe massacre. Each purse had a knife

from the butcher's block through it. The shoes were strewn about the graveyard of expensive accessories, but only the left ones had been violated in some way to make them unwearable. How Lyssa kept her composure she will never know. But she did.

"Can you get me some trash bags please?" she asked calmly.

"You can't throw them out!" Trixie blurted out.

"They're no good anymore."

"But some have a lifetime warranty. No matter what happens they'll replace it."

Lyssa looked down at various little piles of purses. Trixie was right.

"It's just stuff. A big waste of time, money and…stuff."

"Please. Do it for them," she gestured to the purses.

"Ok," Lyssa gave in. "Four bags. Two for returnables, Two for trash."

Trixie ran off to get the bags.

"I'll start pulling knives," Alex stepped into the room.

"No," she quickly stopped him. "Trixie can help me do this. Can you take those two boxes in the corner and throw them out? It's old stuff that I've been meaning to toss. Today's as good a day as any. Do you know where the dumpsters are?"

"Yeah. Chase!" he called him over. "Grab this other box."

They scooped up the boxes and left to perform their errand.

On their way back up they ran into more recruits in the hallway. Two people from graphic design, one from online support and a woman from HR. And thankfully not the woman that Lyssa met with for reviews. This was a young woman who seemed much more relaxed.

"Orders came from the top," she announced. "And we all volunteered."

"Thank you," Lyssa got teary eyed. "Alex can tell you what needs to be done. I don't even know anymore."

As he gave orders, another friendly face arrived to offer his assistance.

"Hello Ms. Winfield."

"Frank!"

She gave her favorite night security guard a big hug.

"I'm so sorry Ms. Winfield."

"Oh, my God. Would you please call me Lyssa?"

"Certainly Ms. Winfield."

She laughed, which made everyone smile.

"I'm here to install your new locks," he held up the Home Depot bag. "And we have some doosies for you this time. After these are put in place, you'll probably have a hard time getting in your own door."

As Frank set about his task, Lyssa returned to finish sorting the last of the mutilated purses. The handles of all the knives had been dusted for prints, making the cleanup that much more messy. Lyssa's hands were covered with powder by the time she was done. All of the knives were slated to be run through the dishwasher, which was currently already running a load. She wanted everything cleaned.

Thankfully the clothes in her bedroom were just scattered about and not destroyed, so she didn't lose everything. It was just the storage collection that had been purposely focused on for destruction. But she still insisted that everything be cleaned.

Everything.

"I wonder if this is washable."

Lyssa looked at the walls closely.

"How about a cleaning service?" Trixie suggested. And for once in her life, it was a good idea.

"Any suggestions?"

"Let me get a name and number of Bryan's service. He likes them, so they have to be good. He's a picky little bastard."

She got out her phone to make the call. Lyssa should have stopped her from calling the CEO for this info, but she was getting tired. Besides, she was also getting the distinct impression that Bryan's fortune and stature didn't make him anymore inaccessible to Trixie than any of her other friends.

And true enough, within five minutes she not only had the info she sought but Bryan's assistant was contacting the service herself to make the appointment.

"What's the point in having a rich fuck buddy if you can't use it to your advantage?" Trixie smirked.

Lyssa's eyes damn near fell out of her head.

Trixie held her finger up to her lips, signifying it was a secret, then snickered to herself and sauntered over to tell her brother about her latest manipulation in securing a cleaning service.

Alex walked over to her.

"You ok?"

"I'm not sure I want to know you people anymore," Lyssa said quietly and walked away, leaving Alex to wonder just what in the hell Trixie told her.

"Oh, are you fucking kidding me?!" Chase suddenly shouted from the bathroom.

"What happened now?" Alex stuck his head in the doorway, then let out a loud laugh. In fact, he was laughing so hard he had to walk away.

Lyssa looked in. One of her two pillows had broken open in the dryer. There was filling all over the place. She tried not to laugh, but she failed miserably at hiding it.

"Not funny," Chase grumbled and proceeded with the unenviable task of cleaning out the dryer.

"Ok, Ms. Winfield," Frank walked over to her. "Here's the keys to your new locks," he handed her the sets and explained how they worked.

"There's a swinging bar lock." Lyssa found this odd.

"Yeah," Frank was embarrassed by it. "My wife made me promise to put it here. She said you would want this most of all."

Lyssa pondered it.

"I love it!" she declared. "It feels like my apartment is a hotel room now. Which is a good thing because I don't really like my apartment at the moment. But this is great! And it might be the only thing that could keep Alex and Chase out."

"No," Alex and Chase both said.

"Or not," she grumbled.

She gave Frank a hug and promised to come over for dinner some night with his family.

Then slowly, one-by-one, people started leaving. The co-workers meandered off as the chores got done.

"Thanks for being here last night," she spoke privately to Chase before he left.

"Oh sure. Anything for you."

"And thanks for understanding... and for taking care of that... *thing*."

"Oh God. Don't even think about it," he gave her a big hug.

"I owe you."

"You know, after Alex finds the guy that did this and rips his balls out through his nose he's probably going to have to go back to Baghdad. That's a few weeks you'll be on your own. I expect you to call me."

She was mortified that he would even joke about her cheating on Alex with him.

"So we can go shopping for toy replacements!" he clarified quickly.

"Oh!" she laughed. "Ok."

He hugged her once more, then left with Trixie, who insisted on taking the purses with her.

"You're distraught right now. I don't want you to do something crazy, so I'll just take these with me."

"Ok," Lyssa smiled at her. "Thank you Trixie."

When it was over... when everyone was gone... when she had no energy left... Lyssa curled up on the unmade bed with the one remaining pillow that hadn't perished in the dryer.

"I just wanna cry for a minute," she informed Alex when he came to check on her.

"Sure."

He spooned up behind her and carefully pulled her hair away from her face. Leaning down, he kissed her gently on the side of her temple.

"I'm sorry I didn't prevent this from happening."

"It's not your fault."

"I should have seen it coming and stopped it."

"How were you supposed to do that?"

She rolled over just enough to look up at him.

"I don't know who gave you the impression that you have these godlike abilities, but I regret to inform you that you cannot predict the future, you cannot stop a car with your face, and you cannot make my ass fit in your pants."

"Well, it only seems fair since you let me in your pants."

She giggled even while the tears were sliding from her eyes and rolling down her face. He caught them before they reached her ears, wiping them away.

She rolled back over and he cuddled up closer behind her, circling his arms around her tighter.

"But I will never stop trying," he quietly promised her.

* * * * *

Lyssa hadn't intended to fall asleep, but she obviously needed to because she had. When she woke an hour later she found Alex in the living room watching football and folding laundry. Or trying to.

"Foul medieval contraption," he was muttering at her bra.

She took it from him and with two flips of the wrist it was tucked up into a neat little off-white, lacy burrito.

"Magic!" she teased.

"They burn witches at the stake here, you know," he continued to mutter.

She sat next to him on the couch and started folding clothes.

"Am I going to have to have protection 24/7 now?"

"Yep."

She stood and walked over to the new apartment keys. She pulled off the duplicate set and handed it to him.

"I'll get you a pass for the building too."

He nodded. She sat back down and he handed her another bra.

"I'm surprised you're not going to argue about that," he said.

"Maybe tomorrow."

He continued to hand her underthings over since she was so much quicker and efficient at folding them.

"I'm sorry you've been saddled with me," she said quietly.

"I know. It's terrible, isn't it? I could be wandering aimlessly around the Gobi Desert in one-hundred-and-sixteen degree heat or playing poker in a diseased third-world country while listening to bugged conversations between crime lords and drug dealers. I've even spent two months living the high-life on an ice breaking ship in the Antarctic once. Instead, I'm being forced to spend all my time with my beautiful lover in the greatest city in the world. Those complete bastards!"

She reached over and playfully slapped him.

"Babe," he laughed, "I don't know what you think I do, but it's not that glamorous."

"You're my James Bond."

"James Bond is a fictional character who in real life wouldn't have made it an hour into any mission. I drive whatever dull-colored, mid-ranged, four-door car the rental service has available. I avoid guns whenever possible. I don't even own a tux much less wear one. And nine times out of ten, I'm in a meeting somewhere being bored out of my mind."

"And the one time out of ten?"

"I'm either sweating or freezing my balls off somewhere while trying simultaneously not to get killed. Those are the times you don't want to know about or that I honestly couldn't tell you about."

"Have you done anything illegal?"

"Of course. I'm constantly breaking the speed limit and jaywalking."

She snorted at his joke. Mostly because it took her by surprise.

"No. I haven't murdered anyone. Well, anyone that didn't deserve it."

She squeaked; he chuckled.

"I'm kidding."

"You are?"

"Not really."

"You wouldn't shoot someone for stealing your Speedos, would you?" she grinned at him.

"You're still wearing it?"

She nodded.

He looked down at her lap.

"Don't make me think about your dirty bits so close to the place where I put my junk."

"If I weren't so exhausted right now I would gladly throw my dirty bits on top of your junk."

"Evil, little witch," he whispered into her ear, making her squirm.

He slowly pushed her over into the couch, nibbling on her neck, rubbing his hand up her stomach to her breast.

YOU KNOW I WISH THAT I HAD JESSIE'S GIRL! I WISH THAT I HAD JESSIE'S GIRL! I WANT JESSIE'S GIRL!

"Let me guess," Alex looked up. "Marlene."

She nodded. "But that's not how she sings it."

"Do I want to know?"

"No."

He sat up and let her answer the phone while he visited the bathroom. By the time he came back out she was off the phone and looking almost ill.

"Everything ok?"

"Marlene invited us over for dinner."

"You broke her heart, didn't you?"

She shook her head slowly.

Alex sighed heavily. "You said yes."

She shrugged. "She made jambalaya. I was weak."

Alex laughed. "Ok. Let's go."

"We still have time for a quickie," she suggested.

"You always get a quickie with me," he mumbled, irritated with himself that his stamina hadn't improved much in the bedroom.

"You're not quick. You're perfect," she stressed.

"Yeah, yeah, yeah," he picked up his jacket.

"I keep telling you anything more than five minutes and it isn't worth it."

He wasn't buying it.

"Seriously. I would rather bounce on you for three minutes ten days in a row than endure thirty solid minutes of aerobics on your taint and be sore for a week."

"Hey, my recovery time is better than a day. I can probably do three minutes three times a day."

"I will test that theory tomorrow."

"Good."

16

"Oh, my God Alex! Yes! Yes! Yes!"

Alex stuck his head into the bedroom doorway where Lyssa was stretched out on the bed in her short satin nightie reading the newspaper.

"There's a new Tandoori restaurant opening up next week near the pier."

"Ok," he nodded, failing to see all the excitement in this news.

"My favorite Tandoori restaurant closed last month and I haven't found another I like as much. Can we go? Pleeeeeease!"

"Uh, sure."

"Yay!"

Alex shook his head in wonder and went back to watching SportsCenter, the one evil sin he allowed himself each morning. And after the 'good boyfriend duty' he put in last night, he'd earned himself a little sin.

"I can't wait to spend the karma points I earned tonight with you," he'd growled at her when they left Marlene's house.

"Oh, don't pretend you didn't love the attention."

His stare was intense.

"Ok, maybe not," she muttered.

Marlene's three eldest children spent the entire night vying for his attention in their own special way.

Myra Templeton, 13, was a tow-head on the cusp of puberty. She was a very thin girl and hadn't developed yet. If Marlene had her way she never would.

"I pray each night that God will make her a lesbian."

Marlene feared the insatiably curious girl would make her a

grandmother before she was thirty-five.

"So, you must work out a lot," she flirted with Alex.

"Yeah," he simply answered.

"Do you go to the gym?"

"No."

"Do you swim?"

"Occasionally."

He slipped his fingers into the back of Lyssa's pants and snapped the Speedos. She gave a small squeak.

Mandy Smith, 11, was a fair-skinned red-head. She was pre-occupied with the fact that Alex had dark brown eyes. Apparently that was a new thing for her. She didn't say anything but stared at him like she was expecting him to jump across the table and bite her. If Lyssa knew how badly Alex wanted to do that just to scare the crap out of the strange child she'd be truly disappointed in him.

Michael Smith, 14, was a red-head. Oddly enough, Michael's dad wasn't the same red-headed Smith as Mandy's father. It was just a huge coincidence that Marlene managed to get impregnated by two gingers with the same last name. This once prompted Marlene to quip, "I should have just dated guys named Smith. Would have made school registration a lot easier, that's for sure."

"Were you ever a bodyguard for Rihanna?" he asked.

"No."

"How many people have you shot?"

"Lots."

"Whoa."

Lyssa jabbed Alex under the table with her foot.

"I just said I shot them. I didn't say I killed them," he explained.

Lyssa rolled her eyes. She had a feeling she'd be doing that a lot tonight.

Marlene's youngest boy Tommy Arezzo, whose father didn't even stay around long enough to lend his last name to the child's birth, didn't seem to be enthused or bothered by the presence of

Lyssa's bodyguard. He was a quiet, bright child who had just celebrated his eighth birthday two weeks prior. He spent most of his time talking to his favorite 'Aunt'.

"Aunt Lyssie," a name he and only he was allowed to call her, "when can I play the new game?"

"I don't know honey. It's not ready yet. This one might be a little scary for you."

"I played the first one."

"Yeah, I know," Lyssa glanced up at Marlene.

"If it were the others, no," Marlene explained. "He's the only one I'm not worried about."

"What about the pirate game we talked about?" Tommy asked.

Lyssa explained, "We have to finish Mutation 2 first and then I'll ask my boss about it."

"Do you still have my drawings?"

"Yes I do. They're safe and sound in my desk at work."

"Ok."

"We have a seven-year-old game consultant?" Alex said to her privately.

"He's eight. And kind of. He's a beta tester. Probably our best one. I take his ideas very seriously."

Alex looked down at the boy who sat on her other side. It was freakish how much the child actually looked like Lyssa. Brown hair and grey eyes. Alex sat back and muttered into Lyssa's ear, "He gives me the heebie-jeebies."

"Did you just say heebie-jeebies?"

"Children have that kind of effect on me."

"What affect is that?"

"A heebie-jeebie affect." He threw back his beer.

"Another?" Jerry offered.

"Please."

He handed over the empty bottle to Marlene's boyfriend, who was a much more calm and pleasant man than would be expected for someone that was sleeping with Marlene.

"Things patched up?" Lyssa asked Marlene quietly.

"Oh yeah. Things are all good between me and my Nubian love prince," Marlene chuckled.

"Ew," everyone else responded.

"Are you sure you're doing ok?" she reached over and patted Lyssa's hand.

"Yes," Lyssa stressed for the fourth time.

"You know you can always stay here."

"No," both Lyssa and Alex replied.

Jerry returned with Alex's beer, which he thanked him profusely for.

"Thank you Marlene," Lyssa added quickly, "But given the security measures involved it would be better if we didn't stay here."

"Where are you staying?"

Lyssa looked at Alex for an answer as this was something they hadn't discussed. She figured he had a plan worked out in his head anyway.

"We'll stop by my place so I can grab my overnight bag and we'll stay in your apartment," he relayed.

"Are you sure?" Lyssa questioned. "It still needs a lot of work. All the clothes and dishes..." she trailed off as she remembered the day's dirt and grime.

"The sooner you move back in the easier it'll be. I need to get you back in your own bed."

Jerry snickered. "Amen brother."

He and Alex toasted their beers.

"It's not like that Jerry," Marlene glared at him. "He's just her bodyguard."

Both men stared at her.

"Right Lyss?" Marlene looked at Lyssa, who was a deer in headlights.

"You didn't tell her?" Alex whispered loudly to Lyssa.

"I assumed she knew. Everyone else knew."

"Knew what?" Marlene was growing dangerously close to screeching levels.

"Hang on." Jerry pulled out his phone and turned on the camera. "I gotta get a record of this." He clicked it and it flashed a snapshot. "That's one for the scrapbook."

"Lyssa?!"

"What?! I'm sorry! I thought you knew Alex and I are together."

"You mean together-together or just together?"

"What's the difference?"

"One is Driving Miss Daisy and the other is *Driving* Miss Daisy."

"That's gross," Michael commented. "She's old."

"Excuse me?" Lyssa turned on him.

"Not you! The old lady in the movie with the old black guy. It's like..." He gestured back and forth between his mother and Jerry.

"Excuse me?" It was Marlene's turn to throw her son some attitude.

Alex started snickering.

"What are you chuckling about?" Marlene turned on him next.

"Don't bother. That doesn't work on me."

"And why not?"

"Because I'm sleeping with your boss."

He and Jerry toasted again.

"Oh, my God." Lyssa put her face in her hands.

Alex wrapped his arm around her waist and pulled her close to kiss the side of her head.

Marlene started screeching and flailing her arms like a mad woman.

"Alex and Lyssa are a couple! Alex and Lyssa are a couple! Hallelujah! Praise the Lord!"

"Marlene," Lyssa reached over and put her hand on her assistant's arm to calm her down.

"I've prayed for this for so long!"

"You've been praying Lyssa gets laid?" Michael blurted out.

"Hey," Jerry warned him with a strong, deep voice.

"Sorry," he immediately apologized.

"But I have! And Lord be praised someone's finally clasped you to their bosom, plowed your fields and planted his seed!"

"Marlene!" Lyssa was near furious.

"It's just an expression," she added quickly, realizing too late that she'd rambled on a bit too much there. "I didn't mean it like that."

"Praise the Lord," Alex mumbled, eyeballing the design Mandy was making with the food on her plate. It looked like a decapitated unicorn.

"Oh, my God." Lyssa grabbed Alex's beer and downed it all in one shot.

"I gotta stop taking her to church with me." Jerry shook his head and stood to get more beer. He paused and pointed to Marlene. "I'm sending you back to the Methodists to have you re-whitened."

"Racist!"

"We can leave now," Lyssa whispered to Alex, and by all accounts she was ready to bolt for the door.

"Lyssa," Marlene started much more calmly this time. "Why didn't you tell me?"

"Maybe it's none of your business Mom," Myra was mortified.

Marlene's eye started to twitch.

"Honestly, I thought you knew," Lyssa continued, ignoring the children. "Everyone else knew and I didn't really have to tell them."

"I'm usually the first to know! I didn't have a clue! And now I've dragged you here when you should be enjoying your lover's honeymoon."

At least two children went, "Ew."

"Oh no. I really wanted the jambalaya," Lyssa stressed.

Jerry came back and put a six-pack in the middle of the table.

"And I really wanted this," Alex immediately took one out.

"So, when?" Marlene asked, trying to be cute about it.

"A week ago tomorrow," Lyssa confessed.

"A week?" Marlene started freaking out again.

"Mom!" Myra was being a little melodramatic at this point.

"Hand me one of those," Marlene gestured to the beer.

"It's been a beautiful week, but a long week Marlene," Alex said as he opened the beer before passing it on.

"I'm sorry. I guess it has," she relaxed again. "And now after what's happened, you'll be stuck up her butt even more now."

"I don't do that," Lyssa mumbled.

Alex, Jerry and Marlene all nearly spit out their beer.

"Ew!"

"I think what you meant is I'll be providing security 24/7," Alex stressed.

"Of course!"

"Well," Mandy started. "I think it's very nice. Don't worry. I won't try to steal him from you," Mandy laughed at Lyssa.

Alex looked at Lyssa like someone was holding a gun to his face. Marlene was silently praying to the ceiling.

"Pray harder," Jerry said to her.

"So, Alex is your boyfriend?" Tommy finally spoke, summing up the long, intense conversation nicely.

"Yes he is."

Tommy held up his plastic cup of Kool-Aid. Alex reached over and tapped the side of it with his beer bottle.

"Oh, my God."

Alex wondered if Marlene adopted Tommy. Not only did he not have a name that started with the letter M, but he was completely different from the rest of them. He was far more mature than any eight-year-old he'd ever met. Hell, he was far more mature than half the people they worked with.

He had been openly pondering all of these thoughts back at her apartment when Lyssa walked away from him in the middle of his sentence and locked herself in the bathroom.

"Are we having a fight?" he asked himself.

Then he heard the telltale sounds of his girlfriend violently purging her dinner into the toilet.

"Ah shit," he mumbled and got out some mugs to make tea. It was the only thing he knew to do in this circumstance. Make tea. Maybe some toast.

Do we even have bread? Or butter?

A couple minutes later…

Knock knock knock.

"Babe? You ok?"

She didn't answer.

"Babe?"

"Leave me alone."

"Honey, please let me in."

"All I wanted was jambalaya and now that's ruined too!"

"I'll make you some jambalaya tomorrow."

"Can you even make jambalaya?"

"Yes."

"Is it any good?"

"Well, to my knowledge no one's thrown it up."

The sound of something solid hitting the door made him jump back.

"Babe, I'm sorry," he tried to say without laughing. This shouldn't have been funny, but everything she did was so cute to him. "It was a joke. Please unlock the door."

"Why are you even asking?! Just unlock the goddamn thing yourself! It can't be too hard! Everyone else in the city can just open any door whenever they damn well please and waltz in! Your apartment! My apartment! It's just a fucking bathroom door!!"

And then she started throwing up again.

"I deserved that," he mumbled to himself, not seeing the humor in this anymore. He felt as if he'd lost control of himself and this entire situation. He needed to re-group. He needed to fix this.

A couple minutes later as Lyssa sat on the floor, knees cradled to her chest, trying to calm herself so she'd stop being ill...

Buzz buzz buzz.

Picking up the phone she'd thrown at the door, she had a text from Alex. It was a picture of a piece of coffeecake and a mug of tea.

Run a bath and I'll feed you cake and tea in the tub.

She glanced over at the spa tub.

"I like cake," she mumbled to herself then proceeded to turn on the faucets and open the bathroom door.

She was undressed and soaking peacefully when Alex entered carrying dishes of cake and tea. He set the little plates on the tub's edge and sat on the floor outside the tub, resting against the wall, facing her so they could talk.

"So, what's your schedule like this weekend?" he calmly asked, wisely choosing the route of ignoring the previous half-hour's trauma.

"I don't have anything planned. Just more cleaning. Maybe a little shopping."

"Sounds good."

"What about you?"

"I have nothing on my calendar."

"How long do these things normally last?"

"Well," he took a deep breath and thought over his answer carefully, "my only other serious relationship was in college. That lasted about two years. So it's hard to tell. If you can put up with me being an idiot once in a while, I'd like to keep you forever."

She giggled and it made him smile.

"I meant the stalking."

He paused, then chuckled. "Yeah, well, that's even harder to tell. I don't think it'll be much longer. I'm sure between Chase and the police that they'll find him soon."

"You too."

He nodded. "Me too."

Alex stood and collected the dirty dishes.

"I'm going to swap out the dishwasher one more time before bed. Don't fall asleep in here."

"I won't. I'll be along shortly."

"Ok," he winked to her and left.

"Hey."

A jiggling set of breasts in his face dragged Alex's thoughts out of the previous night's events and back to the present.

"Huh?" he looked up at his girlfriend, who was wiggling her satin covered chest in front of him.

"Your phone was ringing. You left it on the dryer."

She handed it to him.

"Oh, thanks," he took it from her. She returned to laundry duty as he rang back the caller.

"You called?... I don't know. It might be a rough day."

Lyssa walked thru the room with another basket of clothes for the washer. She stopped and bent over just long enough to show him her bare ass.

"Maybe."

She stood back up and smiled at him. He was smirking back at her with a dirty look in his eyes. The kind of look that made her legs weak.

"I might be working Andre."

At the sound of his gay friend's name, Lyssa bounced over and jumped into his lap.

"Hang on and I'll check," he held the phone against his chest. "Interested in going to Rockport for a little while?"

"Yes!" she smiled.

He chuckled and went back to the phone. "Yeah, sure. We can be there in a couple hours."

"A couple hours and three minutes," Lyssa whispered to him then blew him a seductive kiss. He put his hand on her neck and pushed her over onto the couch; she giggled while struggling to sit back up.

"We'll see you sometime late this morning Andre. Bye."

Standing, he scooped her up in his arms and carried her to the bedroom where he tossed her onto the bed.

"Ok. It's on."

"It's not fair."

"Why not?"

"You know you do that thing with your hips and I'm done."

"Ninety seconds," she grinned at him.

His jaw clenched.

"It's your own fault. You're the one that brought in the timer."

"Ah shit," he mumbled.

"Do you think you can do that six times a day?"

"How do you do that anyway?" he demanded.

"A witch never gives up her secrets."

Somehow his jaw clenched further.

"You know you're kind of sexy when you're angry."

She rubbed her finger over his tight jaw and it made him start to smirk.

"I honestly have no idea how I do that. I just know what I like and I like getting you off."

"No wonder you're happy all the time then." He broke out in an even wider smile.

A couple more miles down the road...

"Do me a favor?" she spoke up.

He glanced over at her.

"Don't try to change anything."

He nodded.

"You're so worried about your performance that you forget the smile you put on my face every time."

"I haven't forgotten. I just wish I had a little more control over it. That's all."

"The moment you can stop it and walk away is when you'll break my heart."

"Babe," he reached over and placed his hand over hers. "Don't overthink it."

"Ok." She swallowed the tears that were building up.

"I don't want it to stop. Quite the opposite. I would like it to last forever."

"Eventually it starts to chafe."

Alex laughed. "They make stuff to prevent that."

"You just make me unbelievably happy the way you are."

"Ditto," he said, pulling her hand up to his mouth, kissing the back of it.

Alex didn't know exactly why she was worried but someone somewhere along the way had broken her heart badly. And he had a feeling it had something to do with the accident and the little scar on her abdomen.

He detested being compared to emotional baggage, but he had some scars himself. And if he was being brutally honest he'd admit his desire to be the ultimate lover was directly related to them. So he could understand the consequences of the past affecting the present. Even if you didn't want it to.

"Ice cream," he suddenly announced and spun the car so quickly into Mom & Pop's Frozen Custard Stand parking lot that Lyssa grabbed for the dashboard and Jesus strap.

"Oh, sorry," he chuckled.

"Maniac," she muttered.

"Want some frozen custard?"

"Yes. And the car keys please."

Their visit to The Waldron Art Gallery in Rockport was an interesting one. Lyssa had never been privileged to watch artists at work. Alex and Andre spent hours trying to decide where everyone's pieces of artwork were to hang.

"You're positive you're going to bring a piece," Andre asked when they got to the blank section his sketch was meant to go.

Alex was the only artist that didn't have his piece in by the previous day's deadline. He was also the only artist that Andre was willing to make this exception for. Mostly because he knew Alex wouldn't let him down on opening night and it would be worth the wait.

"Yes. It's just not done yet. But it will be."

"Did you finally find a more suitable model?" Lyssa inquired. Her voice was sweet, but he saw the fires of jealousy in her eyes.

"Involuntarily," he smirked at her. She cocked her head at him.

"What does that mean?"

"I wasn't looking for one but I had one thrust upon me."

Andre started laughing. "Oh, that's rich."

"Are you referring to me?"

He nodded.

"Eek," she squeaked, placing her hands over her groin.

"What do I need a model for anyway when I live with a nudist?" he winked and walked away.

"I am not!"

"Oh please," Andre rolled his eyes. "You were nude the first time I saw you. I'm surprised you're wearing clothes now."

"I am always appropriately dressed!"

"Are you still wearing my Speedos?" Alex looked back to her as he traveled around reviewing the art placement.

"Um, no."

"Are you even wearing underwear at all?"

"Yes! I always have on underwear with pants."

"So you admit that sometimes you wear none under your skirts?"

"Depends on how short they are?" she teased.

"You need to trim better then," Andre whispered to her.

"I'm trimmed just perfectly, thank you," she said between grit teeth.

"Do you really wear a Speedo?" Andre asked Alex.

"Just in the lap pool," he clarified quickly.

"Are you sure?"

"Yes!"

"What color is it?"

"Dark blue."

Andre pondered. "Yeah, not gay."

"No shit. Jackson and Levitt's pieces should be switched," Alex finally decided.

"I need to get more clips from the basement then," Andre sighed.

"Can I use your bathroom?" Lyssa asked him quickly before he left.

"Of course. Follow me dear."

Alex was pondering the statues in the first and second areas, wondering if they would be better off on each other's pedestals, when he sensed someone behind him. He turned sharply towards the front windows, but no one was there. No one on the sidewalk. No one in the street. Not even a tourist.

He quickly scanned the windows of the buildings on the opposite side of the street. The drug store. The quaint bakery. The tacky souvenir store. Nothing.

But he couldn't get over the feeling there were eyes on him. Watching him. Watching the windows of the shop.

He pulled out his phone and stabbed a single button.

"Chase, it's me. Are you in the hub?... Great. Do you have my GPS?... Run a cellphone scan in a hundred foot radius of my location... Nothing? Nothing at all?... That's not possible. If nothing else, it should at least pick up Lyssa and Andre's phones... Shit. Ok. Keep me posted."

"Sweetie."

He jumped slightly as he turned to her. He'd been concentrating so hard that she managed to sneak up behind him.

"Yeah Babe," he recovered before she noticed.

"If I weren't, um, trimmed to your liking, you would tell me right?"

"Not a chance in hell."

"You wouldn't?" She was surprised and a little hurt.

"I can be an idiot, but not that big of an idiot."

"Are you sure?"

He cocked his eyebrow at her. She giggled.

"You wouldn't tell me if it bothered you?"

"Just don't shave another man's name in your turf and it will never bother me."

She giggled again, then briefly thought that she should probably stop giggling since she was thirty-something years old and not fifteen. Maybe if it didn't make him smirk every time she did it...

"Seriously? Guys don't care about that kind of thing. And the ones that do have bizarre fetishes or fantasies you don't want to know about. As far as I'm concerned, it's sacred land and I am the Chosen One. It's not my place to question the gardener."

She blushed a little and hugged him. He happily enveloped her with his arms. Turning his head, he rested it on top of hers while looking back out the front windows.

I know you were there... I know...

Two hours later, the guys had finished setting up the gallery and Lyssa happened to just finish the book she was reading.

"Sorry that took so long," Alex apologized to her as he polished off his bottled water.

"No problem. I rarely get a chance to just sit and read. It was nice. I love a good sci-fi novel."

"Oh!" Andre gasped. "The boats should be coming in now. Care for an early dinner of fresh lobster?"

"Yummy!" Lyssa's eyes lit up.

Alex shrugged.

"You don't like lobster?"

"I do. Just not the hassle of cracking it open."

She gasped. "You're a traitor to the commonwealth!"

"Hang that man for treason!" Andre declared.

He rolled his eyes at the melodrama.

"Come my dear," he held his arm out to Lyssa, who gladly took it. They proceeded to walk out together.

"You are dead to me," Andre threw his hand up in Alex's face as they walked by.

"Oh for crying out loud... "

17

The next day was quiet. Especially when compared with the previous week. Lyssa finished up the cleaning around the apartment just in time for the cleaning service to arrive and do it all over again.

"Um," Alex squinted, trying to wrap his head about this situation.

"But you—"

"Don't say another word," she warned him.

"Ok," he shrugged it off and did his best to just stay out of the way.

Meanwhile, Lyssa made a grocery shopping list which they immediately went out and purchased after the cleaning service was done.

Later that afternoon, as Lyssa worked on getting dinner ready...

"Sweetie?"

"Hmm... "

"Don't you have Kendo lessons?"

"No."

"Didn't you say once that you practice Kendo on Sunday afternoons?"

"Only if I want to."

"You don't want to?"

"Not today."

"Why?"

When he didn't answer, Lyssa came out of the kitchen and stood between him and the hockey game on TV.

"Uh, Babe?" he gestured with his finger for her to move.

"Why?" she demanded.

"Game's on."

"Why aren't you going?"

"I'm working."

"You're not going because of me."

"No. I'm not going because I'm working."

"Which is protecting me."

"A minor coincidence."

"Alex!"

"When I'm forced to give up something I like, it's for work. When I'm forced to give up something I don't like, it's for you."

"And if I forced you to leave anyway?"

"That's not happening," he snorted.

"How do you know?"

"Because I know exactly where to tickle you to make you surrender to my will."

"I hate you," she mumbled and walked back out to the kitchen.

"Don't let that stop you from trying!"

Ten minutes later her door intercom buzzed.

"This is the front desk. There's a Bill McLean here to see you."

"Oh wonderful! Please send him up."

"Bill?" Alex cocked his eyebrow at her.

"Start packing for the dojo," she smirked. "Your replacement is here." She walked back to the kitchen with her tongue sticking out at him.

"Tricky little minx."

Minutes later she let him in the door with a smile.

"Hi Bill!"

"Hey kids! How's it going?"

"Good! Motivate him please."

"You betcha!"

She went back to the kitchen, leaving the boys to duke it out.

"Here to watch the game with me?" Alex asked, still not having moved from the couch.

"Hell no," he unplugged the TV set.

"Ah shit," Alex mumbled and sat up.

"Get going."

"Bill, it's my job to guard her."

"I know it's been a while since you've had to do this so take the advice of a man that's been married for fourteen years. You do what she wants and she'll kiss you goodbye, make you a nice dinner for when you get home, then ride your big salami later. If you don't do it I'll throw you out the window and Chase will offer to personally console the grieving girlfriend at your funeral."

Alex's eyes flared with anger.

"She thinks she's being a burden," he said quietly so she wouldn't hear.

"It's my duty."

"It's also your life."

"What's the difference?"

"That's the problem. You don't see one and she does."

"Do you?"

"It doesn't matter. You have to learn where to pick your battles. It's not like you're abandoning her drunk on the T headed for Boston College Station during frat week. She's home. She's safe. Make her happy and go kick someone else's ass."

Alex stood. "Alright. I'll go."

"Do it with a smile and maybe she won't make you sleep on the couch."

Alex grabbed a few items then realized he needed some more from his studio apartment. Or was it at work? Maybe he left them at the dojo?

"I might be a little later than expected," he told Lyssa when he came to say goodbye to her in the kitchen where she was making spinach manicotti. "I have no idea where half my gear is. I'm currently sleeping in three different places and I can't remember what's where anymore."

"I'm sorry," she pouted.

"Don't be. I could be sleeping under a bridge but as long as I have you with me I wouldn't care."

"I would!"

He chuckled. "Bye Babe." He kissed her quickly, then started out.

"Alex!" she stopped him, then went to the door to see him.

She slipped her arms around his neck and gave him a long kiss goodbye.

"Promise me something," Alex started. "If anything should happen, don't let Chase bone you on my coffin."

"What?!"

"Bill will explain. Bye," Alex left with a smirk.

"What?!" she turned to Bill.

"I hate you Dane," he mumbled. "Sometimes I really, really hate you…"

By the time Alex returned to Bay Front Apartments, it was well passed dark. He'd already phoned and told Lyssa and Bill to eat without him. He took the opportunity out to do some personal shopping and to pack a few more things. His time at the dojo and Kendo training had really been a good thing for him. He had no idea how much this situation had affected him until he allowed himself to relax and concentrate on something other than protecting her.

But all that went to hell as soon as he walked into the apartment building lobby.

"Good evening Frank," he greeted the usual night guard.

"Mr. Dane. I was hoping you'd return."

"You were?"

"These arrived for Ms. Winfield."

He gestured to a vase of flowers at the end of the counter.

His eyes narrowed; his jaw clenched.

"I didn't think you were a roses-type of guy," Frank commented.

"I'm most definitely not. Let's see who is."

Alex plucked the envelope from the plastic holder and pulled out the card. His jaw grew tense and his eyes were full of rage.

"I'll start pulling the security tapes."

By the time the police were done dusting for prints, reviewing the tape, and talking to the manager of the flower shop where the card came from, it'd been determined that they had no idea who in the hell delivered the flowers. Just that it was a white male anywhere between the ages of 25 and 45.

Frank just remembered that the delivery guy was covered with a rain jacket and baseball cap. Not unusual as it was raining out at the time. The only other distinguishing features about him were very indistinguishable. He was a clean-shaven white guy. The conversation on the video tape was short.

"Kinda late for a floral delivery," Frank commented when the guy entered the lobby carrying the large vase.

"Yeah. These got missed. The boss was really pissed about it too. Hopefully the lady won't be too upset though. Have a good night."

There was nothing distinctive about the voice either. No accent. Not too high. Not too deep.

When Frank saw they were for Lyssa, he set them aside. After everything else that had happened lately, he wasn't about to give her any deliveries without Alex's approval first.

By eleven o'clock the clamor had died down, Bill had left, Lyssa had been told, and Alex was finally able to sit down to dinner.

"This is wonderful," he commented on the manicotti.

"Thanks," she mumbled.

"You gonna be ok?" he looked up.

"Sure."

Personally, she was looking forward to going back to work. She never thought it would be a lot less stressful there.

"What do you think it meant?"

He shrugged. "Rarely does it mean anything except to the person who wrote it. It usually does no good to try and figure it out. Is there more bread, by any chance? After that workout I'm starving."

Lyssa went to the kitchen and brought in the remaining bread.

"Oh, thanks Babe," he mumbled and dug in.

"Do you think it's safe here?"

He looked up, a little surprised by the question.

"I mean, if you would feel more comfortable at Markison or the studio I could stay there with you."

"It doesn't matter. You're only as safe as whomever or whatever is guarding you."

"I didn't mean that you couldn't."

"I know," he added quickly. "If you would feel safer we can definitely stay somewhere else."

He finished his bread and quickly cleaned up the table. Lyssa had moved to the couch where SportsCenter was playing.

"You can change that," Alex pointed out, settling in next to her.

"I'm not really watching it anyway."

Lyssa snuggled into his side. Eventually she was stretched out, her legs over his, her head on his shoulder, her arm on his chest. She became so completely relaxed that she fell asleep.

Minutes later she jolted awake.

"Sorry. I fell asleep."

"I know. You were snoring," he picked.

"I'm a Leo. I don't snore. I purr."

He laughed. "Oh, ok. I'll remember that."

"See that you do."

Another couple minutes later…

"Ok. I'm going to bed," she pushed herself up off the couch.

"I'll be right in. I just wanna catch today's scores."

"Ok."

He tried not to take it personally that she was concerned about the safety of the apartment. She wasn't questioning him. If anything, she was trying to make it easier for him to do his job.

Of course, the fact that she fell asleep in his arms so easily was proof enough that she was fine wherever they were.

Maybe she had a point though…

Alex turned on his phone and looked down at the photo that was still up on it. He'd snapped it just before he called the police.

STOP AND I WON'T HURT YOU.

"You should have thought of that before you scared her. I'm coming for you and I promise it will hurt… "

18

"How's your day going?" Alex asked when he entered her office shortly after lunch the following day.

Lyssa shrugged.

"Not good?"

"I know everyone means well but I wish they'd stop asking me if I'm ok. I was fine when the day started but now I'm just starting to get ticked off."

"You're a popular girl."

"Popularity is overrated."

"All the popular kids say that."

Lyssa crossed her arms at him. He just smirked at her, convinced he could get away with it.

"You're lucky you're incredibly sexy today," she gave in with a smile.

"So if I ask you a personal question do you think you could refrain from getting pissed at me?"

"I think so."

"Good. Are you available tonight for dinner?"

"Um, you're my bodyguard. I don't have a choice."

"I mean to go out for dinner. Not protein bars in your office or leftover crab salad from the cafeteria."

"Oo! Like a real date?"

"Kind of."

"Kind of? Wait a minute. What's the catch?"

"You have to sleep with me later."

"Oh. Ok," she smiled and bounced with delight.

"Here."

"On my office couch? Ok. It'll be kind of tight but I love a challenge."

"Funny, that's what my johnson says every time you pass through the room without your panties on."

"How did you know I wasn't wearing any?" She pulled down on her skirt.

Alex groaned. She giggled and he pulled on the front of his trousers.

"Don't do that to me," he grumbled.

"You started it."

He conceded that point. "So dinner tonight is ok?"

"Uh huh."

"And we can stay in my suite here?"

"Uh huh."

"And you'll keep your dirty bits packaged up neatly until it comes time for me to unwrap them?"

"Uh huh," she squeaked.

He gestured for her to come over to him. She obeyed. He kissed her tightly, slipping his hand under her skirt.

"You little wench," he groaned as he slid his hand between her legs to verify that she really wasn't wearing any panties. "Did you do this just for me?"

"I wish I could say I did. They were starting to bother me so I took them off."

"Oh," he retracted his hand quickly. "Is it irritated?"

"No! I mean, it was starting to. Nothing like before."

"Oh, so I can?" he hinted, pushing her back up against the desk, pulling up on her skirt.

She was about to give him permission when there was a knock on her door.

"Dammit," she sighed heavily.

Alex turned away just as the door opened.

It was Jay.

"Hey boss. Sorry to interrupt but Carlson's on the phone in conference room two and he's ranting and raving like a lunatic."

"Oh, ok."

"I tried to buzz you first," he explained by way of further apology.

"The phone's stuck in 'Do Not Disturb' mode. I can't figure out how to get it off."

"I'll work on that," Alex said. "You go."

"Thanks sweetie," Lyssa smiled to him as she left.

Alex ended up resetting the overly-complicated phone back to factory default settings to turn off the DND light. He started to leave the office and returned to snag a protein bar from the bottom desk drawer.

"Beats tuna noodle casserole."

"I know it doesn't look original... "

"No, I think it's cute you picked Martinelli's for our date."

"Well, since I thoroughly botched our last date here... "

"That wasn't our date. That was mine and Gerald's."

"I'm pretty sure I got further with you that night than he did."

"You're not going to get anywhere tonight by bringing that up," she warned.

"Note to self, do not bring up past dates with other guys that I may have inadvertently —

"Inadvertently?"

"Completely and totally invaded like a small but extremely sexy European country in the middle of a land war."

She stared at him like he was insane. "You spend too much time with Chase."

"Possible."

He opened the door for her as they walked into the restaurant.

"Ah, our beautiful damsel and her brave knight are here!"

"Did you tell them about the land war?" she muttered to Alex, who just kept smirking right along.

Martino and Frederico met her with hugs and kisses.

"Welcome to chef's night!"

"We are so glad you could come tonight!"

"Chef's night?" Lyssa was lost.

"I didn't tell her," Alex confessed.

"Oh, you kept it a surprise?" Martino asked.

Alex nodded.

"I hope a good one."

"She will be elated," he assured the owners.

They explained that once every few months on a Monday -- a night the restaurant is normally closed -- the Head Chef invites an exclusive crowd to try out some new recipes. Patrons are asked to give their opinions of the new dishes.

"Oh, that sounds wonderful!" Lyssa bounced in her shoes.

"I told you my princess loves her food," Alex explained.

Lyssa hugged him around the waist in appreciation.

"I surrender."

Lyssa flopped back onto Alex's bed when they returned to his penthouse suite at Markison. After dinner they'd taken a walk along the waterfront to help digest all the magnificent food they'd tasted. Afterwards they picked up overnight bags from Lyssa's place.

Alex stood at the end of the bed, looking down at her.

"This is comfy," she noted.

He continued to stare. He noticed the rise and fall of her breasts increase with her quickening breath.

She ran her hand over her stomach, rubbing her legs together. She was teasing him.

Tonight, it wouldn't work.

"No," he held up his hand. "You're my present tonight, remember?"

She smiled at him shyly.

"All mine… "

19

When Lyssa woke she wasn't surprised she was alone. She knew Alex liked to do laps in the pool in the early morning. On the mornings they stayed in her apartment, she even got up early to go down with him so he could still enjoy his exercise. Since she still didn't have a bathing suit she used the treadmill in the exercise room next door. She was a little surprised he let her be that far away from him.

(Little did she know, but Alex had the security desk monitoring the room over video surveillance the entire time she was there.)

It was also possible he was also working somewhere in the building this morning doing whatever it was he did when he wasn't protecting her buttocks.

Without much more thought about it, she hoisted herself out of bed and into the bathroom. While going about her morning routine her mind kept wandering back to the previous night.

"All mine… "

Alex carefully peeled off her layers of clothing like he was unveiling a delicate treasure.

"I want to taste you."

He caressed her legs, pushing them back, kissing along her inner thigh.

"Alex?"

He looked up at her and noticed she was nervous, almost scared. He smiled understandingly and crawled up to kiss her on the lips.

"It's just – "

"It's ok," he gently interrupted.

His shower was state-of-the-art and bigger than most people's guest bedrooms. It had eight different showerheads. Some on the ceiling. Some on the walls. It didn't have faucets with which to turn it on. It had a space-age command center.

He settled in next to her; his body half on the bed, half covering hers. He rubbed his fingers over her arm. Even though his voice was reassuring and his touch soothing, he could still sense her nervousness.

"Alex, I – "

He gently hushed her. "I'm not going to rush into something you're not comfortable with. I have all the time in the world to play with you."

He slipped his fingers to the back of her arm towards the spot where he knew she was ticklish. She started squirming in anticipation. He laughed and stopped short of the devilish deed.

It looked so difficult to turn on that she was tempted to skip the shower and load up on deodorant instead, but she really needed to wash up today.

"You work for a software developer. You can handle turning on a damn shower."

She bravely set about trying to work the complicated shower controls.

She drew her fingers over his jaw, running her nails through his course facial hair. He'd trimmed it that morning and it was a little shorter than she was used to seeing it.

"I wasn't paying close enough attention and put the trimmer on the wrong setting," he explained. "I was too busy watching you get dressed from the bathroom mirror."

"You were?"

He nodded, not especially proud of that confession, even if it did make her laugh.

"Well, I still like it."

"That's good because it'll probably take me a week to grow it back

STEPHANIE K. DEAL

out."

It took her a couple minutes to figure out, but eventually there was water coming out of the various showerheads. After making sure the temperature was just right, she stepped into one of the nicest showers she'd ever experienced.

He traced up her arm, over her shoulder blade, and down her breastbone. His fingertips grazing her skin just enough to make them tingle.

"I don't want you to be disappointed," she said quietly.

"I could never," he assured her with a simple smile. "Besides, there are other ways to taste you."

He carefully pushed his legs against hers, opening her pelvis up more to him. He slid his hips up against hers. Slowly. Rhythmically. His erect penis rubbing her clitoris. Stimulating her.

"I can't wait to feel you," he whispered into her ear as she panted.

The showerheads were strategically located for someone over six feet tall. And the water pressure was a little too strong for Lyssa's more delicate skin. Adjusting them to be softer was a simple matter of pressing a single button on the control panel. It was the only button that was clearly marked.

"I want to feel you come on my cock."

She reached down and took hold of his penis. She knew exactly where and how to use it on herself.

"Almost there," she breathed heavy, then suddenly guided him into her vagina. "Yes!" she shouted as she peaked.

He thrust into her, deep, stopping to feel her walls pulsating around his stiff member.

"You feel so good Lyss," he groaned.

"Fuck me Alex!" she screamed, digging her heels into his buttocks. "Hard!"

He fucked her hard and fast. Her nails dug into his arms.

"Alex! Yes!"
He howled.

She noticed his bath products weren't anything too fancy. Glycerine soap. Generic shampoo which smelled surprisingly nice. Probably not like the rainforest it advertised on the bottle, but it was sweet without being nauseating. He didn't have the gamut of male-oriented products that were currently flooding the market. There was one small bottle of Axe body gel. It looked like an unused stocking stuffer.

After, they laid together in the bed, exhausted and fulfilled. He'd driven her mad with lust and all she wanted was to be held by her lover. She silently promised herself she'd personally wash all the linen the next day.
"You are wonderful," she whispered to him.
"Because you are loved," he whispered back.
It was the last thing she remembered before she fell asleep...

She'd just finished her usual shower routine and was enjoying the perks of the large showerhead above on the "gentle rain" setting when movement caught her eye. Looking behind her, she noticed she had an audience of one.

She smiled to her guy, who was appreciating the view from the dry side of the shower partition. He reached up and traced the outline of her curves on the glass with his finger. Then throwing her a quick wink, he walked out of the bathroom again.

Minutes later she exited the bathroom wearing nothing but a towel. She found Alex sitting on the edge of the bed, staring at the floor. He was wearing a pair of jeans and long-sleeved shirt. Her assumption that he might have been working was the correct one. And from the looks of him, he'd been working most of the night.

She stood in front of him letting him rest his head against her stomach. She ran her hands over his head, running her fingers through his hair, massaging his scalp.

"Everything ok?"

He wrapped his hands around her legs, pulling her closer against him, cradling his cheek into her abdomen.

"Yeah. Everything's fine," he answered a little too quietly.

"Why am I having a hard time believing you?"

"Because you know me better than that."

"Alex — "

"Babe," he quietly interrupted, "it's been a long night."

"Why?"

"Don't ask that. Please don't ask that," he got quieter.

"You're scaring me."

"Don't. It's just... just a long night. Thank you for being here."

She wanted to know more, but now wasn't the time. She put on her happy-girlfriend voice.

"Anything for you handsome."

He let her go. "I better let you get to work."

"Get some sleep."

"I'm fine."

"Bullshit. If anyone knows fine around here it's me."

He laughed as he lay back on the bed. He didn't even bother to take his clothes off. Lyssa moved quickly but quietly as she got dressed.

Before leaving, she leaned over the bed and kissed Alex on the cheek.

"Love you," she whispered, hoping her words would reach him in his sleep.

"Rough night?" Marlene asked when Lyssa arrived in their department.

"No, why?"

"You're hair's up and it's still wet. That usually means you're either running really late or you're hung-over and didn't want to listen to the hairdryer."

"Well, you can add another excuse to the list. Boyfriend was sleeping when I left. I didn't want to wake him up."

"Ah," she cooed. "That's so cute."

"I know," Lyssa smiled. "I have to call Marty in New York. It's probably going to be a very loud call because he's half-deaf and I have to yell at him for being late with last month's stats. So, if you hear screaming, ignore it."

"Ok boss!" she saluted.

Lyssa stepped into her office and closed the door. She set up her desk with the usual electronic gadgetry and sat down to make the call.

"Marty," she mumbled as she dialed the phone. "I wish you wouldn't make me yell at you."

She sat back and waited for the ringing line to be answered.

Jay, John, Kevin and Lee were standing at John's cubicle discussing the latest colorations for the final level of the game when a high-pitched scream cut into their conversation.

"Mar?" Jay looked over at the administrative assistant.

Marlene shrugged, not sure what to make of it.

"She did say to ignore her screaming at Marty."

"That didn't sound right."

Lyssa's door opened. She stepped out slowly.

"Get security," she said just before she passed out.

"Why the hell didn't someone wake me sooner?"

"She said not to."

"You still should have."

"She's the boss."

Alex looked down at Marlene. He hated it when she was right. He stepped past her and nodded to the uniformed officer stationed by the door.

"Hey Dane," one of the police detectives inside the office

addressed him.

"Hi Harding. Where's the damage?"

Harding pulled the door partly closed. The intruder's message was written on the back of the door in bright red paint.

DIE BITCH!

"Dammit," Alex muttered.

"This is Alexander Dane," the second detective introduced him to a couple men in suits that Alex had never met before but immediately knew who they were. "These are Agents Lewis and Jenson from the FBI."

He nodded to them sternly. He didn't like their presence here at all, but he knew well enough to keep that opinion to himself.

"Alex works in Markison's security unit. He's also been Ms. Winfield's personal bodyguard throughout this ordeal."

"How long has that been exactly?" Agent Lewis took the lead.

"I was called in to provide extra security for the project three weeks ago today. I wasn't on the books as her bodyguard until the break-in at her apartment, which was last Thursday."

"We'll need all information about the project and the threats."

Alex nodded.

"Including access to emails and the network."

"Approval will have to be given by the CEO."

"I've already given it," Bryan walked into the room. "Bill will handle it."

Alex nodded again. The men in the room didn't notice any difference in his nods, but after twenty years of friendship Bryan was very accustomed to them. That nod was against his will.

"Where's Lyssa?" he asked.

"She's in one of the conference rooms down the hall. I'm not sure which one."

Alex nodded and left before he said something he'd have to

apologize for later, even if he didn't regret saying it.

"Thank you for playing nice gentlemen," Bryan commented to the agents.

"I still think it's foolish you didn't contact us sooner."

"I'm not entirely certain I should have done so now," Bryan cocked his eyebrow at him.

He'd already had a talk with the agents and assured them that if they tried to wield any kind of authoritative power over his staff or the local authorities that they'd be dismissed. Considering Markison's contacts in Washington, they didn't doubt it.

"It certainly went better than I expected," Agent Jenson commented.

"Alex doesn't lose his cool until he has to."

"He's a reasonable man then."

"Usually, but I assure you that today he doesn't necessarily want to be."

"It's understandable. A threat has been made in his home."

"And more importantly, to his girlfriend."

Bryan turned and left, leaving that bit of information hanging in the air.

Alex was looking for Lyssa when he literally ran into her coming around the corner.

"Sorry," they both apologized.

"Watch it, you clod," Marlene blurted out at him.

Lyssa threw a look to the assistant that had been following her.

"Sorry," she pouted.

"Why don't you go make sure the police haven't stolen anything from my office?"

"Do you think they would?" she perked up again. "Those bastards."

She stomped off to frisk some hard-bodied officers of the law. The flabby ones she'd probably let get away with taking the stapler and Post-It Notes.

"Marlene's a little on edge."

"Just a little."

"She's probably gonna get herself arrested."

"I heard you fainted."

"It just took me by surprise. That's all. I'm fine now."

He wrapped his arms around her, giving her a hug. He didn't say it, but she could sense his guilt.

"It's not your fault," she assured him.

"I'm supposed to be your bodyguard."

"You are. I'm still alive. I haven't even been shot yet."

"Yet?"

"The day's still young."

"Don't joke about that Babe."

She stepped back. "What else am I supposed to do?"

He didn't have an answer for that.

"I don't know what to do anymore Alex. He's gotten into my email, my home, and now my job. I'm scared. There. Is that better? Is that what you want to hear?"

He enveloped her again.

"Excuse me Ms. Winfield."

They looked up to find Agent Jenson walking towards them.

"We'd like you to answer a few more questions for us, if you wouldn't mind."

"Sure," she stepped back again and looked up at Alex. "Could you see if you can find me a Mountain Dew? I'm drained."

He nodded.

"Thanks sweetie."

She left with Agent Jenson.

As soon as they were out of hearing range Alex took out his phone and punched the number he'd used most lately.

"Where are you? We have to talk…"

20

Bryan Markison had just finished a very intense board meeting the morning after the break-in and graffiti incident when he found his best security staff member waiting in his office.

"Hello Alex. How's things?" he asked as he entered and sat behind his desk.

"Not good."

"No? Last I heard you were quite enchanted with my favorite production manager," Bryan smiled at him.

"That's the problem."

Bryan's smile quickly faded.

"It's distracting. I can't maintain complete concentration on the job."

"Alex —"

"I respectfully request reassignment."

Bryan sighed and dropped his pen on the desk, sitting back in his chair. He couldn't believe after all these years he was still trying to understand what went on in the mind of Alexander Dane.

"Alex, if this is about what happened with —"

"It's not," he stressed.

"The two situations are nothing alike."

"I know!" he suddenly bellowed. "I know," he added more quietly.

The two men remained silent for a moment while the memories passed between them. Memories that sometimes still plagued their friendship.

"What do you want to do instead?" Bryan finally asked.

"I've discussed it with Chase and he agrees that Lyssa should be placed in his protection and I need to go back undercover, which will allow me to focus on what I do best."

"How is she going to take it?" Bryan asked.

"She'll be fine."

"Are you sure?"

"She always is."

"It's just as well you're going undercover because her posse will storm the castle to lynch you when they find out you dumped her."

"I'm not dumping her. I'm just adjusting the parameters of the mission."

"Jesus Christ Dane. I know you want this to just be another job again but for once can't you at least do it like a human?"

"Do you want this to succeed or not?"

He had nothing to say about that. Of course he did. Instead he took another deep breath before continuing. He sat up straight in his chair again while picking up his pen once more.

"You and Chase do whatever you have to. I'll leave the details up to you two. Just keep me informed."

Bryan always preferred to get the details via email. He had a tendency to find their ideas moronic in person, but in retrospect they always worked. He'd learned to trust their instincts in these matters from a distance.

"Thank you," Alex replied and turned to leave.

"But you have to tell her yourself," he stressed, glancing up at him.

Alex nodded and continued leaving.

Bryan tried to concentrate on the paperwork before him, but his thoughts kept returning to Alex and Lyssa. He'd just spent two hours convincing the board that the situation was completely under control. The FBI was brought in as consultants only. Markison was still running the show. The project was safe and secure and would be released on time. Blah blah blah.

At the time, he believed it. He still did.

He just couldn't get over this foreboding feeling that this

entire operation could be won or lost based on one small, but extremely powerful factor.

Lyssa's faith in Alex.

"Fucking hell."

* * * * *

Lyssa found it hard to concentrate. She was back in her office after the police and FBI cleared it. It took most of the afternoon to clean the fingerprint dust off everything. Plus there was the fact that Lyssa was determined to throw out anything in there that might have been contaminated, including everything in the closet.

"That's a nice scarf!"

"I don't care."

"And you can't throw this out!"

Lyssa damn near jumped out of her skin when Marlene opened up the umbrella.

"See. It's still good."

"Then you keep it. I will not have it anywhere near me. He might have..."

"Might have what?"

"I don't know. I don't want to know. And if it's gone then I won't have to know."

Marlene eyed it suspiciously, then decided to just throw it out with the rest of the trash.

Looking around, Lyssa couldn't help but think that there was something she missed. A tap on her door interrupted her dark thoughts.

"Hey handsome!" she smiled as Alex entered her office. When he didn't smile back she lost her own smile.

"What's wrong?" she asked, concerned.

"We have to talk."

"Ok."

"Come."

He gestured for her to join him. She sat very nervously on the edge of the couch as he sat next to her.

"Effective immediately Chase is going to be your personal bodyguard."

She was afraid of this. That someone -- an executive or an HR rep -- would find out about their relationship and insist they be separated.

"I'm going to be reassigned," he continued.

"Why?" She tried to remain calm.

"I can't protect you anymore."

"You can't?"

He shook his head.

"Did Bryan reassign you?"

"No. I asked to be."

"I don't understand."

"I'm losing sight of what I'm supposed to do. What I'm supposed to be."

"I didn't ask you to change."

"I know. That's the best thing about you. You accepted me and everything about us and you never asked for anything."

She made no sound as the tears which had been building up slid down her cheeks. Alex reached over to her desk for some tissues, pushing them carefully into her hand. She made no attempt to wipe the tears away.

"Please don't do this because of me," she begged.

"I can't promise I can keep you safe and you're more important to me than that. I used to be able to see the villain in the crowd. The hidden enemy in the shadows. I had no blind spots. No filters."

"You can't do that anymore?" she whispered, unable to form sounds anymore.

He shook his head. "All I can see is you."

He couldn't take seeing the tears glistening on her cheeks

anymore. He pulled a tissue from her hand and wiped them away, but more kept coming.

"If I were a normal man with a normal job, then it really wouldn't matter how much you distracted me. But right now it might get someone killed. I won't take a chance that that someone is you. Chase will take good care of you," he assured her.

"Will I still see you?"

He shook his head. "Probably not until this is over."

"What if it's never over? What if they never find him and I never see you again?"

"That won't happen."

"But what if—"

"It won't," he stressed a little stronger than he meant to.

"You're leaving me," she openly cried.

"No," he feebly argued, knowing that's what this was. She didn't see business and personal. Everything was her life. This was leaving.

"I'm not leaving you Babe," he said quietly, rubbing her arm to comfort her. "I'll always be your guy. But we can't work together like this. I work a lot better without--" he caught himself from saying it.

"Without me," she finished for him.

"If by you, you mean a sexy temptress that I can't tear my eyes from and keep my hands off of, then yes, that's you. And ninety-nine percent of the time that's the best place in the world to be. But right now?" he shook his head.

"You're hurting me."

He looked at her.

"I promised to tell you when you're hurting me."

She did. That first afternoon together. In his art studio. In his bed.

He stood quickly and walked over to the trash, throwing away the tissues that were still in his hand. He walked back to her and kissed the top of her head.

"I'm sorry Lyssa."

He left her office immediately, never looking back.

"You're not supposed to apologize…"

21

Lyssa crossed the parking garage with Chase hobbling behind her.

"Ow. Ow. Ow. Ow."

"Oh, shut it."

"It hurts."

"Whiner."

"That was brutal."

"Pussy."

"You're mean."

"Damn straight."

She'd forced him not only to attend the previous night's yoga class with her but dared him into partaking. He'd never done a lick of yoga in his life and at this point he swore he never would again.

"It's good for you."

"It's a racket."

"How's that?"

"Universal peace and calm my ass."

"Good grief."

"My poor abused glutes."

"Oh, it can't be all that bad. You work out every day. You're in excellent physical form. How can you be in that much pain from one yoga class?"

He shrugged, preferring not to tell her that he might have overdone it trying to impress the hot chick who was on the yoga mat behind him. A middle-aged blond with nearly no cleavage, but she could lock both legs behind her head. An act that made his groin cry.

"I don't know. Must be different muscle groups than I normally hit when I work out."

She stopped and glared at him. "There's something pervy in that, I know."

He sighed. "No. Ow."

They continued to the elevators.

"You really think I'm in excellent physical form?"

"Don't push it," she groaned.

"Yeah. Ok," he dropped it immediately. This was not the week to be joking around with Lyssa.

Wednesday night they'd spent at her apartment. He ate most of the leftovers in her fridge and she polished off a pint of Ben & Jerry's Dublin Mudslide.

"Really? That's gonna make you sick. And fat," he commented at the time.

"Fuck you Chase."

"I was kidding...sort of."

"It's mandatory. You get dumped. You eat ice cream with your best girlfriend and cry."

"He didn't dump you... sort of. And I'm not a girl."

"You are now, Chelsea."

He rolled his eyes and handed her the box of tissues on his side of the sofa.

It was a long night.

Thursday night after yoga wasn't nearly as bad. She didn't cry much. And they ate a healthy broiled haddock dinner.

"Maybe there is something to this cosmic purging bullshit after all," he contemplated.

"What are you mumbling about?" Lyssa asked as they rode up in the elevator to her office.

"Ah, nothing. So, what's on the schedule today?"

"I don't know. I can't remember anything anymore."

"What's in the planner?"

"I don't put my plans in the planner."

"Whaaaa?"

She pulled it out and showed him. "I jot down ideas that pop into my head during meetings so I don't forget them. It's usually just... "

She trailed off as she'd flipped thru the planner and landed on the page with Alex's bridge drawing.

"Damn. That really is good," Chase noted, taking the planner from her hand to inspect the picture closer. "I tried to convince him years ago to quit the security gig and be an artist full-time."

"Why didn't he?"

"I don't know. I think he secretly enjoys the pain and suffering of working for a thick-headed Jew."

Chase knew it was a lot more than that, but this wasn't the time or place. Those stories would have to come from the man himself, if he even wanted her to know. Chase had already said too much about his past. He just closed the planner and handed it back to her without further comment.

As they reached her office, they were met with a smiling Marlene.

"I don't trust that smile," Chase frowned at her.

"Can the FBI arrest you for mooning the security camera?"

"Probably."

"Oops."

Chase shook his head at her and entered Lyssa's office to do a quick scan.

Ever since the message was left on the back of her door they'd quadrupled the security on the floor. Cameras were added everywhere, which only succeeded in making everyone even more nervous.

Lyssa's office had its own camera, which on Wednesday morning recorded an armed Marlene coming in early to look for intruders. When the landline on the desk buzzed, she destroyed the phone with the Louisville Slugger she was carrying around with her.

Chase replaced the phone and told Marlene to stay out of Lyssa's office until he got there.

Thursday morning she snuck in with pepper spray and ended up dousing the computer monitor when she accidently jostled the mouse, waking the PC from sleep mode.

Chase replaced the monitor and gave her another threat.

"Stay out of her office, Agent Double-Ds."

"I'll have you know these are all-natural Fs, which are Triple-Ds."

"Stay out or I'm telling everyone they're falsies."

Marlene gasped in horror.

"You wouldn't!"

"Try me," he snarled.

Now with Friday morning's admission that she'd entered the office again he should have followed through with his threat, but he kind of liked the idea of the FBI seeing Marlene's chunky bare ass on tape. He hoped they reviewed the recordings over breakfast.

"It's clear," Chase reported when he came back out of the office.

"Do you think they'll put me on some FBI watchlist now?" Marlene asked.

"I'm sure you're already there for kicking Agent Lewis in the shin when he asked Lyssa to confirm if she was having a sexual relationship with Alex."

"Well, it was none of his goddamn business."

"They probably have to re-ink the stamp that says Hostile on it just because of you."

"Awesome! Hey boss, are you coming to the party tonight?"

"I don't know."

"Oh."

"I'll let you know later. Depends on how today goes."

"Ok. I'll check with you later."

Later…

"Are you coming to the party tonight?"

"I still don't know Marlene," Lyssa replied honestly. "It's been a long week and I still have a lot to do."

"What's the party again?" Chase asked.

"A Miche party," Marlene answered.

"Miche?"

"It's purses."

"A purse party?"

"Yes. You talk about purses; you look at purses; you buy purses."

"You know they have thousands of those things in the store already right?"

"Well of course I know," she was getting annoyed with him.

"But you girls still have to bring them into your homes to buy more there? And you talk about them even more than you already do?"

"Yes," Marlene snarled.

"I don't get it." Chase shrugged and dug back into his food.

The three were eating a late lunch in the cafeteria. It was so late that they were currently the only people in the large hall. That was common on a Friday as most people just wanted to get work done so the weekend could begin.

Today Avery had very kindly stayed later than usual and made them a small hot meal. He still felt a bit guilty about the incident with the car in the parking garage even though Lyssa had explained to him time and again that it wasn't his fault.

"You should come," Marlene turned her attention back to Lyssa. "You don't have to buy anything. It'll at least get you out of the house."

"Yes, but into your house," Chase noted.

"Can I hit him?" Marlene asked Lyssa.

"Yes."

"Now wait a minute. Only you are—ow! Dammit woman! That hurt! Lyssa doesn't hurt."

"You don't?" Marlene looked up at her boss.

"Apparently not."

"Oh. How's this?" She slapped him again.

"Ow!"

"That still hurt?"

"Yes! You hit the same spot as before."

"Ok then, give me your other arm."

"Lyss," Chase whined.

"Stop hitting him Marlene," she mumbled, not especially caring if she did or not.

"Poop," Marlene pouted.

"Who's coming to the party?" Lyssa looked up finally.

Marlene rattled off a list of about a dozen women.

"Oh, and my sister Wendy is coming."

"I didn't know you had a sister," Lyssa looked up, finally interested in something in this conversation. "I thought you just had a brother William."

"*Had* a brother is right."

"You lost me."

"William is now Wendy."

"Say wha girlfrien'?" Lyssa screeched.

"Don't go all Janice Kelty on me," Chase warned her.

"Sorry."

Marlene finished her mouthful of beef & broccoli before continuing.

"My brother William had a little snip-snip tuck-tuck stuff-stuff. And now he's my sister."

"That's wrong," Chase grumbled.

"Don't pass judgment," Marlene pointed her finger at him.

"I'm not passing judgment. I'm just saying to snip-snip..." he paused and put his hand on his junk to reaffirm to himself that it was still there. "No, I'm sorry. That's wrong."

"Honestly, except for the name change and the giant 34Ds, he's exactly the same to me. Oh, except for the weirdness with the shrimp."

"Shrimp?"

"He never liked seafood before but ever since the surgery she craves shrimp and scallops and crab and all kinds of stuff they drag from the ocean. What's the tentacle thing again?"

"Octopus?" Chase guessed.

"Squid," Lyssa corrected him.

"Yeah, squid, but when you cook it, it's... um... "

"Calamari."

"Yes! Will, er, Wendy eats it by the bucket."

"I can't stand that crap," Chase commented.

"It's not crap," Lyssa argued. "When prepared correctly it's very good. Especially the calamari at the Martinelli Brothers' restaurant. Alex and I went there last Monday and..." Lyssa trailed off as the memory came back to her. "Excuse me," she whispered tearfully and left for the bathroom.

"Look what you did?" Chase accused Marlene.

"It's not my fault! All I did was mention... what's it called again?"

"Calamari."

"Yeah, anyway, it was your fault for saying it was crap!"

"How was I supposed to know it would remind her of Alex?!"

"You work in security! You're supposed to know these things!"

"Forgive me for not being as psychic as The Great Dane!"

"Totally not forgiven!"

"I CAN STILL HEAR YOU!" Lyssa shouted from somewhere unseen.

"SORRY!"

A couple minutes later she came back, completely recovered

from her mini-breakdown.

"I'll come to the party Marlene," she announced.

"Yippy!"

"Is that ok?" she asked Chase.

"I still don't get it, but if it makes you happy..." he put on a huge smile for her.

"Smart thinking. You'll be married before you know it."

"No thank you. Following you around is marriage enough for me," he grumbled.

"Excuse me?!"

"Nothing dear."

Slap.

"Ow. Now that's a good slap."

* * * * *

Marlene said a dozen people would be there. It was two dozen.

"I forgot about Jerry's family," she confessed.

There were so many people that Lyssa could probably have disappeared and no one would have noticed. Chase must have been afraid of that because he stuck to her shirt sleeve like they were sewn together.

"So, is that your new man?" Marlene's Aunt Dora asked her as they circled the snack table picking at cheese and crackers, fruit, and cookies.

"No." "Yes."

"Sounds like someone's in denial."

Dora let out a horse-like braying laugh that scared three people who were currently picking out food that had fallen off their wooden skewers and into the chocolate fondue.

"Get over here!" Marlene showed up out of nowhere, grabbed her Aunt by the arm, and dragged her off.

"You said yes?" Lyssa turned to Chase.

"I panicked."

"I can certainly understand that but can you please refrain from spreading anymore gossip around here."

"I'll try."

"And get off my sleeve."

"Please don't leave me," Chase desperately begged her.

"Oh, my God. You and your brother really are just alike sometimes."

"Don't worry. You'll get used to it," Jerry walked up to him and handing him a beer.

"That's what scares me the most."

Jerry just chuckled, kissed Lyssa on the cheek in greeting, and took her drink order.

"I don't think I have any arsenic stocked in the liquor cabinet," he said in response to her sarcastic request for a margarita rimmed with poison. "How about vodka and cranberry juice?"

"Close enough."

Eventually everyone moved into the living room to listen to the purse presentation. It was cramped but Chase still managed to force his way onto the couch between Lyssa and Aunt Genevieve, who was about ninety going on nineteen.

"You're cute," she grinned up at him.

"I'm gay," he said without hesitation.

"The cute ones always are," she sighed.

Chase tried to turn towards Lyssa.

"In all my years working security this is by far the most uncomfortable position I have ever been in. And that includes the time I served as the personal shield for a Moldavian prince during a peace summit held in Thailand."

"So go wait in the kitchen with Jerry and his brother."

"A true Markison man never abandons his post."

The words weren't barely past his lips and he was regretted them.

"Lyss—"

"It's fine."

"But—"

"Forget it Chase."

"Have you?"

"I'm trying to."

Luckily for both of them the presentation was beginning. Patty was a new rep for the Miche company and Marlene's third cousin four times removed, which is why Marlene agreed to this party in the first place.

Patty was doing well and had just gotten to the part about the lifetime warranty when everything went pitch black. Women started screaming.

"Ladies! Please calm down!" Chase shouted, but his voice was drowned out by the hysterical screams.

"SHUT IT BITCHES!" Jerry's voice boomed over them all. Amazingly enough it was followed by complete silence.

"Who you calling a bitch?" Marlene spoke up a second later.

"You woman," he growled.

"Oh, well," she softened, "that was very forceful of you, my Nubian prince. Let me bow to your—"

"Whoa!" Chase shouted. "That's not his royal staff you're grabbing!"

"Oh, sorry Chase."

Then a lamp broke.

"Marlene!"

"Oh, sorry Boss."

"Maybe you better just keep your hands to yourself for now!"

"Yes boss."

Lights from cellphones began to illuminate the room. Lyssa found she was sitting on Chase's lap, a spot only slightly less dangerous than being next to Marlene. With enough light now for her to track Marlene's wandering hands, Lyssa slid back onto the couch.

"Do not move from this spot," Chase warned her quite seriously and stood, pulling out his own phone.

Text announcements started to flood the room...

"Hey, my cousin says there's no power in her house either and she lives on Maple Ave."

"Neither does my mother and she's in Burmingham Towers on the South Side."

"My sister's brother-in-law's girlfriend doesn't have power either. I have no idea where that ho is."

The front door opened. In the moonlight, Chase could see a tall man leaving. It was likely Jerry. He came back in soon.

"Whole street is out. Maybe more," he reported.

"Looks like a citywide problem," Chase announced, based on the texts he got from his unknown source. "Crap, it's actually coastal. All along the seaboard the power is down."

"Oh thank God," Marlene sighed. "I thought maybe I forgot to pay the power bill. Again."

"Just in case, you better stick with me," Chase said quietly to Lyssa, sitting next to her.

"I'm not goin' anywhere with that creep on the loose."

"You talking about the stalker or Marlene?"

"Um, both, actually."

Chase chuckled. Lyssa smiled at the joke, but her hold on his arm tightened all the same.

Marlene got candles out and soon they had enough light throughout the house to see into the corners of the rooms. Patty started up her purse spiel again. With all the women surrounding Lyssa, Chase was comfortable moving around again. He wandered to the kitchen to make some phone calls in private.

By the time the girls were left to play with the samples and browse the catalog, Chase had the answer.

"Power grid failure. Should be fixed in an hour."

"How do you know?" an attractive young woman who now sat on Lyssa's left asked him.

"I have friends," he said mysteriously and winked to her.

"This is Marlene's sister Wendy," Lyssa said.

"Ah, oh, yeah, friends are good," he mumbled and hurried away.

"He's cute," Wendy commented to Lyssa after he was gone.

"He has herpes," Lyssa added quickly.

"Still worth it."

"And a seafood allergy."

"Drat. Skip," she sighed, disappointed.

By the time the party was over Lyssa had purchased almost $250 in purses.

"That's a lot of purse," Chase commented as he drove them back to her apartment.

"Shut it or I'll email Wendy your phone number."

"You wouldn't!"

"Probably wouldn't matter. I told her you had a seafood allergy. She won't call you."

"That's brilliant!"

"It's only because she didn't seem to mind when I told her you had herpes."

"Not funny."

"Not kidding."

"You told her I had herpes?!"

"I'm sorry. Let me call her right now and tell her it was a lie—"

"No!" he reached over and clumsily knocked the phone from her hand. "Sorry. I panicked. Please don't call her... him... it. Whatever that he-she-thing wants to be called. I'm sorry, but I find it so unnatural. I love my cock so much I can't imagine being parted from it. If God had meant for man to be a woman, He would have evolved us that way. I mean, have you seen my cock? It's a beautiful thing. Well, of course you haven't seen it. No matter how many times I've offered it to you, you haven't seen it. And now you can't because that would be just wrong. You're like a sister to me. Like Trixie or Marie. Or even Joshua sometimes because he's a flamer. And I have no qualms about gay guys. I really don't. Do what you want with your tallywacker, I don't care, but at least leave it attached at the root. Lyss? Hello? Are you even listening? Lyss?"

In truth, she stopped listening about four sentences into his speech and was staring out the front window. Most of her co-workers knew what this meant. Chase had no clue.

She was forming an idea. And idea that took... hold... now!

"Oh, my God! Chase! You are magnificent!"

She reached over and kissed him so hard on the cheek he almost veered into a parked car.

"What? What'd I do?"

"That's it! It's perfect!"

"What's perfect? What'd I say? I forgot already. Was it tallywacker?"

Lyssa frantically grabbed her phone off the car floor and jabbed a few buttons until she found the number for Patrick Kelty.

"Patrick! It's Lyssa!... It is? Ten? Wow. Were you asleep?... You were? When did you get to be such an old fart?... Oh, yeah! Get the gang together tomorrow at your house! Tell them to bring their laptops. I have a huge announcement to make... I got the name!"

22

"I'd like to thank everyone for giving up their weekends to be here," Patrick addressed the group gathered around the family room in his finished basement.

"Anything for you, Boss-Boss," Jay spoke for them all.

"Boss-Boss?"

"Well, Lyss is Boss. You are her boss. That makes you Boss-Boss to us."

"Yeah, ok. Anyway, I'm sure it wasn't easy to break your commitments, well maybe except for Kevin."

"Damn you Kelty! Making me miss my sister-in-law's fourth wedding! Curses!" he mocked.

"Yeah, I bet," Patrick laughed. "This weekend isn't about the game or Markison. It's about Lyssa. Most of you know the stories by now. I can tell you they are pretty much all true. Someone's trying to stop this game from being released and they've decided the best way to do that is to attack its production manager. We've only had to give up a weekend while she's lost her privacy, her sense of security, and a lot of sleep."

"God, you wouldn't know it," Jon commented.

"She's a very strong woman. It just makes what we do here ever more important. And before she gets back with the coffee and donuts, I'll answer the big question on everyone's mind. No, her boyfriend Alex did not break up with her. He's just on another assignment. It's undercover though, so she doesn't get to see him. Don't bring it up and she'll be fine."

"Hey, we're back!" Chase shouted very loudly through the house. Perhaps too loudly, but he knew they were going to have a quick pre-meeting while she was gone and wanted to give them ample warning.

Patrick ended with, "So remember, we're doing this for the woman who gave up everything for us."

He was pretty sure they still didn't want to be there (with the exception of Kevin, of course) but he hoped they would keep the grumbling to a minimum, especially around Lyssa.

Before the day was over, they would surprise him.

They all grabbed something to eat and returned to their places in the living room, ready to give it their all.

"Ok," Lyssa addressed them. "Thank you for being able to be here. I know it's wicked short notice and I'm so grateful all of you could come."

She had no idea that Patrick and Jay practically ordered them to be there. Thankfully not one of them showed it. How could they be mad at her? Especially since she kind of looked like shit.

"Did you get some coffee?" Chris asked.

"I will in a little while."

"Make sure you get some before Kim drinks it all."

"Mmmm. Coffee." Kim caressed her cup a little too much.

Lyssa ignored her and continued. "This weekend the goal is to finish up the preview and trailer so they're ready for release Monday."

"Are we really going to release this with the title Game of Hearts?" Harry asked.

"No. We finally have a title."

Her laptop was hooked up to Patrick's large screen TV. She brought up the slide she created the night before using a game test shot.

Mutation 2: Evolutionary Divide

They were silent. Lyssa was starting to doubt her idea until Jon yelled out…

"That's awesome!"

They all suddenly shouted out similar opinions.

"Are they lying because it's me?" Lyssa asked Patrick. "Did

you tell them to do this?"

"No, I did not."

When she told him last night he told her it was a good name, but even he was a little surprised at how much they liked it.

"We need the nickname," Chris pointed out.

"M2ED..." Kevin pondered.

"How about just ED?" Harry said.

"Evo D?" Kim threw out there.

"Evo D!" Jay became animated. "I love it!"

"Sounds like a rapper," Simon suggested.

"You're thinking of Heavy D."

"Can we get him to do a song?"

"Dude! He's dead!"

"Oh. How about Tenacious D instead?"

Jay chucked a small throw pillow at the laughing lead art designer's head.

"Hey, stop it," Lyssa smacked them both in the head and put the pillow back. "Janice will have a fit."

"You are brilliant," Chris hailed her with a truly honest smile.

"Now I know how Stage 3 needs to end!" Kim shouted out. "I love you! This is totally worth my weekend."

"Wait a minute! Wait a minute!" Jay stood on the couch, gesturing with his hands for them to shut up. "Why Monday?"

"Oh, well, we've arranged for the teaser video to be played during halftime at the Celtics last regular season home game."

Another moment of silence was followed by an even bigger roar of excitement.

"Oh, my God!" "We're playing the New Boston Garden!" "Can we finally put the zombie basketball team in the game? Please?"

Lyssa sat back down to talk quietly with Patrick while the staff started blurting out all kinds of ideas, only about 2% of which would actually be usable.

"What do you think? Is the title really ok?"

"It's better than ok. It's perfect," he smiled at her.

It had been a long, but productive day. They got more done than any of them expected to, which was a good way to head into Sunday.

After dinner, Chase found Lyssa sitting on the garden wall in the backyard. She was looking up at the stars. He sat quietly next to her. He remained silent until she spoke.

"Chase."

"Yeah?"

"Have you talked to Alex?"

"A couple times."

"How's he doing?"

Chase shrugged. "I'll be honest, it's hard to tell with him sometimes. And as you know I can't give you a lot of detail about his work. It's called undercover for a reason. Hell, I don't know the details myself most of the time. He is working his ass off, that much I can tell you."

"Can you tell me what country he's in?"

"He hasn't left the country. Work's kept him close to home this time. Actually, I think he was in Pennsylvania yesterday. That's like a foreign country. I'm pretty sure it's entirely populated by orange traffic cones."

Lyssa smiled at his joke.

"By the way, I'm sorry about the comment I made yesterday about Markison men not abandoning their — "

"Don't worry about it," she interrupted. "I know you didn't mean it that way."

"I sometimes open my mouth before I think about what's going to come out. I'm truly amazed I haven't been shot yet."

"I think we all are."

They laughed lightly.

"Someday we're gonna laugh about this whole thing," he

added. "You'll see."

"I can't imagine it, but I hope so," she said quietly.

After another moment of silence...

"Is Alex still participating in Andre's exhibit?"

"I don't know if he'll be at the opening, but I do know he dropped a sketch off for it."

Then after an even longer moment...

"Chase."

"Yeah?" he looked up at her, bracing himself for what he knew she was going to say.

"I want to see it."

"I'll get the car."

* * * * *

Andre Waldron sat on the bench in the middle section of the exhibit. The gallery had been closed for almost twenty minutes now and he still hadn't moved. The contributing artists and their guests were upstairs enjoying champagne and catered delicacies. He could occasionally hear the eruption of laughter or the sharp click of a woman's heels crossing the hardwood floor above him.

He was hungry. He was thirsty. He was tired. But still he remained downstairs, admiring the exhibit selections before him. They really had done a good job with the placement.

Well, Alex did a good job.

He glanced over at Alex's sketch. It had mysteriously shown up during the night in its spot on the wall. Andre knew by now not to be surprised, and more importantly, not to question his longtime friend and fellow artist. He led a strange and complicated life.

"Here."

Andre looked up to find his partner David holding out a bottle of water to him.

"Thanks."

He took it, downing half of it immediately. David proceeded

to close the front window curtains, whose primary purpose was to block out sunlight during the morning. It not only caused artwork to fade but the glare would interfere with the viewing experience.

This fact prompted the gallery owner to ask, "Do we really have to close those? It's night."

"He said to. It's for security purposes."

After he closed the last one, David disappeared behind the partition again.

Andre recapped the bottle and set it on the bench next to him, then returned to staring at the wall. He was so tired. And he'd worried so much about tonight. This was the one last drama for the day and then maybe he could go upstairs, greet the guests, drink too much, and start on tomorrow's regrets.

When the gallery phone rang an hour ago he was determined not to answer it. He didn't know why. Of course David had no such intuition and he answered it straight away with his usual pretty customer service voice.

"It's Chase," David announced, holding the phone out to Andre.

"I don't want to talk to him."

"Why?"

"I'm busy. What does he want?"

"He's bitchy. What do you want?" David said instead, which made it instantly true. "Oh, well in that case we certainly will be... Ok, I can do that... Can't wait to meet you both."

David hung up and went about his business.

"Well?" Andre grew animated.

"He's bringing Lyssa to see the exhibit, but they're just leaving now. I'll let them in when they get here."

"Oh," Andre's tone changed. "Ok. You don't have to. I'll do it."

"I'd rather be down here than upstairs watching your ex try and stick his tongue down your khakis."

"Now who's being bitchy?"

David raised his eyes to try and glare at him. He wasn't very good at it though.

"Don't be jealous. It gives you lines."

Andre drew his thumbs over his partners forehead to straighten the skin.

"By the way, why did you tell them they could come?"

"I want to meet the woman that stole Alex away from you."

"He was never mine!"

"Maybe not, but admit it. You were jealous at first."

"Maybe a little." *He tried to pretend he was pouting but he ended up just snickering. "She's adorable though."*

"Another good reason to meet her. She makes you laugh."

"Ok. But I'm still staying down here with you. Sandy's got the role of hostess upstairs down pat. They don't need me."

"He said they should be here in an hour."

"Good. By the way, you have no reason to be jealous yourself. Ollie is an ex for a reason."

Andre squeezed David's butt cheek just before slipping away to greet a new patron.

There was another burst of laughter from above and the slow clicking of woman's shoes. Except this time they were behind him.

"Hello Andre."

He stood and turned to greet the woman he'd been expecting for the past hour. He immediately smiled at her. How fresh and lovely she was! He felt a little guilty for the temper tantrum he threw when he'd called Alex earlier that week about the opening just to be told that Alex was no longer her bodyguard. It couldn't have been an easy thing for him to do, giving up this woman.

"Hello Lyssa," he practically cried as he hurried over to her. "How are you my dear?"

"I'm ok Andre. How did the opening go?"

"Oh, much better than I expected."

"Always does," David mumbled.

"Did you meet David?" Andre scowled.

"Yes," she smiled back at his partner, who stood attentively by with his own calming smile. "I'm sorry for being a bother, but I really wanted to see the exhibit."

"Oh! No bother! Please," he gestured for her to continue through.

Chase walked around the partition at that time. The two nodded sternly to each other.

"Andre."

"Chase."

Their relationship was defined many years ago when Andre accused Alex of sleeping with Chase and Chase punched him. It was during a horrible phase in which Andre drank a lot and cried over the men he couldn't have. The worst part was Andre could never recall which one of the two extremely buff men he was pining for at the time. Perhaps both! (Another phase in his life that he thoroughly enjoyed but wasn't necessarily proud of.)

They'd since made up, but it had never been a warm friendship between the two. It was mostly tolerated for Alex's sake.

Chase followed Lyssa to the opposite partition to walk thru the exhibit. He wasn't gone two seconds and he was back again.

"Alright, come explain this to me," he said, gesturing with his head.

Andre reluctantly followed him while David snickered and slunk back upstairs to make sure the guests were behaving.

"What in the hell is that?"

"It's supposed to be the view from a fetus."

"That's a womb?"

"Yes."

"I thought it was a decaying eggplant."

Andre shrugged. He was an artist, a gallery owner, and had once interned as a museum curator, but he didn't always get modern art either. He knew enough to value the artist's vision though, even if it didn't make much sense to him.

"Why is this statue missing a penis?" Lyssa asked.

"The artist's dog apparently chewed it off and he decided to leave it as is."

"Ew," she curled up her nose at it.

"I told you it was wrong to chop it off," Chase grumbled.

They found several pieces of artwork they liked amongst the stranger ones. Chase eventually trailed behind as Lyssa and Andre chatted amongst themselves. The Gay made her laugh and somehow her laugh made him even gayer.

When they got to Alex's piece they grew uncomfortably silent again.

"Is that..." she started to ask.

"Yes," he quietly answered her unspoken question.

"It's... "

"Perfectly you."

"Uh huh," she nodded, amazed.

It was the time Alex had caught her in his penthouse suite shower and she'd looked back at him with an alluring smile. He'd captured the moment in pencil and charcoal on paper, safely encased in a silver and glass frame. Every detail was there. Each curve, each drop of water, even the twinkle in her eye.

"I had no idea," she whispered, trying not to cry.

"I gave him an out. I told him he didn't have to submit a piece. I have several of my own I could have hung in the spot. But he insisted and I can see why. It's probably his best work."

She smiled and wiped her eyes.

"It'll all work out," he added sensitively.

"Everyone says that. I don't see it."

"You don't now, but you will. He isn't the type of guy to let someone down unless he has no choice or it's for a greater cause."

"I think that might be the problem. I don't want to be in the middle of his To-Do list. Below save the planet and cure cancer. Is that selfish?"

"No. That's called love. He loves you too. You can trust me

on that. I'm gay."

"You sound like my mother," she laughed.

"Oh my gawd! Your mother was gay too!"

"No, but she used to say—"

"Wow!"

They looked back to find Chase had caught up with them.

"No you don't!" Lyssa threw her hand over his eyes.

"Oh yes I do!" he tried to fight her off, but she was vigilant that he not see it.

"No!"

"Why not?!"

"It looks just like me!"

"Exactly!"

"Andre!" she screamed at him.

"It's down!" he announced.

Lyssa let Chase go and they turned to find Andre had taken the sketch off the wall and placed it on the floor with the back towards them.

"Oh," Lyssa sighed. "Very good. Thank you."

"Bastard," Chase grumbled.

Lyssa stomped on his foot.

"You bi—" he cut himself off before he finished that thought because she'd hurt him some more if he did. Instead he limped away to walk it off.

Andre couldn't help but snicker.

"Congratulations. It's a very lovely exhibit," Lyssa smiled to Andre.

"Thank you my dear."

They gave each other quick pecks on the cheek, then she turned to leave.

"I'll give you ten grand for a print."

Andre looked up at her adolescently grinning bodyguard.

"Chase!"

"Coming dear!" he called out cheerfully, "Maybe just a little

267

peak before I — "

"CHASE!"

"I'M COMING! Jesus, it's like we're divorced or something."

He meandered off, still grumbling about nagging ex-wives.

After he heard the gallery front door open and close Andre carefully hung the picture back up on the wall. Satisfied with the placement, he stared at it.

"I hope you know what the hell you're doing Dane?" he mumbled.

"You ok?"

Andre turned to find David crossing to him again. He nodded to him.

"Finish your water." His boyfriend picked up the bottle and handed it back to him. "You don't want to get dehydrated. It's bad for your complexion."

Andre laughed, but did as was asked of him and drained the bottle completely.

"Thank you."

"Sure."

"You're a dream David."

"I know," he gloated. "Now stop being a nervous nelly and come up to the party. I'm about to make my famous sangrias."

"Oh, I just love you."

"I know that too."

Andre dimmed the gallery lights and they traveled upstairs to a much more lively reception.

* * * * *

He waited several minutes after the lights dimmed and the couple had retreated to the party above before crossing the street to the front door. He needed to make sure one of them hadn't forgotten something at the last minute and come back down to retrieve it.

Opening the door was a simple matter. It wasn't a complicated lock and the security system hadn't been turned on. No one would have expected a burglar with over thirty people in the apartment upstairs. Plus, someone was liable to wander back downstairs to the exhibit and trip the alarm. The last thing a late-night party needed was the arrival of the police to a possible break-in call. Another damn good reason to leave the security system off.

Not that any of it really would have mattered since he's the one that installed the security system in the first place. A system which included the video surveillance that was currently streaming to his laptop in the car. At the time he thought it was an excessive feature, but now he was glad for it since they closed the front window curtains.

The intruder found it easy to enter and even easier to travel about as the sounds of the party above more than adequately covered up his movements. Crossing to the sketch which had been a hit with everyone who'd seen it that night, the dark visitor reached up to adjust it just slightly to the left. He was adamant to the point of nausea that the sketch's placement be perfect. Just as perfect the sketch's subject.

Reaching up, the talented, deft fingers traced the woman's curves along the frame's glass. The glass was cold and unforgiving, but his skin retained the memory of her warm, soft flesh.

Eventually he was forced to lower his eyes, allow his hand to fall back to his side, and walk away from her.

Just like he'd done that morning he caught her in the shower.

And every morning since.

Soon Babe. It'll all be over soon.

23

Tonight on ESPN, it's the New York Knicks at 46 and 35 visiting the Boston Celtics, who carry a record of 52 and 29. Here in Boston it's a rainy, cold night outside but inside the New Boston Garden it's a dry, packed house as the Celtics enter the last game of the regular season against the Knicks. Good evening. I'm Mike Tinesco and with me is Hall-of-Famer Huey Brownell.

The New Boston Garden was sold out and almost every seat filled. Two notable seats in Section 312 Row A were occupied by a couple of Markison employees.

"Any one of these people could be him."

"Possible."

"It's an arena full of suspects."

"Well, I think you can rule out the women and children."

"That white guy down there looks suspicious. He's pacing. I don't trust him."

"What guy?"

"The one in blue. On the court."

"Jeremy Lin?"

"You know him?"

"Not personally, but I don't think anyone from the Knicks is a suspect."

"Oh," she squinted.

"Are those glasses real?"

"No."

"Maybe you should have your eyes checked."

"Maybe."

Lyssa was nervous about today. She had no doubt that the video would play flawlessly. She was even less slightly concerned about being found in the crowd by her stalker. Her fears were mostly focused on the possibility that the crowd wouldn't be impressed with the video at all.

"Are you sure you don't want to sit in the club box?"

"No. Absolutely not. I want to sit here. Blend in with the crowd. The box is kind of obvious."

"You know, you probably don't need the disguise."

"You don't like my Gloria Vanderbilt rims?"

He shrugged. "Only you would wear glasses as an accessory."

"All the cool kids do it."

He snorted and looked at the new text on his phone. "Good. My substitute is on his way."

"Substitute?"

"So I can go up to the control box to make sure nothing goes wrong with the video."

"Do I happen to know the substitute?" she hinted.

"Oh yes. You do," Chase pointed.

"Hello Ms. Winfield."

"Frank!"

Lyssa jumped up to hug the security guard, whom she otherwise might not have recognized in his everyday clothes.

"Thanks for covering for me." Chase shook his hand.

"Thanks for the tickets for the family!"

"No prob. You be a good girl," he pointed at Lyssa and hurried off.

"Yeah yeah yeah," she mumbled as they sat back down. "Your family's all here?"

"They're courtside."

"Oh, and you have to sit here with me?"

"I prefer it up here. My son gets a little too into the game. Last month we went to a Bruins game and thanks to a bad call I ended up with both his soda and nachos all over me. I like my sports from a safe distance. And preferably not so sticky."

The game began and before the first quarter was over Lyssa had removed the annoying glasses and Frank had a shoe full of beer. It'd spilled three rows back and trickled down to him.

"I just can't win."

When halftime came, there was a Best Buy Shoot-Out Contest featuring three fans from the crowd each trying to make half-court shots for a chance to win a 3D TV. (None of whom were even remotely close to making the basket.)

There was a kids' challenge where ten fans had to dribble a ball through a maze of orange cones for Pizza Hut gift certificates. (Which they all received regardless of how they did.)

This led to Lyssa receiving a text from Chase...

Tried to get them to say sponsored by Pennsylvania. Wouldn't do it.

It made her chuckle. Her response didn't show it though.

CONCENTRATE ON THE VIDEO!!!

Yeah yeah yeah. Oops. I spilled my beer on it. Ok. It's fine now. I licked it clean.

NOT FUNNY!!!

In the last few minutes of halftime, the video began...

Coming this June
From Markison Industries

Lyssa had seen the video dozens of times by now. She wasn't watching it. She was watching the crowd.

The video began with a clip from the original game Mutation. Even though it was only a few years old, it looked ancient and dated. The scene changed to show it was actually a scientist watching this clip on a monitor. The scientists turns and it's a snarling, blood-thirsty zombie. The crowd jumped slightly, then laughed nervously.

The action in the video continued through the halls of the laboratory to the anarchy on the streets of Boston during a zombie invasion. It traveled on the T to North Station, which was right below the New Boston Garden. Eventually the zombies invaded a Celtics game. Familiar faces filled the screen, like Rondo hanging from the rim while a zombie tries to grab his feet, and Pierce hitting another in the face with a ball. Even Doc was in it.

When it ended, only the title remained...

MUTATION 2: EVOLUTIONARY DIVIDE

The crowd loved it. They cheered and shouted.

The first text she got when it was over was from the only person whose opinion really counted when the day was done. Bryan Markison.

Good job.

"You guys did that?" Frank asked. "That video? That game?"

"Yeah."

"That's neat. I cannot even fathom how you do it, but that is amazing."

"Thanks Frank. Sometimes I even amaze myself."

Bryan was still smiling after he sent the text. He looked over at his friend's phone. Alex's finger was paused on the Send button. Bryan reached over and took the phone from him. He deleted the message before handing it back.

"She doesn't do things half-assed. You're either with her or not. You can't expect her to understand why we do what we do. Not yet, anyway."

"She would say you're being melodramatic."

"She would probably be right."

Bryan crossed to the food table to finally get something to eat. While he was calm and ever-cool on the exterior, his insides were a churning mess today. Now that the video was out he could relax and get something to eat.

Meanwhile Alex continued to stare out the club box window at the court below. He'd been called in for security today as the department was stretched thin throughout the Garden. While he preferred to be out in the crowd, looking for the bastard that caused this situation, he was needed to protect Bryan in the event of an emergency.

When they announced on the website about today's release at the game they almost hoped the stalker would make some kind of move. Reveal himself so they could finally take him down. But he didn't. And now that the video was shown, it wasn't likely he'd do anything. That window of opportunity was now closed.

Or it's possible he was going to do something and couldn't. They were extra sneaky about this operation. Extra serious. Extra protected.

Now all he wanted was to tell her how special and brilliant she still was.

You did it Babe. I'm proud of you.

But he couldn't.

* * * * *

Later that night after Lyssa returned to her apartment she reviewed the ESPN coverage which she'd recorded…

Mike Tinesco: And we're back here at the New Boston Garden where the Celtics are leading the Knicks 56 to 52. It's been an exciting first half. Almost as exciting as that halftime.

Huey Brownell: Wasn't that great?

Mike: Fans in the Garden were treated to a special video on the Jumbotron at the end of halftime. It was the trailer for the upcoming

Mutation 2: Evolutionary Divide. A video game that's due to be released next month.

Huey: The video, it was like a mini-movie really, featured a zombie invasion here in the Garden!

Mike: My favorite part was when zombie Huey Brownell tried to take a bite out of Celtics' Coach Doc Rivers! And Doc protected himself with a folding chair!

Huey: Oh, my grandchildren are gonna love seeing that!

Mike: You look good as a zombie Huey!

Huey: I don't look that much different than I do now!

Mike: Probably why they picked you!

Huey: Probably.

Mike: Well, Markison Industries, the makers of the Mutation game series, has its headquarters in Boston so it makes sense that they would pay tribute to their hometown team in the video. For the viewers at home, if you want to see the video you can go to their website www.mutation2.com. It should be up online after the game.

"Is that normal?" Chase asked Lyssa as he sat next to her on the couch, shoes kicked off, feet stretched out on the table. "For the announcers to do that?"

"No."

"How did you get them to announce that on air? Or didn't you."

"Maybe I did."

"Confess!"

"Jon's brother Aaron went to college with Mike at SU. Jon called in the favor. Mike said he'd do it if we put Huey in the video."

"That had to be very last minute though."

"Not really. Originally it was zombie Jeff Van Gundy whom Doc was smashing over the head with the chair. Substituting Huey wasn't really all that difficult."

"Sweet. ESPN won't care that he gave us a shout-out?"

"I promised ESPN we wouldn't put the video up until after the game is done. We gave them a little ad space in the side banner as a plus. It'll stay up until the final game thing is done."

"Final game thing," Chase laughed. "You crack me up."

"Hey, I don't really like basketball. Especially pro ball."

"Really? Because Frank said you were screaming like a lunatic when Garnett fouled out."

"It was a stupid call!"

"Ok. Relax. I agree."

"Blind jackass ref," she continued to mumble.

"Yeah. You don't like it at all."

24

Rarely is Tuesday morning a good morning, but for the Gaming Software Department at Markison Industries Tuesday morning was unusually sweet.

"Reviews are still pouring in Boss," Jay came over, all smiles.

"The most anticipated game sequel of the year. Sequel? Why sequel?" Kevin asked.

"Leaves them an out for whatever new game Blizzard puts out this year."

"I didn't think Blizzard was putting anything new out this year."

"They're not."

"Well, that just doesn't make sense."

"It's a marketing thing. Don't worry about it. Since another Call of Duty sequel is coming out this year, consider it a good thing."

"Ok," he said but continued to pout, still not liking it.

But every good thing must come to an end...

"Dr. Lyssa Winfield?"

"Hey, you have already been warned." She shook her finger at the FBI agents that approached her.

"Sorry. *Ms.* Winfield."

"Better. Good afternoon Agent Lewis, Agent Jenson. What can I do for you?"

"We'd like to ask you to come downtown with us to answer a few questions."

"Questions? About what?"

"It would be better if we could talk downtown at the Police Station."

"Why? What happened? Where's Chase?"

"He's already downtown ma'am. We picked him up in the lobby on his way in."

"I don't know about this," Lyssa was growing very nervous. "I'm not supposed to leave without him. Maybe I can call Alex for this."

"You know where Mr. Dane is?"

"No, but I'm sure he'd answer the phone if I called. I mean..." she trailed off, wishing she hadn't mentioned his name now.

"We'd be very interested in knowing where he is."

"Why?"

"He's wanted for questioning also."

"I haven't seen him in almost a week. He's working on another assignment."

"I'm not so sure about that ma'am."

"Why is that? And stop calling me ma'am, you damn punk."

Lewis looked at Jenson, then decided he'd just better tell her.

"The last threatening email sent to your account at nine p.m. yesterday came from the IP address of Alexander Dane's computer here at Markison Industries."

"Alex would never do that!" She became very defensive.

"That may be, but we'll still need to speak to all of you downtown."

"Hi ya!"

A karate scream cut through the air as the department's administrative assistant climbed up onto her desk and jumped off onto Agent Jenson's back. Before she even landed, Jay was making her a new nameplate for her desk.

Marlene Arezzo: Oompa Loompa Ninja.

Jenson was trying unsuccessfully to reach over his back and pluck her off.

"Put her down!" Lyssa berated him.

"I'm trying!"

"Run boss! Run!" Marlene screamed.

"I'm not running! Stop spinning around, you're gonna—"

Too late. Marlene and Jenson went sailing into the nearest cubicle wall, knocking off all the Star Wars action figures that lined the top.

"You bastards!"

Harry pulled out his Nerf rifle and proceeded to assault everyone and everything in sight.

Meanwhile, Kim crawled around from behind her cubicle wall and bit Jay in the leg.

"Ow bitch! What are you biting me for?"

"I wanted to get in on the fun."

"Fair enough," he nodded and turned into a zombie, chasing her around while she screamed. Occasionally she'd pull off an article of clothing in her perilous escape.

By the time Jenson had freed himself of the motion-sick Marlene...

"I'm gonna hurl!"

...Kim was running around shirtless, hands over her enormous breasts.

"ENOUGH!!!"

Lyssa's voice brought everyone and everything to a halt. Even the clocks stopped running when she yelled.

Until...

Ding.

The elevator doors opened to reveal the CEO of their company and Boston's Chief of Police.

"Ah fuck."

To this day no one knows you said it but everyone was thinking it.

"Good afternoon," Bryan said calmly when they reached the stunned group.

Everyone mumbled hello.

"Running a simulation, I assume," he glanced around.

"More like giving me ideas for a future game," Lyssa responded.

Bryan's eyes paused momentarily on Kim, then continued back to Lyssa.

"I look forward to the proposal on that one."

"I bet you are," she said, trying to keep her tone at bay.

"This is my good friend Chief O'Malley."

"Hello Lyssa," he shook Lyssa's hand. "I met Chase earlier today. He asked if I'd be so kind as to escort you to my station."

"He did?" she glanced quickly at Bryan, who was nodding. "Ok."

She turned to the FBI agents.

"I'm gonna ride with him."

They shrugged, not really caring. They just wanted to get out of the building at this point. Lyssa left with Chief O'Malley, Bryan left for his board meeting, and Marlene was left with a mess to clean up.

"Let's get the hell out of here," Lewis said to Jenson.

"Ok, but I'm driving."

"No way."

"It's my turn."

"It's my car."

"It's a rental!"

"My name's on it."

"Oh really. Is your name Toyota or Corolla?"

"Piss off. I'm driving."

* * * * *

"Again?"

"Again."

"Ok. Here's the short-short version. Alex and I met for the first time a month ago when he was assigned to increase the security measures on project Game of Hearts."

"I thought it was called Mutation 2: Evolutionary Divide."

"It is now, but then it was called Game of Hearts."

"Please continue."

"We became very close quickly and a week and a half later we gave in to the inevitable and entered into a sexual relationship. A week ago he came to the realization that banging the woman he's supposed to take a bullet for was not working out, so he had himself reassigned to another project more suited to his talents. An undercover project."

"What undercover project?"

"Busting a ring of puppy sweater smugglers in Provincetown."

"Really?"

"No! Duh! The entire point of him being undercover is that no one knows what he's doing. It would kind of defeat the purpose of unnnnnndercooooover!"

"So you're no longer in contact with Alexander Dane."

"Not while he's undercover."

"And you have absolutely no idea what he's doing?"

~~~

"Nope."

"You haven't talked to him at all Chase?"

"Nope."

"Has Ms. Winfield?"

"Nope."

"How can you be sure?"

"I'm with her 24/7."

"She might have talked to him in the bathroom. Surely you don't follow her in there."

"Of course not! What kind of pervert are you?"

"I just meant — "

"I don't want to know what you meant! Lyss is like a sister

to me. How you think about her bathroom habits is between you and your psychiatrist."

"Her relationship with you is like that of a sibling?"

~~~

"I don't have a relationship with Chase."

"You spend all day and night with him. You must have some kind of relationship."

"I tolerate him just enough to annoy the hell out of him."

"He refers to you as his sister."

"Well, it sounds like his feelings are mutual then."

"Chase refers to many people as siblings. Including Mr. Dane."

"That's because they're brothers."

"Adoptive brothers."

~~~

"Same diff. A brother is a brother. Whether by birth or by chance."

"So if your brother came to you and asked your help to bring down his tyrannical corporate employer – "

"Tyrannical? Bryan's not tyrannical. He's Jewish."

The agent stared at him.

"Sorry," Chase sighed. "You were saying?"

"If he asked for your help no matter what it was--"

"It would matter. Believe me. And no, he didn't ask me to help him take down Markison. He would never do that. Bryan's a brother-from-another-mother too."

"Almost."

~~~

"It's still the same thing. They're family. They wouldn't do that to each other. And he wouldn't do that to me."

"Think about it Ms. Winfield. He had ample opportunity. He could have entered your apartment building while you were at work or at yoga to make it look like someone broke into your apartment. He certainly has access to paint messages on your office door. He possesses the technological knowledge to send the emails through a proxy. Hell, my nephew can do that."

"So arrest your nephew."

"He doesn't really have a motive."

"Neither does Alex."

"That you know about," he said darkly.

~~~

"Whose idea was it for Alex to head up the security enhancement project?"

"Bryan asked him about it. He reviewed it and gave him his recommendations. I agreed."

"But whose idea was it for Alex to head it up. Be the lead. Be Ms. Winfield's bodyguard."

"His," Chase sighed.

"Why?"

"He loved her."

"Seriously?"

"Have you seen her?"

"Of course."

"She's fucking hot."

"She is quite attractive, I'll admit."

"You'd kill to bang her," Chase leaned over the table with a big smirk. "We all would."

Lewis shrugged.

"So how come you get to question me?"

"Excuse me?"

"Whose idea was it for your buddy Jenson to interview Lyssa?"

He paused.

"Exactly. That's why Alex got Lyssa. She already shot me down."

"Then why did he turn the assignment of being her bodyguard back to you?"

~~~

"He found it hard to work with me around. He liked playing with me too much. It was distracting."

"I would have been tempted to say to hell with it and just play."

"He'd be playing with my life at this point. He didn't want that to happen."

"He didn't want the responsibility for it."

"On the contrary, he's all about responsibility. He's smart enough and man enough to know when it's time to turn it over to someone else. That's all."

"Do you miss him?"

"Of course. He said he'd be back when his undercover job is over."

"Do you believe him?"

She paused. She'd never really thought about it.

"You doubt him."

"I don't doubt that he wants to. I just don't know if he will. He has strong work principles and if I get in the way..." she trailed off.

"I just don't understand how a man that loves you can leave you. Especially during this time."

~~~

"He didn't really want to go."

"But you said he asked for reassignment."

"Sometimes we do things we don't want to because we think it's for the better. Like you being here questioning me. You have to do it even though you know you're wasting your time."

"Why did he send the threatening email?"

"He didn't and it's a preposterous theory that makes no sense whatsoever that he would."

"Maybe he doesn't have a direct grudge towards Lyssa, but he might towards Bryan Markison. And what better revenge than to break the heart of the woman that's managing one of the biggest software sequels in your company's history."

Chase sighed, growing quite irritated with the same line of questioning over and over again.

"Break her heart? Do you know how incredibly stupid that sounds? Not to mention complicated! First you have to get her attention, then make her fall in love with you, then you can break her heart. Besides, in case you haven't been paying attention, it hasn't stopped her. You'd have to kill her to get her to stop working.

"Or kidnap her, which honestly would have been easier than sending emails and trashing her apartment and leaving death threats on her office door. And with her missing the project would have been massively delayed, thereby ruining Markison financially.

"You know, I'm starting to think I'm working for the wrong side. I should consider turning to a life of crime. I bet I'd be really good at it."

Lewis was getting especially annoyed at this point. Mostly because he was right. It was a shit theory, but it's all they had and all they would ever have thanks to the restrictions on this case.

What fucking case?

"So, is the FBI always in the habit of hiring bathroom fetishists?"

And that comment would keep Chase locked up as a suspect

until well after the dinner hour.

* * * * *

When Jenson was done talking to Lyssa he left her in the Chief's office while he went to find out about Chase's release.

"The FBI thinks Alex is being paid by an outside source to do this," the Chief began. "To destroy Markison internally. To break your heart and weaken them."

"That really doesn't make much sense."

"You don't think Alex is capable of it?"

"Oh, I think he's perfectly capable of it. I just think he'd do a better job of it."

O'Malley snorted. "Yeah, I suppose so."

"He's my secret agent and a proud artist. He wouldn't have sent an email using the Ransom font. It's not original and it's beneath him."

"It could have been part of the ruse so you wouldn't suspect him."

"We never in a million years would have suspected him. There was no track for him to throw us off of."

She picked up her purse and pulled out her wallet. Opening it to the credit card holders she pulled out one of the cards and handed it to O'Malley.

He looked up at her with a smile.

"It came with the flowers he sent me the day after... "

She didn't have to finish the thought. He knew exactly what she meant.

"A man who does that does not spray 'Die Bitch' on the back of an office door."

"I agree. Which brings me to one question... what did you bake that captured the attention of that man?" He handed the card back to her and she tucked it safely back in its protective plastic cover.

"I baked him a cake."

"What kind?"

"Carrot."

"I'll assume it had cream cheese frosting."

"No other kind."

"Well, my dear, I can tell you that I've dealt with Alex a few times over the years and I quite like him. He's been fair to me and my men in some very sticky situations. He certainly doesn't strike me as the type of man that would break a woman's heart for money. Or anything else."

She smiled. "I'm glad you agree."

"Excuse me," a detective stuck his head in the door. "Here's the case file you asked for sir."

"Thanks."

"I should let you get back to work," Lyssa stood. "I can wait for Chase in the lobby."

"Are you sure? You're more than welcome to wait here."

"No. You have far more important things to do than babysit me."

"Probably, but none as lovely."

She smiled to him. "You smoothie."

He laughed and shook her hand goodbye.

When she was gone, the Chief picked up the case file that was brought to him and walked out into the squad room.

"Burns! Get me the D.A.'s office on the phone. Tell him it's about last week's robbery spree on Kensington Ave. Then do an internet search for carrot cake recipes."

"You think that's a clue to the robberies?"

"No, I think my anniversary's next week and I want to surprise my wife."

* * * * *

Lyssa said she'd wait in the front lobby, but after ten

minutes she decided she'd had enough waiting. It felt like she'd been waiting all her life. She needed to move. Besides, Chase could call her when he got out.

So without a word to anyone, she slipped out of the police station and caught a taxi back to Markison. Instead of going up to her floor, she picked up her car from the parking garage.

Lyssa drove aimlessly around outer Boston. She'd deduced that maybe if she kept moving no one would find her. She felt safer in her car than anywhere on Earth right now.

"Maybe I'll drive to Portland or Buffalo," she pondered. "I have my laptop. I could work remotely."

After three hours of wandering, which included a jaunt out to Concord for a latte to go with the small assortment box of chocolates she picked up from the Priscilla Candy Shop, the gaslight came on. Lyssa stopped to fill up and decided she'd actually had enough driving. Normally she enjoyed spending time alone in her car, but her thoughts were still too frantic. She decided she needed to visit Val. Maybe even take part in her Tuesday night class.

"Where the hell is my yoga bag?"

She filed through her memories in search of the last time she used it. It was a week ago Tuesday. The day her office was broken into. The last night she was with Alex.

"Ah dammit."

The bag is in Alex's car.

She'd changed at the yoga studio and gone out for dinner with Val and Alex. He'd thrown both their bags in the trunk of his car. It was probably still there.

Now the big question was...where's the car? Is it at Markison, the studio, or places unknown? He could be using it for a stake out. He could be in it right now. Maybe he's rendezvousing with his silent partner. She was probably a beautiful, voluptuous owner of a rival software company. Maybe she was entertaining him in the back seat. Payment for a job well done in making Markison's production manager go completely insane. A bonus blowjob for all his hard work.

Her thoughts were on a rampage, and soon so was her car! After crossing three lanes of traffic on 93 at an unsafe speed and nearly taking out the off-ramp speed limit sign, she slowed considerably.

"Ok. Probably should calm down a little bit," she laughed nervously to herself.

Taking a guess, she stopped at the studio first. She parked on the street and punched in the code to let herself in the garage door.

"Bingo!"

There were two cars. One was the Porsche Boxster. They'd taken it to the art gallery the weekend after the break-in but other than that Alex said he rarely got to use it. At the time he'd mentioned he'd hoped they could take it out on a weekend jaunt to the Cape someday.

She felt her stomach clench when she thought back to it. The smile on his face when he told her his plans for the trip; the glow in her heart to make future plans with this man. His words sounded so sincere.

The second car was the silver Honda Civic. The twin to her own Civic and the world's most invisible car. Perfect for the spy that doesn't want to be found in the crowd, and less likely to be broken into or stolen, so it was the car of choice during the week. It was this car they were in the last Tuesday they spent at yoga together.

The one thing that was missing was his bike. The Ninja.

"So much for the backseat blowjob theory," she mumbled to herself, disgusted that she'd let herself get jealous of her own imagination.

She dug out the studio keys from her purse and opened the back door to grab the car keys from the hook on the wall, then came back and opened the trunk of the Civic.

"Ah ha! Found it!"

She pulled her yoga bag out from alongside a box and was about to shut the trunk when something about the box caught her eye. Shoving the sheet covering it aside she found it was two boxes. Specifically the two boxes from her apartment she'd asked Alex to throw out. The two boxes that contained painful memories from her past.

Why are they in his trunk? Why didn't he throw them away?

Her mind raced as quickly as her pulse.

Oh my God! What if the FBI is right?

Her heartbeat was pounding so loud in her ears that she didn't hear the garage door open.

"What are you doing here?"

Jumping, she turned to find Alex calmly walking in.

"Yoga."

She held up the bag that was still in her hand.

"Oh yeah. I forgot that was in there," he shut the garage door.

"Something else you forgot was in there?" She gestured down to the boxes.

He walked over and carefully closed the trunk, taking the keys out of the lock, tucking them in his pocket.

"I didn't forget."

"Why?"

"I just wanted to be sure you meant it."

She was confused.

"You weren't in a good place mentally that day. I figured when this was all over I'd ask you if you really wanted to throw it out or if you were just in a moment."

"I meant it."

"Ok. But it's not wise to throw out such personal items when you're being stalked. Stalkers are like raccoons. They love to root through trash. We'll shred it. Or better yet I'll take them out to Ron and Shirley's farm and burn them in his bins. Then neither one of us will have to see it."

She nodded.

"I didn't go through the boxes," he stressed. "I swear."

She nodded again, not entirely convinced though.

"Why are you here alone? Where's Chase?"

"With the FBI."

"Still? Well, that explains some things."

He ran his hands through his hair, obviously not happy with that piece of news.

"They're looking for you."

"I know."

"They said you did it. Sent the emails, broke into my apartment, wrote on my office door."

"I bet they did," he snorted, amused by the idea of it.

"They can make a pretty convincing case for it too."

"Lyssa," he reached for her and she stepped back, "you can't possibly believe them."

She shrugged. "I'm not really sure who I'm supposed to believe anymore."

The color drained from his face. He put his hand on top of the trunk to steady himself.

"I would never... "

"I didn't think so, but I've been wrong before."

"Not this time. You were right all along. We know who it is, but the problem is we can't find where he's hiding."

"So, it's—"

Her words were cut off by the sound of a car pulling up to the curb outside. They both immediately knew who it was. Alex snapped back to attention.

"Go," she urged.

He didn't move.

"Alex, go!"

"If staying proves to you that I'm not the stalker, then—"

"Dammit! Go before I change my mind!"

He reached around her head and pulled her close to kiss her

quickly. Then he darted into the studio, closing the door behind him. Thankfully she'd left it open because she planned to return the key.

She opened the garage door to leave just as Agents Lewis and Jenson were exiting their car.

"Are you following me around or something?" she walked out and closed the door behind her, making sure it was securely locked.

"Trying to," Lewis scowled at her. "You drive like a maniac."

"You should see me drive when I'm in a good mood. It's worse."

"I told you to let me drive," Jensen grumbled. "I could have made the exit." Lewis threw him a dirty look before turning his attention back to Lyssa.

"This property is listed as belonging to Bryan Markison."

"It is," Lyssa nodded even though she didn't actually know that. She assumed it was under Alex's name, but now that she thought about it, it was infinitely wiser to keep it under Bryan's name.

"It's an art studio?" They glanced up to the second floor windows.

"Yes. It's like summer camp. We come here and do arts and crafts. Finger painting, macramé, boondoggle. If the weather's nice, we make smores on the roof and tell ghost stories about the killer hook."

She smiled evilly for dramatic effect. They weren't impressed.

"Is Alex up there now?"

"I have no idea. I didn't go up there. I just got my yoga bag from the company car in the garage."

"You drive a company car too?"

"I drove it while mine was being fixed." She mentally smiled at herself for coming up with the quick, believable cover story. "I forgot I left the bag in the trunk."

Lyssa happened to look up over Agent Jenson's shoulder and spy a black Ninja motorbike turning the corner and head off down the street in the opposite direction.

"You know, rumor has it that Bryan Markison uses the studio to host parties. With his lady friends," she strongly hinted with a big wink.

"Really?"

She nodded. "I know some of those women and I wouldn't suggest you go up there without a tetanus shot and a blue light."

They cringed slightly.

"Now, if you gentlemen will excuse me I have a yoga class to attend. In case you get lost again, it's at The Lotus Blossom on East Concord."

While Lewis grew irritated with her, Jenson was more understanding and personable about it.

"We're just concerned for your safety."

"I imagine that you are. Him?" she pointed to Lewis. "Not so much."

Jenson snorted; Lewis glared.

"Bye!"

She smiled, waved, and bounced over to her car. Hopping in, she sped off down the street, nearly hitting a trash can on her way by.

"Maniac."

* * * * *

From the rooftop of the art studio Alex watched Lyssa talking to the agents. He couldn't hear them but he could read the body language clearly. She was teasing them, picking on them, giving him a chance to escape.

"Good girl," he mumbled to himself as he climbed down the fire escape on the opposite side of the building and made his way through the alley behind the building to Dartmouth Street where he'd parked his bike around the corner from the studio.

He started up the Ninja and cruised quietly around the corner, spying her glance in the rear-view mirror. He swore he saw a smile from her to go with it.

He didn't know what was worse. Seeing her and not being able to stay to protect her, or leaving her with the FBI agents. He knew Lewis and Jensen by reputation and they weren't bad agents, but he didn't necessarily trust them with her safety. Thankfully neither did she. He knew she'd climb back in her car and be gone to yoga as soon as he was out of sight.

Once she was at yoga she'd be okay. There was something soothing about The Lotus Blossom. You just couldn't imagine something going wrong there. Val, despite being as horny as Chase, was a hub for tranquility and peacefulness.

Meanwhile, Alex had another lead to follow. A lead that might bring an end to this pain and frustration that plagued their lives.

Eleanor Partridge's house. A tiny marshmallow-green split-level in Greater Boston. It stood out from the other houses not just in style and color but in smell.

Alex hadn't gotten three feet from the front door and recognized the faint distinct odor of decaying flesh. He pulled his collar up over his nose and bravely picked the lock to the front door.

Entering the house, he was hit violently with the scent. He left the front door open to vent the foul stench as he nearly heaved up in the front yard. He allowed his mind to recall images of his crying girl to harden himself to the tragedy that lay within the house walls.

Stolidly he traveled thru the house, to the basement where the scent was stronger. Upon the floor next to the chest freezer he found a huge pile of decaying meat. It appeared to be store bought and weeks old, rotting on the floor.

Why is this here?

He crossed to a chest-freezer that was heard easily running.

He opened the chest-freezer and stood frozen himself at the site of the two bodies. An elderly woman, whom he assumed was Eleanor Partridge, and signs of the body of a younger woman underneath her.

Alex closed the freezer and left the basement, exiting the house as quickly as he came.

He rode back into town until he found a pay phone. Once there he dialed a number he kept in his cellphone but never actually dialed from it.

"Chief O'Malley, this is a call from a mutual friend. I have a lead you might want to follow-up on... "

* * * * *

Lyssa arrived in plenty of time for yoga class. Before anyone else came, she was able to sit down with Val for an hour to talk about life. Surprisingly, Lyssa had very little to say. She didn't want to talk about the FBI or Alex. She wanted a break from thinking about it.

"So, have you seen him?" Val asked anyway.

"Once. Briefly. He looked tired."

"That's all?"

She nodded. "I think he misses me. He gave me a kiss goodbye."

"Well, that's a good sign."

"It is."

And it really was. Lyssa didn't really think he was the stalker, did she? It just made no sense in the world. But when she thought about everything the Agents told her, it made her doubt him. Hell, she was even starting to doubt herself at this point.

But his reaction when he realized she had doubts is what brought her back to reality. There are things you can fake. The look on his face at that moment was not one of them. It was why she let him go.

Val could sense Lyssa wasn't in the mood to talk about it, so she regaled her with stories about her dates that weekend, all of which turned into daytime soap opera style storylines. Lyssa nodded and laughed at the appropriate places, but mostly she was just going through the motions. She was too emotionally drained to really apply herself to anything more.

After class, Lyssa sat in her car wondering what she'd like to have for dinner. She wasn't particularly hungry. The donut she had at the police station while waiting to be questioned was still sitting in the pit of her stomach like an intestinal road block.

Glancing down at her phone, she noticed one voicemail. She was pleased to see who the caller was and after listening to it she decided to go for a happy drive to meet up with him.

"Hey, it's Lyssa. I'm on my way. I'll be there in...hello?... ah dammit. Good timing phone."

The battery died.

"Oh well, at least he knows I'm coming."

He did. And he was ready...

* * * * *

After Chase was released by the FBI, he raced back to "the hub", or the Markison Network Center as it was officially known. It wasn't just the system administration for the penthouse and indeed, the entire building, this room was also their eyes and ears to the world. The FBI certainly wouldn't be comfortable if they knew all the connections they had from this room.

"Where the hell are you Lyss?" he mumbled, working frantically to find her. He tried calling a dozen or so times only to go to voicemail immediately. He figured her phone was shut off. At least he hoped that's all it meant.

The network room phone buzzed. He glanced at the digital

display.

Ah fuck.

"Hey Alex," he answered it.

"Where is she?"

"I don't know. I just got out from the police station not five minutes ago. Her phone's not answering. She's left me no messages. You haven't seen her?"

"I caught her at the studio about two hours ago. She was getting her bag to go to yoga. But the Feds followed her there and I had to leave quick."

"She's at yoga then."

"She's not there anymore. It's been over for a half hour."

"Damn."

"It gets worse."

He told him about the bodies he found recently.

"I called it in anonymously to the Chief."

"That's good. Meanwhile, I checked her email and there's nothing. Her phone is off because it goes right to voicemail. Well, it goes right to a message that her voicemail is full."

"Full?"

"You haven't heard it?"

"I haven't tried calling. I figured the Feds are monitoring her phone calls now. They'd expect you to call but not me."

"Oh, true."

"Lyss is far too organized to let her voicemail get full. Someone filled it up today."

"You wouldn't happen to know the code for her phone."

"No."

"The last time we tried to crack one it locked up."

"I know."

"Do you even have a guess?"

"No," he sighed. "I wouldn't even know —"

Alex suddenly stopped.

"Know what dude?" Chase urged him to continue.

"I'll call you back."

Alex hung up and accessed her internet from his smartphone. He pulled up Google Drive and plugged in her email address. Now for the all-important password. He was embarrassed to do it. Ashamed that he even could. But her life depended on it at this point.

"What's the password?" he pondered to himself while accessing the spyware program he installed on her pc.

alexdane1

He typed it into the webpage.

Accepted!

"Awesome Babe," he mumbled, almost giddy to see that he was her Google password. In the age of technology that was a sign of true love.

Flipping to the spreadsheet he'd seen her briefly use on her PC at home...

Addresses and Websites.

The first tab was a listing of personal and work addresses, phone numbers, and emails. There were additional tabs for birthdays, anniversaries, and just things in general to remember about certain people. The third tab was websites. A huge list of them, and her username and password for each.

Yes, she was unbelievably organized.

The last tab was the one he wanted. Personal banking info. Credit card info.

Phone pin number = 3325.

He called Chase back.

"Try 3325."

After a couple seconds...

"Yes! How the hell did you guess that?"

"I didn't. She gave it to me."

"What?"

"Later."

"Ok, we got three calls from work. Six from me. Twenty-seven from a 978 number?"

"978 is the exchange for Rockport. Andre, maybe?"

Chase googled it quickly.

"Yes. That's from the Waldron Art Gallery. Why would he call her twenty-seven times?"

"I don't know. It's Andre though, so I wouldn't doubt it."

"There's only one voicemail though."

Chase played it loud enough for Alex to hear.

"Lyssa, it's Andre Waldron from the gallery. Alex called me and asked that I get in touch with you. I guess he's in some kind of trouble and he's worried the cops will come get the portrait. He wants you to come get it. I didn't really understand all of it. You might know more than me at this point. If you stop by we can chat over tea and biscuits. Love you dear!"

But the message didn't stop there. It sounded like he set the phone down but never hung up. They could hear muffled voices in the background.

"What's the rest of that?" Alex asked. "I can't quite hear."

"Me neither. I'm going to have to see if we can clear it up. I'm assuming you never talked to Andre."

"No, I certainly did not."

"Well, she called him back. For a whopping three seconds. I bet her phone died. She never plugs that thing in. Do you think that's where she went?"

"I'm going."

"I'll meet you there."

* * * * *

"Andre?" Lyssa walked into the art gallery.

"Hey," the proprietor waved to her from the other side of the room.

"You ok?" she noticed he looked frazzled.

"Oh sure."

He crossed to her, gave her a hug, and whispered, "I'm so

sorry. I didn't want to call you."

"What do you mean?"

She stepped back and saw a man standing right behind Andre's shoulder. He lifted his arm and brought it down on the back of Andre's head.

Lyssa reached for him, but his body was too heavy for her and it slid to the floor.

"Leave him bitch!" a voice snarled at her.

A strong, cloth-covered hand clamped over her face. Lyssa struggled for a few seconds before her world went black.

* * * * *

When Lyssa opened her eyes again she was staring down at a cement floor. She was tied to a chair in a dimly lit room. A mechanical hum next to her caused her to turn her head. She groaned at the sting in her jaw where she'd fought against the attacker's grip. After the pain subsided, she recognized the hum was coming from a dehumidifier.

She slowly surveyed the rest of the room. The single workbench lamp that was on shed very little light but she could make out stacks of paintings and frames lined up against the wall. The workbench itself had paint and brushes scattered about. The unopened box just to the right of her was addressed to Andre. She guessed this was the basement of the gallery.

"Hello Dr. Winfield."

Standing across from her was someone that she recognized. Someone that she knew for sure had sent the emails, broken into her apartment, and had been terrorizing her. And now he was going to kill her. At this point in the game if he wanted to call her doctor she would let him.

"Stephen? Stephen Brooks?"

"You remember me," he seemed genuinely surprised.

"Of course. You were one of my best programmers."

"Don't patronize me, Doctor," he snarled.

"I'm not trying to," she said quietly.

"I broke the program."

"You broke it?" Lyssa struggled to remember.

"The fatal 463 error message!"

She started to recall. It was a troubleshooting message that got left in the game after an update was put out. It wasn't that big a deal. It caused issues for a handful of gamers but it was corrected within hours with another online update.

"Just because you made a simple mistake — "

"Simple?!"

"Yes. We've all made them. And it wasn't anything that couldn't be fixed."

"Do you know what they said about me? The things the players called me online?"

"I did read some of them, but it wasn't about you. They didn't even know you. They were just lashing out at the game. Most of them are just ugly little pre-pubescent teenagers anyway."

"Sophia was so embarrassed by it she left me."

"Left you?"

"I came home that night. I told her about my day. I confessed to her about the error. And she left me."

Lyssa didn't know what to say. Surely it couldn't have been because of that! It was probably because Stephen was clearly off his rocker, but she sure as hell wasn't going to tell him that now.

"I'm sorry Stephen."

"You're sorry!" He flexed his fists in rage. "I lost my wife and my job because of that!"

She looked at the floor, praying he would calm again. He did so quickly. After a quiet moment Lyssa spoke again.

"You didn't lose your job. You quit."

"I couldn't stay there after that," he said as if it was the most obvious thing in the world.

"We had no intention of firing you. Most of us had forgotten about it the next day."

"It's too bad really," he started to pace the room. "I really *am* brilliant. Much more brilliant than your buddies in the security department."

"You did all of this?"

"Oh yes. Don't you think I'm capable?"

"Of course!" she quickly agreed. "How did you get in my apartment building though?"

"I waited in the parking garage until an elderly tenant with groceries needed assistance. I ever so kindly carried the bags while she let us both in."

"Oh."

"I kept my head low for the cameras and said I was Greg from 315D. We look similar so security didn't suspect a thing when they reviewed the tapes."

"And my office door?"

"Used my wife's ID to get in the building. If you come during rush hour and swipe it quick they have a hard time matching every passer-by's face with the one that pops up on the screen. Most of the time they're just waiting for the beep of an invalid ID anyway and not even checking the good ones."

"Isn't your wife on worker's comp leave though? Wouldn't that trigger something?"

"Normally, but her physical therapist is on the sixth floor. And she has a lot of appointments. Thanks to governmental patient privacy laws even your goons couldn't verify with the office that she actually kept them. I'm sure they didn't think it was suspicious enough to break the law and find out for themselves."

"And the car?"

"Oh," he frowned, embarrassed by this story, "I don't want to talk about that."

"Why?"

"Because it didn't go according to plan, ok?" he got upset again. "The car was supposed to hit yours directly in the passenger door. Instead it barely nudged your car and hit that ape that was following you around for a while. The one you were sleeping with. Slut."

"I am not a slut," she defended herself.

"You *are* a slut. And a lying bitch!"

He pulled out his gun. It wavered in his hands. He was clearly not an expert with it, but he was probably crazy enough to try and use it.

"Stephen, please," she pleaded quietly, tears in her voice.

"Don't do that! Don't beg me!"

"You're scaring me."

"All you lying bitches are the same! Sophia. My mother. You. Mother never lied to me until she married him."

"Him?"

"My stepfather. Jerry Partridge. He always hated me because I was smarter than him. Nothing was as important as physical strength to him. The faster and stronger you were, the better you were. Mother said he was just intimidated. That he really cared for me. That was the first lie she ever told me."

He leaned over to look directly into her face.

"Aren't you going to plead with me? Tell me how wonderful I am, and how much you love me? Just so you can get your way."

"I never said I loved you Stephen."

He stood back up, surprised. He wasn't expecting that.

"You didn't. The others did. The others begged for my love and to be forgiven."

"But I never said I hated you either."

"No, you never did."

Lyssa gave him a little smile, all while she was nonchalantly working her hands out of the shoddy knots he tied them in.

"But it's too late now."

"Too late?" Lyssa's smile faded.

"Yes. I still have to kill you."

"Why?" Lyssa's lip started to quiver.

He got right in her face.

"Because you're still a bitch!"

Pulling her left arm free, she took him by surprise and boxed his right ear with her fist. He fell to the ground, curled up into a ball and cradled his ear in his hands, screaming like a small child. The gun had flown from his hand and landed somewhere unseen. Perhaps under the worktable.

Lyssa wrenched her right wrist free. Thankfully he hadn't tied her feet to the chair so she was able to scramble away as soon as she was free. She'd never been in Andre's basement so it took her a moment to spot the stairs. As soon as they were in her sight she ran for them.

Stephen was recovered and up on his feet by now. He caught her ankle halfway up the stairs and started to pull her back down.

"No!" she screamed and kicked at him.

"Come here you bitch!"

One of her feet connected with his shoulder, throwing him off balance. He lost his grip and tumbled off the bottom of the stairs. Lyssa kept climbing.

The door to the basement exited near the bathroom so she knew exactly where she was now. She stopped as she neared the counter next to the front door. There was a foot sticking out from the end.

"Andre?" she whispered, full of fear.

Looking around the end she could see him stretched out on the floor. Thankfully he was still breathing. He'd only been knocked unconscious.

She debated what she should do at this point. Stay with Andre and phone the authorities from the gallery phone on the counter? Or make a break for it and pray she can get help before Stephen decides to take revenge on poor Andre?

Before she could even decide Stephen found her first.

"Die. Bitch."

His head slowly rose over the counter. He seethed with anger. Lyssa let out a short scream then bolted from her spot.

She darted around the first exhibit partition. He dove for her but slipped on the newly cleaned floor and fell into the wall, knocking one of the photographs off the wall.

Lyssa rounded the corner and made a beeline for the front door.

Locked!

And it wasn't the kind you could just unlock with a twist of a knob.

Lyssa turned and slipped on a wet spot on the floor. She fell on her side hard. Groaning, she turned over to see Stephen standing over her. He was holding the eunuch statue overhead.

"DIE! BITCH!"

She raised her arm, preparing to block the blow.

But it never came.

His strike was interrupted by a loud crash as someone came hurtling through the front window. Startled, Stephen turned and dropped the statue. It just missed landing on Lyssa's foot.

A hooded man rolled to his feet, stood, and turned to face them. Lyssa's heart leapt in her chest.

Alex.

"You bastard!" Stephen shouted and raised his fist in anger.

The inexperienced fighter was no match for the Kendo-trained bodyguard. Alex caught his flying fist easily and twisted his hand, snapping his wrist. Stephen screamed in pain. His screams were silenced soon when Alex punched him across the jaw. Stumbling back, Stephen fell against a nearby pedestal, cracking his head wide open on the corner of it. The vase that was perched atop fell off and shattered on the floor.

Lyssa didn't know if Stephen was dead or not, but judging from the amount of blood that was pouring from his head wound if he wasn't he would be soon. She pushed herself up off the floor to avoid the red river that was flowing towards her.

Alex looked down at himself. The hooded sweatshirt he was wearing was covered with slivers of glass. He unzipped it and carefully peeled it off, tossing it into the growing pool of blood, glass, and ceramics.

He quickly surveyed his head, arms, long-sleeved shirt and remaining clothes for any stray shards of glass. After finding none he could finally turn his attention to Lyssa.

"Are you ok? Did he hurt you?" he walked over to her.

"Alex," she whimpered and wrapped her arms around his chest.

"It's ok Babe." He held her close, rubbing her back, grateful to have her in his arms. "It's over. It's all finally over."

She allowed herself to do the one thing she wanted to do all day long.

Cry.

Alex silently held her against his chest and let her.

* * * * *

Chase arrived mere minutes after Alex.

"Dammit. I wanted to be the hero this time."

Rockport Police and Fire arrived next. The ambulance left with Andre, who was awake long enough to declare, "I never thought I'd be happy to see you," when he recognized Chase.

The FBI arrived soon after. They'd put a GPS marker on Chase's car and followed him there.

"Ass," Lyssa spouted at Agent Lewis, who was forced to admit his theory about Alex might have been wrong.

Alex said nothing. He didn't have to. She was taking care of it for him.

Much to everyone's surprise, Chief O'Malley arrived just after the FBI. He supplied the information about the bodies they found at Brooks' mother's house.

"Don't tell me you put a marker on my car too?" Chase

asked after the FBI left.

"I did it the old fashioned way."

O'Malley gestured for them to look up. As the FBI car drove away they could see a small driveway reflective marker taped to their license plate.

They laughed.

"You rock Chief!" Chase clapped his shoulder.

"Since we got a helpful tip of where to find Brooks' first victims, I thought I could help you boys out by clearing your name personally with the Feds."

"Very kind of you," Alex said.

The Chief nodded to him, then walked away.

"Did you—"

"Later," Alex quietly interrupted Lyssa. "I'll tell you everything when we're done."

An hour later, when things had finally calmed down, Alex and Lyssa sat on a bench a block down the street. It was close to where Alex had left his bike to make his silent approach to the gallery when he arrived that evening.

"How did you know I was here?"

"The voicemail Andre left you. I didn't call him, so I knew either someone had impersonated me or he was coerced into calling you. Either way, someone wanted to get you here."

"You checked my voicemail?"

He reluctantly nodded. "You weren't answering your phone. We needed to find you."

"How did you do that?"

He explained about the Google document and her pin number. He conveniently left out the part about the spyware on her PC and silently reminded himself to remove it as soon as he could.

"Am I that obvious?"

"Only to me. No one else could have figured that out."

"Did Chase warn you about the FBI?"

"He didn't have to. I knew they would be looking for me. I purposely left my computer IP wide open so Brooks could find it and send the email. Then we could track him down. It worked. Kind of. We found where he was hiding out, but he wasn't there."

"Was that Chase's idea? You were already undercover so might as well make you the fall guy for the email."

"It was my idea."

"Didn't that put your undercover job at risk though? What if they found you?"

"Honey, I never really went anywhere. I've been with you the whole time, you just didn't see me."

"You were?"

He nodded. "Chase and I just switched jobs. That's all. It's just when I go undercover I don't hang around the office as much as he does."

She was stunned and a bit hurt by the news.

"I would completely understand if you wanted to hit me right now."

"I'm not going to hit you."

"I wish you would."

"I'm not letting you off that easy."

"This isn't easy Babe."

"You don't get to call me that anymore."

"I'm sorry."

"And stop saying that," she brushed the tears from her cheeks. "You lied to me."

"I didn't," he stressed. "I just didn't tell you that you were the one I was going undercover for."

"Not telling me the truth isn't any better than telling me a lie."

"I'm surprised you didn't figure it out. You figured everything else out. You were practically a step ahead of us the entire way."

"I've been a little distracted lately," she said angrily.

"Please," he begged quietly, reaching out for her. She slapped his hand away and this time she meant it. There was no playfulness in her touch today.

"Why did you accept this assignment in the first place?"

"Bryan called me after the first few emails and asked my opinion. I told him it was worth investigating. So he sent me all the details, including your personnel record. All one hundred and twelve pages of it."

"A hundred and twelve? Really?"

"Well, the FBI file was eighty pages alone."

"I have an FBI file?!"

"You were involved in a terrorist bombing in London. Yeah, the FBI has a file on you. It was them that had the workers' comp case, which was well over sixty pages."

"Oh, my God. And you read it all?"

He nodded, then snorted. "My favorite part was when the FBI referred to you as non-complacent and argumentative because you disobeyed the doctor's orders and took a transatlantic flight home."

"I didn't do much to change their opinion about that today either."

"I might have normally skimmed that page but Bryan had circled it with a red pen and wrote 'Hire Her' next to it."

"He did?"

"He knew from day one how special you were. And so did I. So when I told Bryan he needed to beef up security on the project I told him I wanted the assignment."

He pulled out his wallet and removed a picture from the inside flap.

"Because I didn't want anyone else in security to get their hands on her."

It was a picture of her taken on her first day at Markison. It was for the company interoffice email introducing her to her fellow employees. Admittedly, it was a good picture. She was so happy to be working there, starting a new life and career. The excitement showed in her eyes.

"Of course that's not what I told anyone else. All I wanted was a few weeks back home to relax; a break from the travel; a simple in-house security job. About two seconds after I met you in your office I knew I'd been lying to everyone, including myself. I said something obnoxious and the look in your eyes made me realize immediately that it wasn't the job and traveling that I needed a break from. It was pretty much the last decade I'd spent in near solitude just doing my job and shunning life. I wanted to start enjoying my life."

"Is that wrong?"

"It is when it put you at risk. That's why I decided to let Chase do his job and I needed to go back to doing mine."

"But you're a wonderful bodyguard. Bryan said you're the best."

"He's usually right, but I've never really had such a vested interest in the body I'm guarding. I got too personal and couldn't focus on the professional anymore. I was having too much fun with you, if that's possible."

"You could have told me."

He shook his head. "If you knew I was still there it wouldn't have worked."

"But—"

"Babe...Lyss. This is the part where I have to ask you to trust me and I know you don't feel you have a reason to, but undercover operations never work if the subjects know it's an undercover operation. *Never*," he stressed. "In order for Brooks to slip up I needed him to think he was winning. I needed him to think you were broken. I needed him to stop watching for me."

"You don't think I could have done that?"

He looked up at her. "Less than twenty-four hours after your apartment had been ransacked you were running around the art studio apartment in my Speedos and grabbing my johnson. No offense, but I don't see you as the type of woman that can pretend to be unhappy for too long."

"Ok, you might have a point there," she was forced to admit.

"Plus, you would be looking for me too, and if you saw me you'd probably smile at me. Flirt with me. And I'd just lose it all over again."

"Probably," she quietly admitted.

"I would rather have you alive and hate me than dead. So I risked losing your love, but I wouldn't risk losing your life."

She wiped her eyes again.

He sat in silence for a moment, bent over staring at the ground. Then, much to her surprise, she heard him sniffle. He wiped his face with his hands quickly, then turned to her and kissed the side of her head. Holding his forehead against her, he whispered.

"Breaking your heart was the hardest thing I've ever had to do and not one minute of the day goes by that I don't regret it. But you're alive and that's all that matters because I still love you."

He nearly choked on his final words. He kissed her one more time, then stood and walked away. She could see him rubbing his face again.

He was crying for her.

Chase came over and sat next to her.

"You ok?"

"No."

"Do you want me to offer to take the bike so you can ride home with Alex in the Beemer?"

"Yes."

Chase started to stand and Lyssa put her hand on his arm, holding his sleeve tightly, stopping him from leaving. A minute later, Alex rode off on the bike.

"I don't understand," Chase said.

"Me neither. That's why I need you to take me home."

"Whatever you want kiddo."

25

It was nine a.m. when Alex sat down at the clean sheet of paper.

It was ten a.m. when Alex gave up staring at the clean sheet of paper.

The inspiration just wasn't there today. Yesterday had wiped him out mentally, physically and emotionally. Bryan ordered him to take two weeks' vacation, but he had nowhere to go and no one to go there with.

He put away his pencils and slipped off his linen tunic that he created art in. While he had only intended to do a pencil drawing, it was still habit to throw on the top he favored when painting.

He debated looking up airline fares to Tampa. Maybe visit his adoptive parents. Then his brain silently reminded him that he'd have to face his mother. If she didn't know what happened yet she probably would soon. Chase was a complete security leak when it came to their parents. And her questions and disappointing looks would be relentless. Not to mention his father would be the one made to suffer with her comments after he was gone.

Nope. Better stay away from Tampa for the time being. Maybe Christmas would be safer.

He was reaching for his t-shirt when he heard footsteps crossing the studio floor. The sound came from the clicking of women's heels.

I really gotta change the number on the garage keypad.

He mentally kicked himself.

Trix is gonna chew my ass out.

He was lucky to have avoided his sister until now. He was

dreading the lecture she was going to give him.

I should have stayed undercover.

"Hello Alex."

Alex looked up so sharply he almost wrenched his neck.

"Lyssa?"

Sure enough, it was his girl standing in the middle of the room. She looked prettier than ever in a little lavender and white flowery sundress. She was carrying a wicker picnic basket.

But the best part was her smile. It was so sweet and carefree.

"I came to see how you were doing," she said, crossing towards him.

"I'm fine."

"Your shoulder's bruised," she cooed over him and instinctively reached out to touch him, only to pull her hand back at the last second.

"Oh, it's fine," he assured her. "You know. Fine."

He mentally kicked himself for sounding like an idiot and quickly threw on the navy blue t-shirt in his hand.

Lyssa tried to avoid staring at his firm pecs and biceps, but his physique was so incredible. Somehow the addition of the tight t-shirt had made it just so much more irresistable.

She looked up at the easel instead.

"New work?"

She glanced around the side at the blank tablet.

"Like it?" Alex snorted. "It's a polar bear eating vanilla ice cream in a snowstorm."

She picked up a pencil and poked at the paper in a small circular area.

"French vanilla," she declared, setting the pencil back down.

He chuckled. How he missed the way she made him smile!

She noticed a little picture paper-clipped to the upper-left corner of the page. It was the same picture he showed her before. Her picture. Alex carefully picked it off and tucked it back into his wallet.

"I thought it might inspire me to create something new," he said quietly.

"Give it time. I'm sure you will."

He nodded to her. "Oh, Andre wanted me to tell you how sorry he is."

"How is he?"

"Doing much better. He's got a mild concussion. I visited him at the hospital yesterday. They discharged him early afternoon. David's playing nursemaid."

"Poor David."

"I'm sure Andre will make sure his recovery takes the full week."

"Probably."

She'd spent the previous day thinking long and hard about their relationship. So long and hard that she didn't get a damn thing done at work. A fact that didn't go by unnoticed by anyone.

"What are you doing out of work anyway?" he asked.

"Marlene told me she heard from Jay who heard from Patrick who heard from the guy at the newspaper stand that you're being forced to take a vacation."

He nodded.

"Me too."

"Bryan's making you take two weeks' vacation?"

"Two weeks? I got two days! That bastard!"

Alex chuckled.

"Anyway," she straightened up again quickly, "if you haven't made any plans and you still have the Porsche, I thought it might be a nice day to go to the Cape. It's supposed to be warm out."

"That sounds nice," he started to smile.

"I made a picnic lunch," she set the weighty basket on a nearby chair. "Nothing fancy. Chicken salad sandwiches and broccoli slaw."

He carefully lifted the flap on the basket to peek inside. "I'm sure it's wonderful."

"I also made carrot cake," Lyssa added with a little smile and a twinkle in her eyes.

The same smile and twinkle that weakened him the first time she'd entered this very room.

"With cream cheese frosting?" he asked.

She nodded.

"Does this mean..." He was afraid to finish the question.

"My mother once told me that when you surprise a man you see the truth in his eyes."

She walked up close to him and put her hands on his jaw, keeping his head tilted down towards her. Looking into his eyes now, she was confident that she'd made the right decision.

"I still love you too," she said and pressed her lips to his, giving him a simple little kiss.

"Lyss..." he started and choked on his words.

"You can call me Babe," she whispered.

He wrapped his arms tight around her waist and picked her up off her feet.

"My Babe... my beautiful, beautiful Babe... "

~ THE END ~

Stephanie K. Deal is an electronic claims submission manager for a medical billing software company in Central New York. Her first novel *Game of Hearts* shocked the hell out of her co-workers, friends, and family. They'd heard for many, many years that she was a writer but had yet to see any proof to substantiate such a claim. To all of them she'd like to say, "Na na-na na boo boo. I told you-u. Phlebt." Stephanie is married to Drew and they have three cats --- Sweetpea, Fuzzy, and that other one which won't come out from under the bed.

To find out more about this series and her author,
visit online:

Blog ~ skdeal.blogspot.com/

Facebook ~ www.facebook.com/StephanieKDealWriter

Twitter ~ twitter.com/StephanieKDeal